Garfield County Libraries
Carbondale Branch Library
320 Sopris Avenue
Carbondale, CO 81623
(970) 963-2889 • Fax (970) 963-8573
www.GCPLD.org

ellen booraem

TEXTING

THE

UNDER
WORLD

Dial Books for Young Readers
an imprint of Penguin Group (USA) Inc.

DIAL BOOKS FOR YOUNG READERS
A division of Penguin Young Readers Group
Published by the Penguin Group
Penguin Group (USA) Inc., 375 Hudson Street, New York, NY 10014, U.S.A.

USA / Canada / UK / Ireland / Australia / New Zealand / India / South Africa / China
Penguin Books Ltd, Registered Offices: 80 Strand, London WC2R 0RL, England

For more information about the Penguin Group visit penguin.com

Library of Congress Cataloging-in-Publication Data
Booraem, Ellen.
Texting the underworld / Ellen Booraem.
p. cm.
Summary: Conor O'Neill faces his cowardice and visits the underworld to bargain
with the Lady who can prevent the imminent death of a family member,
but first Ashling, the banshee who brought the news, wants to visit his middle school.
ISBN 978-0-8037-3704-4 (hardcover : alk. paper)
[1. Supernatural—Fiction. 2. Banshees—Fiction. 3. Death—Fiction.
4. Future life—Fiction. 5. Middle schools—Fiction. 6. Schools—Fiction.
7. Humorous stories.] I. Title.
PZ7.B646145Tex 2013 [Fic]—dc23 2012032488

Printed in the U.S.A.
1 3 5 7 9 10 8 6 4 2

Designed by Nancy R. Leo-Kelly
Text set in ITC Korinna Std

For Shelly Perron,
Goddess of Logic and Language

Chapter One

Death stalked the spider, pre-algebra book in hand.

The spider was slightly bigger than a pencil eraser and definitely wasn't poisonous, this being 36A Crumlin Street, South Boston, Massachusetts. But it skittered and it scuttled all over the ceiling—if Conor didn't squash it now, who knew where it would be after supper.

He thought about getting his sister to kill it. But Glennie would call him a wimp and would tell all her ten-year-old friends at school. And they'd tell their older brothers and sisters who went to Conor's middle school. There would be sniggering, maybe even a new nickname, and he hadn't quite lived down the old one.

Which was "Pixie," by the way. Who nicknames their baby boy "Pixie," for cripes' sake? Brian and Moira O'Neill, 36A Crumlin Street, that's who.

The spider was over his bed, preparing to drop itself and hide in Conor's actual, personal sheets. He weighed the book in his hand—three-quarters of a pound, easy. It would squish twenty spiders that size. But what if he missed? He pictured the vibration shaking the spider onto his face or, worse, down his neck.

Standing on the bed, weapon at the ready, he imagined himself high in the mountains, Conor the Bold versus the Invader from Planet Arachnid, humanity's fate on the line.

If only it *were* a humanoid invader. That would be something resembling a person, and people weren't scary.

Not like spiders or snakes. Or heights.

Or depths.

The world was a lethal and unpredictable place. He felt this in his bones, in spite of the twelve totally uneventful years that had been his life so far.

The bedroom door slammed open. "Supper," Glennie said, then saw that her brother was standing on his bed with his pre-algebra book. One side of her mouth curled up in a half smirk, hot pink with her mother's lipstick. "What are you doing?"

"Nothing."

She stepped closer. "Oooo, a big scary spider. Want me to get it?"

"Shut up."

"Wimp. Javier's here, if you care." She left. The spider scuttled away to the corner, where Conor would have to clear off his desk to get at it.

Defeated, he headed for the stairs.

Grump was coming in from 36B, the other half of the

house. "Hey, kiddo," Grump caroled as they headed into the kitchen together. "How's the Land of Shanaya?"

Conor's hand-drawn maps—some of real places, some not—took up fourteen extra-large spiral-bound notebooks. Grump loved the troll-infested Land of Shanaya, partly because its existence annoyed and baffled Conor's dad, but also because it was proof that Conor had what Grump called "the O'Neill Spark." Which went with the O'Neill Blue Eyes. And the O'Neill Black Hair, at least on Conor, his father, and Grump before he went bald.

"Shanaya's good, thanks, Grump." With his grandfather standing there—big, beaming, confident, glasses perched on the bulbous end of his nose—Conor felt braver about the spider hovering over his desk. It was, after all, roughly the size of a pencil eraser. He took his place at the kitchen table with head held high.

His dad shook his head about Shanaya but would never criticize him in front of a guest, even if it was only Javier. Everybody said Brian O'Neill would be elected to City Council within five years. Tact and relentless cheer were his campaign strategies.

"How about them Red Sox, Pop?" said Dad, no doubt choosing the most un-Shanaya-esque topic he could think of.

"Bums." Grump tucked his napkin into his belt.

"It's only April. They lose early, they win late," Dad said.

"Baloney," Grump said. "I'm telling you—"

But then Grump shut up tight and listened as a car alarm went off on the other side of town, faint but with that echoing, anguished-yeti quality so common in the Irish neighborhoods of Southie.

The sound made Conor shudder. His dad frowned but said nothing. Everyone stayed quiet until the noise faded.

"What does it take to turn off a car alarm?" Dad's tone was fiercer than you'd expect from a tactful, cheerful person.

"That," Grump said, "was no car alarm."

Dad dished up the green beans and canned corned beef hash. "How was school today, kids?"

Grump stuck to the topic of yeti-like noises. "Burt Kavanagh thinks he had a screech owl outside his house Saturday."

Glennie eyed her hash and made a beautifully accurate retching sound, violating the house rule on disgusting noises at the table. In the name of her mother—out at nursing school, and therefore present only in spirit—she was banished to the front hall for ten minutes by the kitchen clock.

Conor took a bite of hash and commenced to chew it fifteen times, a house rule that everybody ignored except him. His mother said digesting unchewed food was the chief cause of flatulence in the American male. Conor didn't think chewing made him fart any less often, but a rule was a rule.

"Of course," Grump continued majestically, "that was not a screech owl."

"So, Javier," Dad said, "what badge you working on in Adventure Boys right now?"

"That was a banshee," Grump said. "Kavanagh's uncle died in his soup Saturday night. He lived right next door to Kavanagh."

"I'm going to die in my hash," Glennie's disembodied voice contributed from the hall.

Javier, who normally would have been eating something home cooked and spicier two streets away, smiled into his green beans. His parents and two older brothers had gone to the airport to greet a visiting cousin from San Juan. Javier had stayed behind to do homework. The reward for his virtue was eating canned hash with Conor.

Also listening to Glennie, which Conor could have told him was no reward. But Javier didn't have a younger sister. He thought Glennie was a barrel of laughs with fluffy blond hair.

In reality, Glennie was a soul-sucking demon warrior.

Conor reached chew fifteen and swallowed. "How'd Mr. Kavanagh's uncle die in his soup?"

His father sighed.

"Heart attack," Grump said through a mouthful of un-chewed hash, in direct violation of house rules. "Supper-time. Fell over with his face in the shinbone stew."

"Cripes," Dad said.

"Cool," said the spectral voice from the hall.

"Tell us about banshees," Javier said, even though he'd certainly heard Grump talk about them before.

"There's no such thing," Dad said. "I heard a cool fact today. Did you know—"

"A banshee," Grump said, "is an ancestral spirit, often a girl who dies too soon and then she comes back and keens when somebody in her family's about to bite the big enchilada." Grump liked to use Spanish terminology when Javier was around, to show he was okay with the neighborhood not being all Irish anymore.

"Enchiladas aren't Puerto Rican," said Javier, who hardly ever spoke Spanish outside the home. "They're Mexican."

"Ain't Irish," Grump said. "But that's perfectly fine."

"Keening is Irish mega-weeping," said the spectral voice. "Like if you had to eat hash all the time."

"Glennie, get in here and eat your supper," Dad said. "And wipe that lipstick off your mouth." He gave Grump a change-the-subject-or-else look.

Which Grump ignored. "Only the very oldest Irish families have banshees. The O'Neills, naturally, but also the Kavanaghs. And Conor's mum's family, the O'Briens."

"Grump has a birthmark shaped like the map of Ireland on the back of his leg," Glennie told Javier, taking her place at the table.

"I know. Purple, with a red spot for Dublin."

"Everybody thinks they're so cool if they've heard a banshee." Dad forked a green bean as if he were killing it. "Then it turns out to be a screech owl or a car alarm."

"Funny how the Irish seem to attract screech owls and car alarms," Grump said. "Especially Irish hospitals and nursing homes, anyplace people kick the bucket."

Javier was frozen, fork suspended halfway to his mouth.

"Javier-silence," Glennie announced. That was their term for when Javier was processing data.

Javier reached a preliminary thesis. "Doesn't anyone ever *see* a banshee? Then they'd know if it was an owl or not."

"They maybe saw one before the keening started, but they didn't know it," Grump said. "Some of the tales say a banshee looks like a regular girl. But then the Death draws nigh"—you could always tell when Grump was quoting from folklore—"and the banshee assumes her true form, the wraith, a wispy ghost in the form of an old hag. No one who sees the banshee's wraith lives to tell about it."

"They *die*?" Javier said. "Just because they *saw* it?"

"Oh, *cripes*." Dad slammed down his fork.

"Yup," Grump said, proud that his ancestral tales were so gruesome. "Drop dead, right on the spot. And that's not even the death the banshee came for originally—she gets that, too. There's stories of whole neighborhoods keeling over, and all because of one little—"

"That's enough," Dad said.

"I'm satisfying the boy's curiosity. He's on a quest for knowledge."

"It's dumb and it's garbage, and I'm sick of hearing it."

"It's your heritage and you should respect it."

"I respect my heritage. Garbage is garbage."

Grump furrowed his brow and drew a debater's deep breath. But he never got a word out, because Brian O'Neill, future councillor, was too fast for him. "A-a-anyways," Dad said. "How about them Bruins?"

They had fruit for dessert—house rules had banned sugar ever since Conor's mom had studied nutrition in nursing school. To her children's regret, house rules saw nothing wrong with canned hash.

After supper, Conor hustled Javier to his room for homework. Someone like Javier was handy to have around when you did pre-algebra—particularly if you needed help faking a sudden inability to determine the speed of Train A in relation to Train B. The right answer required brains, but a believable wrong answer? That took real talent.

"I don't get it," Javier said. "Why do you want to blow pre-algebra? I thought you wanted to get into Latin School."

"*Dad* wants me to get into Latin School." That was all Conor was prepared to say.

Javier narrowed his eyes. "Are you just trying to stay in Southie? You gotta leave sometime."

"You didn't go to math and science school when you got in."

"My mom decided I'm old enough to commute now," Javier said. "If I even get in again."

"You'll get in. They're not nuts."

If you kept your grades up and did okay on the entrance tests, the city would send you to an "exam school": the ancient Boston Latin School or another college-prep academy. Not one of them was in South Boston—also known as Southie, the familiar grid of narrow streets between Fort Point Channel and Boston Harbor. Nor had Conor located any of them in *Comprehensive Maps of Greater Boston,* although he had to admit he hadn't tried all that hard to find them.

Conor didn't believe in going places that weren't obvious on maps.

"Why you worrying about it now, anyways?" Javier persisted. "The tests aren't 'til fall."

Conor blew air out his nose. Javier was so dumb about some things. "Right. So I'm supposed to be a math genius now and then totally flunk the exam next fall?"

"Don't worry," Javier said. "You're not a math genius."

Which was true. If Conor was going to blow an entrance exam, algebra was the clear choice.

Here's what Mrs. Namja posted in her math classroom when they started word problems:

1. Understand the problem.
2. Translate the problem into an equation.

3. Solve the equation.

4. Double-check your answer.

Well, Conor's problem was staying out of Latin School. Which translated into blowing an exam. For now, the solution was screwing up just enough homework to maintain credibility without ending up in summer school.

Truth to tell, the whole idea made him breathe funny, even though he kept telling himself he wasn't breaking any rules doing this. *You can't get caught,* he told himself. *It's foolproof.* To make himself feel better, he filled out his complete name and grade and the date on his algebra worksheet, which nobody else ever did because it was too much work and also uncool.

The bedroom door crashed open. "I'm doing homework in here with you," Glennie said.

"No, you're not," Conor said.

"I can sit right here on the floor." Glennie flopped herself down in Conor's Boston Celtics beanbag chair. "I just have to read."

"Where's Javier going to sit?"

"Right here." Javier heaved his backpack up on the bed. Conor almost said "Watch out for the spider," then thought better of it. The spider was nowhere to be seen, although he did plan to strip his bed and shake out the sheets before he went to sleep.

Something revealing must have shown on his face. "Where's the big scary spider?" Glennie said.

Conor strode to the door. "Da-a-ad! Glennie won't leave us alone."

"Glennie." Their father was in the kitchen, working on his Internet accounting course. "Go to your room and do your homework."

Glennie threw back her head for better volume. "I can do homework here. It's reading."

"Go to your room."

"Da-a-ad."

"Glennie, I have homework myself. If I have to come up there . . ."

Glennie kicked her book to the door. "If I had a little sister, I'd let her do homework with me."

"No you wouldn't," Conor and Javier said in unison.

She slammed the door behind her. Then she slammed her own door. They heard her throw something against the wall.

"That book's going to be a wreck," Javier said.

They settled in to work, Javier on the beanbag chair because he could concentrate anyplace, Conor at the desk. They worked their way through five algebra problems. Conor screwed up one in such a complicated way that Javier actually whistled in admiration.

The door banged open again. Conor was about to call his father, but the visitor turned out to be Grump. "Doing anything?" Grump asked.

"Algebra," Conor said.

"Great, great. Listen, kiddo, I'm gonna need a hand with mixing fuel tonight. Mr. Danson can't come, and I figure you're old enough to start taking some responsibility around here."

Ever since Grump sold his convenience store, he and a friend had built model rockets and shot them off at the park. Grump said rocket science was an important educational tool for children, but nobody's parents would let their kids come within a hundred yards of the launch site.

"Grump, I—"

"How about you sneak out around midnight and I meet you in the backyard? Can't do it in the daytime because . . . well, let's say your mum's not that big on rocket fuel. Javier, you're welcome to come, too."

"Grump, it's a school night. They'd never let me—"

"What part of *sneak out* don't you understand?"

"How'm I gonna sneak? They'll hear me go down the stairs."

"Conor, kiddo, do you or do you not have a fire escape right outside your window? Best alternate route known to man or boy."

"It creaks. It's not safe. It's too high. And . . . and it creaks."

"Not if you go at it the right way."

"I don't know what the right way is."

"Time to find out." Grump headed for the door. "I'll see you later, kiddo. *Hasta la vista,* Javier."

"That means 'see you later,'" Javier said carefully. "You

will not see me later. I'm going home and staying there."

"Suit yourself," Grump said. "Sayonara."

Javier's mother called just as the boys finished their algebra. On his way out of the house, Javier stopped to help Conor's dad get rid of a virus on his laptop. Then he was gone and Conor could relax into his customary B+/A– work on social studies and language arts. He got it all done in time to pull out his notebook of maps and create a seaport for the Land of Shanaya. His mom came home, so he scurried into his pajamas before she swept in to say good night.

When she was gone, Conor settled onto his window seat to battle soul-sucking demon warriors on his cell phone. He was about to turn off his phone and go to bed when a black dot slightly bigger than a pencil eraser emerged from the far corner of the ceiling. It skittered and scuttled until it was over his bed again. And then it halted, preparing to drop.

Conor almost thought he'd wait until his parents went to bed and go sleep on the couch. But that would be wimpy, especially for someone with the O'Neill Spark. Instead, he made careful preparations: took off his slippers for increased agility, buttoned his pajama top up to his neck, then opened the window so he could throw the spider out, in case it was only playing dead and had revenge on its mind.

Pre-algebra book in hand, Conor climbed up on

the bed, never removing his gaze from the enemy. He bounced slightly on the mattress, willing himself to slap the book on the ceiling before the spider saw what was coming.

The spider froze, sensing danger. Conor had to do it now. No, now.

Now. Really. Go!

AhhAHHahhAHHahhAHHahh . . . ! A sudden wail—monstrous, insane—exploded outside Conor's window.

It was as if all the sorrows of the universe had erupted at once. It was a car alarm from just north of hell, a jet screaming into Boston Harbor, all souls lost. Subway wheels shrieking on a track known only to rats and zombies.

Every nerve in Conor's body twanged a great twang, and he found himself on his back on the carpet. He watched the spider scurry across the ceiling, unharmed.

The wailing stopped. The universe righted itself.

Somebody on the street below bellowed, "*Another* car alarm? Are you *kidding* me?" The front door slammed downstairs as Conor's parents ran out to confront the owner of whatever vehicle was wreaking havoc on Crumlin Street. Glennie, of course, slept through it all—nothing woke her up unless she wanted it to.

A red-blond head poked through Conor's open window. "Sorry, boy," the girl said, floating. "And now, I suppose, that's a cry wasted."

She drifted, steadying herself with a hand on the window sash.

Conor blinked, thinking maybe he'd hit his head.

Because he was pretty sure the streetlight was shining through her shoulder.

Not behind it. Not around it.

Through it.

Chapter Two

The girl wafted in over the window seat, her body solidifying. By the time she'd settled herself in his Boston Celtics beanbag, she was as totally there as a middle school principal—except for her right foot, which remained translucent. As he watched, the foot floated up as if she were sitting in a swimming pool.

"Look at you now," she said to the foot. "Why ever would you be doing that?" She used both hands to press her leg down and trapped the wayward foot with her other one. "There. All fixed." She looked brightly at Conor. He lay there on the carpet, organizing his thoughts.

She couldn't have floated in the window, he decided. There must have been a ladder out there. It was nighttime and his room wasn't lit very well and he hadn't seen her right.

"Who are you?" He sat up, so he'd look like he was taking charge.

"Oh good, you speak the Tongue. I was afraid we'd not understand each other."

"What tongue?"

She frowned. "Our own, of course."

"English."

"I never heard it called that. Is that what you call it?"

"It's what it is." Conor stood up, wobbled, and sat down on his bed, forgetting to check for the location of the spider. It could be crawling up his back for all he knew. "Who *are* you?" he asked again.

"I beg your pardon, you asked that already, didn't you? I am the daughter of Maedoc, called Ashling, I don't know how many years dead." She pointed at his cell phone. "That is a little computer, is it not? I was watching you from outside. What are the little creatures that jump?"

"It's a video game," Conor's mouth said, although his brain yelled *DEAD? She thinks she's DEAD?*

"Vid. Ee. Oh." Ashling tasted the word, rolled it in her mouth. "Vid-ee-oh game." She surveyed the room. "This is strange and lovely. So clean! Is it that you're noble, or is it that everyone lives in such a way?"

"We're not noble."

Concern flickered across Ashling's face. "Not a son of the Ee Nay-ill?" Or that's what it sounded like, anyway.

"My father's name is Brian. Brian O'Neill."

Ashling's face brightened. "A son of the Ee Nay-ill, then. Descendant of kings."

Grump talked about O'Neills being kings, back in the

dawn of Ireland. "There are a million O'Neills," Conor said, feeling he should apologize. "I don't think we're noble anymore."

Ashling stuck her pointy little nose in the air. "The Ee Nay-ill," she said, "are always noble."

Conor thought of Uncle Ralph drinking Budweiser and belching the national anthem.

Ashling stood up and walked around his room. She was wearing a green ankle-length wool tunic with a thin leather belt, a red wool cloak open in front, and rough leather shoes. Her red hair hung to her waist in a thick braid, a green ribbon woven through it.

She floated up for a closer view of the solar system map on his ceiling. She seemed real—sturdy and solid and muscular. But she was totally floating.

"*What* are you?" Conor asked. Why wasn't he freaking out? He should be running out the door.

The girl landed in front of him. This time her hand stayed in the air, raised as if she were the brainy kid in class. "Did you see that? How I floated? And, mark you, I just learned this . . ." She faded to invisible, then unfaded, except for her left foot. "An amazing thing, yes? Yes?"

Conor's rear end seemed to have become part of his mattress. "What are you?" he whispered again.

Although he was beginning to think he knew.

"Not supposed to tell what I am." She wasn't very tall—Glennie's size. Standing there, she could stare straight into his eyes as he sat on his bed. Hers were a merry blue—O'Neill Blue—but with an odd wedge of gray at the bottom of each iris that for some reason made him cheerful. She smelled of woodsmoke on a chilly night. "But I don't see why I cannot tell *one* person. Promise not to distress yourself?"

"I . . . I don't know." He thought he might be distressing himself already.

Ashling startled him with a wide grin, gleaming white except for one brown tooth on the side. "I am a banshee, of course. Your family's banshee. Sent by the Lady to . . . to . . . *Ach,* you *will* distress yourself, will you not?"

Sent to . . . what?

To keen—like mega-weeping.

Before a death in the family.

Conor's nerves erupted with another mighty twang. "Am I going to *die*?"

"You are distressed. I knew it." Ashling patted his shoulder. "Calm yourself. It's not so bad. I died once upon a time, and now here I am, all new clothes with a ribbon in my hair." She gazed earnestly into his eyes. "Anyway, it might not be you. I've no idea what Death I'm sent for, see. I'll feel it when it's about to happen. At least, I hope I will. In the meantime, I'm compelled to keen for any death that happens near you, the Ee Nay-ill. It's part of my training." She frowned. "At least, I think it is."

"You haven't always been a banshee?"

"Of course not. This may be my one and only time. But I shall be very, very good at it. The Other Land will talk of me long afterward. They'll say, '*Ach*, if only she'd stayed, what a wonder she—'"

"I was about to kill a spider before."

"I know it. That's why I keened. And a marvelous keen it was, worthy of—"

"The spider didn't die."

"I know it. That was odd."

She's a screwup as a banshee, Conor thought. *No matter how great she says she is.*

But he was dreaming, of course. He must have fallen asleep over his video game. He should yell for his mother, have her tell him, "It's only a nightmare, go to bed." *I am Conor O'Neill. I live at 36A Crumlin Street, South Boston, Massachusetts, thirty-two hundred feet from Boston Harbor.*

Ashling's raised hand fell to her side. Her foot reappeared. She crossed the room to inspect his wall map of Greater Boston, Massachusetts. "I wasn't supposed to appear to anyone," she commented. "What a strange design this is on your wall! But you had the little men jumping, and I so, so, so wanted to find out what they were." She knuckle-rapped on his window, then tested the heft of his hockey stick.

He pinched himself.

Ow.

He hadn't believed Grump's Irish fairy tales for years—

24

not since the one about the kelpie, the fairy horse that drowns and eats you. He'd stayed out of the water one whole sweltering July until his mom figured out what was going on and made Grump say that kelpies were another of his old stories.

His dad said a boy Conor's age should be ashamed to believe such baloney.

Maybe kelpies were real. Maybe Grump *did* smuggle guns to Irish rebels.

Another pinch.

Ow.

He was pretty sure this banshee was real. Weird.

He wasn't a shivering scaredy-cat. Weirder.

The spider didn't die. "Nobody here's even sick," he said. "You've made a mistake."

Ashling raised the hockey stick over her head, brought it down in a vigorous chopping motion. "*Umph.* Odd shape, but a good club nonetheless." She shot him a look—analyzing him, amused, with a touch of lofty pity for his fate. Conor might have been a fly struggling in a web. "You may think what you like, but the Lady does not make mistakes."

"Who's the Lady?"

"I don't know that she's a *who*. She rules the Other Land, where the Dear Departed pass through and are counted. Where I've been until now. She it was who offered me my trade."

"What does that mean, *your trade*?"

"She kept me to entertain her—oh, I don't know how many lifetimes—when everyone I knew had been reborn many times over, lost to me, lost, lost, lost in the World." Her voice rose. "And I am no bard, and yet I must tell the same old tales over and over and over and over. *Ach!* What a fate for a daughter of the Ee Nay-ill!"

"Shhh."

"And now at last, at *last,* the Lady has said if I serve her once as a banshee she will send me back to the World. I will have a new human life." She tightened her grip on the hockey stick, fixed him with an intense gaze. "I would do anything—*anything*—for a new life."

"You mean . . . Cripes. You mean you'll be reincarnated?"

"I have heard it called that, yes. And this will make up for the life so cruelly taken from me by the dreaded raiders of the Dahl Fyet'ugh."

Conor's brains went floaty. "Dahl Fyet'ugh," he repeated, trying to match the funny guttural sound she made at the end.

Ashling scrunched up her face and slammed the hockey stick down on the beanbag chair as if beheading someone. "Curs!" she shouted. "Sons of no mother!"

I am Conor O'Neill, 36A Crumlin Street . . .

A chair scraped in the kitchen. "Pixie? What are you doing? Are you all right?" The stairs creaked.

Conor leaped to crack open the door. "I'm fine, Mom," he said in a loud whisper—Glennie was most likely to wake up exactly when you didn't want her to. "I dropped my pre-algebra book. I was killing a spider." *Why don't I tell her we have a banshee?*

Because there's no such thing as banshees. He imagined the expression on his dad's face. Good enough reason to keep this to himself.

His mom's blond head appeared at the top of the stairs, her brow furrowed. "Go to bed, Pixie. It's late."

"Yeah. Okay." *Don't call me Pixie.*

"Moira," his dad said from downstairs. "The kid's fine. And stop calling him Pixie."

"Good night, Pixie."

Conor sighed. "Good night, Mom."

When he turned around, he half expected the room to be empty. But Ashling was still there, still brandishing the hockey stick like an ax. She grinned, showing off her one brown tooth. "'Pixie'?"

Conor was embarrassed. "My name's Conor, but they started calling me 'Pixie' when I was little. Because I was so scrawny"—*like I'm not still*—"and sometimes my eyebrows peaked up so high Grump said I looked like . . . well, a pixie."

"Your eyebrows peak up when you're unnerved." Her grin broadened. "Like now, Conor-boy."

"I'm not unnerved." But then he saw himself in the

mirror. The eyebrows never lie. *Cripes. They're practically in my hair.*

He got his eyebrows under control and tried to deepen his voice. "So, these Dahl Fyet'ugh. They killed you."

"And my brother before me, demons that they be. Maybe the rest of my family, too, but I was too dead to know."

"How . . . ?"

"A raiding party as we drove our cattle home from afar, an ax in my head as I defended the little ones."

She didn't look much older than he was. Conor rubbed the back of his head, which felt like it had an ax in it. "Holy macaroni. I bet that didn't tickle."

"Didn't *tickle*? It was an ax in the head!"

Conor felt his eyebrows peaking up. "It probably hurt a lot."

His visitor dropped the hockey stick on the rug and replunked herself down on the beanbag. "But then I appeared before the Lady to be praised for my bravery, which bested any in the history of . . . What is *holy macaroni*?"

"Something my grump says." But there were bigger questions, weren't there? "Does . . . does everybody get reborn after they die?"

"Not everybody." Ashling kicked at the hockey stick, peevish. "Not me, for example."

"Most, though?"

"Most. They go through a gateway and we see them no more."

"Do people know that they lived before?"

"No. *You* know it now, of course."

Conor's eyebrows shot up toward his scalp. "How . . . how many times have I . . . ?"

"How should I know that? I am Ee Nay-ill, I don't hang about keeping records. That's Nergal's task."

"Nergal?"

"He's Babylonian." She said that as if it explained everything.

"But . . . I don't remember any other lives."

"Of course not. Look at you, you're white as a new bone knowing what you know now. Imagine if you knew *everything*. You would be holy macaroni."

It was time for bed. The world was more out of control than he'd ever suspected.

"You want to sleep," Ashling said. "I shall sleep, too."

"Banshees sleep?"

"It seems we do. I'm tired, in any event." She pondered for a second, then said, "I don't seem to be hungry. That's good, because I'm not supposed to eat anything."

"You don't know much about being a banshee."

"It all happened in such a rush. The Lady said I'd learn as I went along. Considering how new I am, I am doing the best of anyone in the world's memory." She peered at him. "Don't you agree?"

"Yeah, yeah. You're doing great." *You're a total screwup.*

"We usually stay in our family's home. Have you a small space, a bit confined? I'm used to being under-ground, see."

Conor opened the door to the game cupboard under the eaves. "Is this okay?"

She peered in at the shelves of games and retired toys, Glennie's threadbare Mother Goose rug on the floor to sit on while deciding between Mario Kart and Pokémon. A shelf in the back had a bunch of old board games: newish Clue, oldish Monopoly, ancient Trivial Pursuit.

"This is very fine," she said. "Have you any straw?"

Conor felt around under his bed—momentarily con-cerned that the spider might be under there, but not want-ing to be a wimp in front of the banshee. He located his regulation Adventure Boys sleeping bag and pad and spread them out on the Mother Goose rug. He even gave her his extra pillow.

"One thing everyone says about the Ee Nay-ill." Ash-ling flung herself down on the sleeping bag. "Since the world began, no one has seen the match of our courtesy to guests."

Conor shut her into the cupboard, knowing she could get out easily enough—ever since his mom studied child-hood suffocation, house rules decreed that all closet doors have inside latches.

Something skittered across the ceiling—the spider, once again over his bed. Conor watched it dully, willing it to go someplace else. He wasn't about to try killing it again, with a banshee in the cupboard waiting to wail. Maybe he'd get a glass from the kitchen, try to trap it and release it out the window. Maybe . . .

But the spider solved the problem all by itself.

It fell off the ceiling onto his pillow.

Stone dead.

Chapter Three

Conor couldn't sleep. Every time he dozed off, he startled awake because he thought he'd stopped breathing. He took his pulse . . . Was it slower? Faster? What would it feel like if he were dying?

Sometimes he concentrated so hard on his heartbeat it pounded in his ears. That couldn't be healthy.

A little after one in the morning he got up and settled in the window seat with a flashlight and his notebook of maps. He flipped straight to one of his real maps— South Boston, comfortably familiar. Thanks to a friend of Grump's who worked at City Hall, he had written in the names of every homeowner for three blocks north, south, east, and west of 36A Crumlin Street. He had measured the distance to the corner market, the mailbox, the Italian deli, and Glennie's favorite cupcake store.

Finger tracing the three blocks from home to the nearest park, then six to the skating rink, Conor almost laughed out loud at himself. A banshee in the game cupboard, for cripes' sake. He must have been asleep after all. What a bizarro dream.

A door slammed somewhere in the night. A bright light blasted in the window at the head of his bed.

Something clanked out there. Somebody said a word forbidden in 36A Crumlin Street.

Grump. He expected Conor to meet him. *Cripes.*

Conor clambered onto his bed and knelt on his pillow to slide the window open. He held his breath, hoping he hadn't awakened anyone—not Glennie, and certainly not the banshee in the game cupboard.

Who was totally a dream, by the way.

He stuck his head out, weaving it to see through the grating of the fire escape that served his and Glennie's rooms. Below him, a portable floodlight lit up the back-yard. A dark, rangy figure hunched over an object on the ground.

The object fell over with a clank. The dark figure lunged. The forbidden word sounded again.

Conor crept halfway out onto the fire escape, support-ing himself with hands on the rusty grating, his cowardly thighs still clamped to his windowsill. "Grump," he whis-pered. The fire escape gave an ominous creak and he froze, so busy praying for stability that he almost forgot to worry about waking up Glennie.

Grump lumbered to the fire escape. He peered up at Conor through the grating. "Hey, kiddo. Comin' down?"

"Shhh."

Grump flashed one of his big, doggylike grins, which always made you want to grin back. "Relax, kiddo. Everybody's asleep."

Well, yeah, Grump. That's the point. Conor summoned the worst possible threat. "You'll wake up Glennie."

What if Grump's the one who's going to die? What if he blows himself up? Maybe Conor should go down there after all.

The banshee was a dream. Get real.

Grump jiggled the fire escape. "So what if we wake Glennie up? A girl needs a little moonlight in her life. So does a boy. Come on down. I gotta mix up the fuel and put it in the mold to harden, and the stove's all teetery."

"It's a school night." *And you're mixing rocket fuel on a teetery camp stove at one in the morning.*

"You're awake, ain't ya?"

"How would I get down there? Mom'll hear the door."

Grump paused the way he did when something in the modern world—a grandson, for example—perplexed him beyond all hope of understanding. Conor could hear his sigh two stories up. "Conor. If I'd had a fire escape outside my window when I was your age—"

"It *creaks.*"

"So go slow and find the uncreaky parts."

"It's not safe." *Not to mention . . .*

"Hey, kiddo, *I'm* not safe." *Exactly.*

Conor inched his hands forward, putting a little more of his weight on the fire escape. *Screeeeek.* It sounded like a banshee. Or like a metal fire escape parting company with a wooden house. Even though he was close enough to see Grump's angular face, he still felt dizzy looking down.

He inched one knee onto the metal grating. *Screeeeek.* The fire escape shivered.

He couldn't do this. "It's . . . it's a school night, Grump. I'm going back to bed." He inched himself backward until he was almost inside.

"Suit yourself, kiddo." There was no ignoring the disappointment in Grump's voice. As Conor shut the window, he thought his grandfather muttered, "School night. Cripes." But maybe he heard wrong.

Conor sat down on his pillow, struck by the shivers. *It's still April, for cripes' sake. It's freezing out and I'm in my pajamas.* Something fell over again out back, and the forbidden word made it through the closed window.

First a dream, then Grump in the backyard. What a crazy night. And a *school* night, for cripes'—

The cupboard door creaked. Out crawled the banshee.

Conor's heartbeat pounded in his ears. The banshee yawned and settled into the beanbag chair. Conor breathed in and out, very slowly, very carefully.

"You people don't sleep much," Ashling said.

She's a dream. Dream, dream, dream. I'm dreaming.

Ashling yawned so loud this time she sounded like a hyena.

"Shhh." *Okay, she's a noisy dream.* "You'll wake up my little sister."

"Ah. So we are supposed to be asleep now. I wondered."

"I *have* to go to sleep," Conor said. "I have school tomorrow. Today."

Ashling's face lit up. "School! Sock hops!"

"Shhhh. Wait . . . what?"

"Sock hops. You dance."

"I don't know what a sock hop is."

"I know everything about school. You take off your shoes and dance jitterbutt."

"I think that's when Grump was a kid." Conor clambered off his bed to the floor near Ashling, so she'd remember to whisper. "And I think it's jitter*bug*."

"How old is this grump?" She was not whispering.

"Shhh. Eighty-one." No more swearing from the backyard. Maybe the camp stove was behaving itself.

Ashling shrugged. "Not so old. There could still be jitterbutt."

"Anyways," Conor said, "school isn't about dancing. We learn stuff."

"I learned to tend cattle, the best in my whole family. When the beasts saw me coming, *ach*, how they—"

"We don't have cattle around here. We buy meat in the store." Maguire's Market, three and a half blocks due east.

It was on his map, lying on the floor by the window seat.

"Store! You trade with coin, get a hi-fi and a smart phone!"

"Keep your voice down."

"And some gee." She peered to see his face in the moonlight. "You are wondering how I know so much. I got it all from talking with the Dear Departed. I have an unquenchable thirst for learning, the Lady says."

"What . . . what is *gee*?" Conor asked.

"You wear it on your legs. Blue gee." She eyed his red pajamas, with the hole where he'd cut away the Space Rangers emblem the day he turned twelve. "Not like what you have on."

He wished he still had that Space Rangers emblem on him. The years before age twelve seemed so orderly and safe. "You mean *blue jeans*?"

"I don't know. Do you have coin? I would like to see coin."

He pointed at his dresser, where he put his change. Ashling jumped up, took a quarter and sniffed it. "Silver, yes?" She came back and held it under his nose until he took it. It was a Mississippi state quarter, with magnolia blossoms on it.

"No. I think it's made of nickel. It's not that valuable in itself. It's . . ." He searched what he remembered from social studies. "It's a unit of exchange."

"What's that, then?"

He gave the quarter back to her. "I don't really know."

The light went out in the backyard. The door slammed again.

Ashling paid no attention, tracing the magnolias on the quarter with her finger. "Beautiful craft. I once knew someone who could work like this." She sighed. "Gone now. Gone, gone."

"Keep it," he said. She was making him sad, for no reason he could identify.

She shook her head and put the coin back on the bureau. "The craft of this World prevents me from becoming a wraith when I am supposed to. I must not have Worldcraft on my person when the Death approaches. That I *do* know."

Conor tried to imagine this sturdy, red-haired girl turning into a wispy ghost in the form of an old hag.

She poked him in the chest. "If I should transform—"

"I know, I know. Anyone who sees you will die." Conor's spine turned to ice. "You keened before, outside. Did anybody see you?"

"If they did, they're before the Lady now. Dead, I suppose you'd say. Dear Departed."

Forgetting to be quiet, Conor rushed to the front hall window. He hurled it open and thrust his head out. No corpses on the moonlit sidewalk. He almost cried with relief.

"Pixie?" His mother, from his parents' room, sounding sleepy. "What are you doing?"

"Just . . . just throwing a dead spider outside."

"Another one? Why didn't you throw it out your own window?"

There was no good answer. "I don't know."

"Go to sleep, Pixie. It's late."

As he closed the window, he heard his father's blanket-muffled voice. "What does he think, the dead spider's going to crawl in his window and get him back?"

"Go to sleep, Brian."

Conor crept back to his room and shut the door. *I have to get some sleep. It's a school night.*

"Nobody dead?" Ashling was standing on his bed for a closer look at his Grand Canyon poster.

"You don't care?"

She regarded him calmly. "Why should I? They go to the Lady, get another life."

"You said your life was cruelly taken from you by the dreaded raiders of the Dahl Fyet'ugh. Other people don't like losing their lives, either."

Ashling lifted off from the bed and floated to the floor. This time, her braid stayed in midair. She looked like she was underwater.

Exhaustion dropped on Conor like an ax. He wanted it to be four hours ago, when all he had to worry about was pre-algebra and a spider in his sheets. "I'm going to bed. See you in the morning."

"Good night, Conor-boy." She crawled back into the

cupboard and pulled the door shut behind her.

Conor got to sleep at daybreak. When he woke an hour later, he again convinced himself it had all been a bad dream. But he peeked into the game cupboard and there was Ashling, sound asleep, red hair unbraided and spread out on the pillow, red cloak over her like a blanket, her shoes stashed on top of Monopoly.

The game cupboard smelled like woodsmoke and wet earth. As he crouched there, watching her and wondering what would happen next, Conor thought he heard . . . something, a lone flute, the tune just beyond the reach of his memory. The back of his neck prickled.

Somebody coughed, down in the kitchen. Conor froze. Was somebody sick?

Out the bedroom door, down the stairs in a panicky blur. He skidded into the kitchen to see his parents standing back to back near the coffeemaker, shoulders tense, each with a folded section of the newspaper in hand. His mother was dressed for work at the clinic. His father was in his mailman uniform, his feet pointed toward the back door.

Glennie was ready for school, peering hopefully into the granola sack even though she knew the contents never had been and never would be Honey-Glazed Nutsos.

"It's seven-oh-five," his mom said when she saw Conor. "Where are your clothes?"

"Who's sick?" Conor panted.

40

Everybody stared at him as if he were some kind of Nutso himself.

"Nobody's sick," his dad replied. "My watch says seven-oh-seven."

"Somebody coughed."

"That was me," said his mom. "I choked on some granola."

"Stuff could kill ya," his dad said. "Why're you still in your pj's? What time you think it is?"

"There's . . . there's a thing," Conor said.

"There's always a thing," Glennie said darkly, pouring granola into a bowl.

"She says she's a banshee," Conor said. "One of us is going to die."

His dad let out an exasperated breath. "Conor, my pop's stories ain't real."

"Dad, come upstairs, okay? Mom?"

"Pixie, it's seven-oh-six. I have to get in to the clinic early today. I'm already late."

"Mom. Please."

Dad sighed and put his coffee cup in the sink. "Go ahead, Moira. Con, I'll give you two minutes. Then I gotta go."

"I'm coming, too." Glennie abandoned her granola even though she'd already poured milk on it. This was a bad omen: Glennie hated soggy granola. She probably thought there was a good story in the offing to tell her friends.

"You can't say anything to anyone," Conor said.

Glennie half smirked, flicking a bit of granola off her pink skirt. Glennie often wore skirts, as well as ruffles and hair ribbons, in order to distract everyone from her soul-sucking true identity. Today's temporary tattoo, on the back of her hand, was of a pink bunny with a wolf looming behind, ready to spring.

"Mom," Conor pleaded.

"Glennie, you stay right here and eat your cereal." Mom swooped past the sink to give her smoothie glass a drive-by rinsing, then headed for the door. "And no telling the girls." Glennie's jaw jutted out, making her look like a fluffy blond version of Dad and Grump. Her parents ignored her and steamed out of the kitchen, Dad to the stairs, Mom to the coat closet in the front hall.

Hand on his bedroom doorknob, his father fidgeting beside him, Conor hesitated. What if the banshee got mad? Would she turn into a wraith, bringing death to all who saw her? But Ashling hadn't said *he* couldn't tell anyone. So she wouldn't mind, right?

Still, he found himself tiptoeing across the carpet to the game cupboard, his father close on his heels.

"Must be a pretty small banshee to fit under the eaves," Dad said.

"Shhhh." Conor pulled the door open and stood back so Dad could see.

"How small is this thing, Con?" His father stuck his head

in the cupboard to scope it out, reemerging with the baffled look he reserved for his children. "Do I need a magnifying glass?"

Conor almost whacked his head on the doorframe swooping in there. Empty. He jumped out again, and the banshee wasn't hovering near the ceiling or outside the window. He flung himself on his knees to look under the bed. Not there, either.

"Conor," his dad said. "There's no such thing."

"She's gone." A thought occurred to him. "Or she's invisible. Hey, Ashling, if you're here anywhere—"

"Oh, cripes, Con. You were dreaming." His dad turned for the door.

"No, look, there's her butt print on the beanbag."

His dad took him by the shoulders, gazed deep into his eyes. "Listen, kid, Grump's nuts about this banshee business, and I know you think a lot of him. But it's all an old man's stories . . . like the kelpie that summer. I'm not letting this garbage take over your life, okay?"

"WooOOOoooOOOoooOOO . . ." Glennie, out in the hall. "I'm a baaaanshee and you're going to crooooooak . . ."

Conor's dad lifted his eyes toward the solar system on the ceiling, seeking calm. "Glennie, pack up your stuff for school." He headed for the hallway. "Get dressed, Con. I gotta go and you're gonna miss your bus." Almost out the door, he turned back. "Oh, hey . . . I got the money together for hockey next winter. Tryouts in six weeks, Katie

43

Miller says." His face was aglow with sudden enthusiasm, never a happy sight for his children.

"Dad, I'm lousy at hockey." Every day in a skating rink, all summer long. He'd rather die.

Except not really.

"Katie says there's twenty-six kids trying out, but you skate pretty good, so I wouldn't worry." *Glow, glow, glow.*

"I don't *like* hockey." *Don't let him talk about Boston College. Don't let—*

Too late. Worse luck, his father for once had actually heard what he said. "Listen, Con." The glow gave way to fatherly seriousness. "My grades didn't get me a BC scholarship, but yours might. You go to Latin, play hockey, you'll be golden."

"I know that, Dad, but—"

"Plus, your college fund's growing—ain't huge, but I'm not blowing it on trips to the old country like *my* pop did."

"I know, Dad. I really appreciate it, but—"

"I'd like to see you get out there, Con. Off your beanbag and out of the house."

"I go to Adventure Boys every week."

"Because of Javier. Something on your own, that's what they're looking for, these admissions people."

"My maps are my own," Conor ventured. *Unlike hockey,* he might have added if house rules permitted talking back.

Dad looked baffled again. "Half of them maps ain't even *real,* Con. I gotta go. Give it a try, son, okay?"

Conor watched the door close, then turned around and—"Gah!"—inches from his nose, Ashling was RIGHT THERE, her face solidifying. He stumbled backward, landing on the beanbag chair.

"You told," Ashling said. One of her hands was missing.

Conor got his breath back. "You didn't say not to."

"I trusted you to use the wits you were made with." Ashling pulled a large comb, intricately carved out of bone, from a leather bag pinned to her tunic. She dragged it roughly through her hair with her invisible hand. "The Lady said to me, Show yourself to no one, tell no one what you are, but did I listen? No, for there was a vid-ee-oh and a lovely human and I wanted to see and feel and find out. Then the next thing I know he's told MORE humans and one of them may be the dying one." The comb caught on a knot. She worked at it. Her hand reappeared. "It's a tragedy, that's what it is. A disaster. A horror. A cata—"

"You didn't say," Conor insisted, but then he thought, *Lovely human?*

"You didn't SAY, you didn't SAY," Ashling mimicked. "Potent Mother Maeve, what a hare-head." She untangled the comb so she could waggle it in his face. "I shouldn't have told you, and you must not tell anyone else. Best if they don't know what's coming, boy, you see?"

"But what am I going to do?" Conor wanted to keen like

a banshee himself. "Sit here and let somebody die?" *What if it's me? Mom and Dad would think of a way to stop it.*

"Nobody can stop it," Ashling said, as though reading his thoughts. "And the Lady has sent the best of all possible banshees to see it through. That's that."

The kitchen was empty when he ate his breakfast—which was nerve-racking, because what if he choked? He chewed each bite of cereal twenty-five times and didn't drink any juice until he'd swallowed what he had in his mouth.

His heartbeat kept pounding in his ears. He could feel weak spots in his brain, ready to pop. Congestion was building up in his lungs, he knew it was.

Back upstairs, he sat down on his bed and opened his map notebook. But South Boston did nothing to calm him this time, nor did the Land of Shanaya—not even the anti-gravity vehicle port and the Twelve Mountains of the Skull.

He shoved the notebook into his backpack. Then, strictly observing house rules, he descended to the front door with a tight hold on the banister, every footfall safely centered on its stair.

Chapter Four

Which is worse, mockery or death? After a profound inner struggle, Conor decided he'd rather be teased than dead. So he put on his bicycle helmet before he went out the front door.

"Hey!" Grump was on the porch, hanging wet socks on the railing. "Lookit you with your helmet on! Your mum finally letting you ride your bike to school?" Apparently, the helmet made up for Conor's cowardliness at one a.m.

"Uh."

Inside, Glennie shut the hall closet door and thumped around putting on her backpack. Time was short. She'd be out in less than a minute.

"Ha!" Grump winked at Conor. "Moira doesn't know, does she?" He slapped Conor's shoulder. "I knew you had it in ya, kiddo. So where's the bike? Gonna ride it with the backpack on?" Beaming, he leaned over and whispered conspiratorially, "You done with the Mountains of the Skull? Come by and show me after school."

Conor nodded and sidled toward the steps. "I'll see you later, Grump." He made it to the sidewalk. Glennie opened the front door.

"Hey, kiddo," Grump said. "You forgot your bike."

"He's taking the bus," Glennie said. "Why's he got his helmet on?"

Conor pretended he didn't hear them. He kept his helmeted head down and aimed for the city bus stop.

Which was 1,276 feet from 36A Crumlin Street. He knew this because he'd measured it.

He had walked approximately 750 feet by the time Glennie caught up with him. "What the heck?" she said. He didn't reply. When they met the other kids at the corner, he told them he had a slight concussion and had to be extra-careful for a few days.

"Yeah," Glennie said. "Pixie's got a soft head."

She had a sneezing fit before she and her friends set off on their 823-foot walk to the elementary school. Conor made her promise to have the school nurse take her temperature as soon as she got there. "Dweeb," she said. Her friends giggled.

"What the freak is the matter with you?" Javier said as the bus headed for the next stop, his calm, precise voice barely audible over the chatter. "You don't really have a concussion, do you?" He leaned in and whispered: "Is this about staying out of Latin School?"

I can tell him. Ashling'll never know. Conor whispered

back: "There's a banshee at our house. Somebody's going to die."

"That is very awesome." In a lightning change of character, Javier clutched his throat and made a gagging sound. "Oh no! It's me!" He slumped against the seat in front of them.

"Quit fooling around." Conor thumped Javier on the shoulder. "This is real."

"Sweet," Javier said. "Hey, look out there! It's an Arcturian slime creature. Ready phasers!" He aimed his finger pistol at the drooling bulldog tethered outside the newsstand.

"Nerd alert," Andy Watson, a large and cool eighth grader, said from the seat behind them. His cool friends snickered.

"Ignore him," Conor said.

"I am," Javier said, shooting. *"Pshoo. Pshoo."*

"Try ignoring this, Pixie-poop." Andy punched out his fist, stopping it an inch from Conor's nose. "You better keep that helmet on."

"Oh, shut up, Andy." It was one of the mysteries of Conor's life that fists didn't scare him. You never knew what a spider was going to do next, but Andy was totally predictable. His fist never made contact with your nose if you stared at him hard enough.

"Shut up, Andy. Shut up, Andy," Andy said in a baby voice. "Big brave Pixie-poop wif his helmet on."

"Pixie-poop, Pixie-poop, Pixie-poop," Andy's friends chanted.

Fists were one thing. People chanting "Pixie-poop" was something else again.

"Ignore them," Javier said.

Conor stared out the window, the rims of his ears burning. An old lady in front turned around and glared at him, as if the noise were his fault.

"I got the slime creature, by the way," Javier said, relentless in nerdiness. "Twenty battle points. Your turn."

Conor marveled for the gazillionth time at Javier's total lack of concern about people making fun of him. Nobody took Javier seriously—he was way too short, his face too angelic, his eyelashes too long. He often spent recess fixing the computer in the principal's office—an act that was so far beyond nerdy that it left most of his classmates speechless. Javier didn't care one way or the other—call him a name, he'd shrug it off and keep talking.

"Are you coming to Adventure Boys tomorrow?" Javier asked him, upping their joint nerdiness factor by about ten. Fortunately, Andy was busy harassing a kid across the aisle and didn't hear.

"Yeah, I guess." The Adventure Boys leader, Mr. Phillips, was going to ask how Conor was doing on his American heritage badge, and all he'd done was check a history book out of the library. He'd managed two badges so far: house painting and family life. He'd chosen them carefully—he'd had to paint Grump's kitchen anyway to earn his new cell phone, and that counted for both badges.

The cell phone had a GPS mapping application that told him exactly where he was in the world at any exact minute, so that was one good thing that came out of Adventure Boys.

Javier had seven badges and was working on two more, aiming for the coveted designation of Bravest and Best Adventurer. He hoped this would impress the scholarship committee at computer-geek heaven, the Massachusetts Institute of Technology. He'd learned first aid, built a digital circuit, and observed live insects in their habitat (the dumpsters behind the school). He'd wanted a bugle-blowing badge, but his father put his foot down.

"We're going to learn how to make doughnuts tomorrow," Javier said.

Great, Conor thought. *Maybe I can die from a heart attack.*

Walking into school (one-point-seven miles from 36A Crumlin Street), shoving his helmet into his locker, Conor tried not to worry about who might be dying at that very moment. He distracted himself by crumpling up a school dance poster somebody had taped to each seventh-grade locker and chucking it at a wastebasket six lockers away. He missed, but at least that was one normal thing in this horrible day.

"Oh thanks, Conor," Olivia Kim said. "We worked hard on those posters."

"Right. Like I'm going to a *dance*." Conor snorted. Javier, however, folded his poster carefully and stored it in his back pocket.

"What're you doing?" Conor asked.

Javier smiled at Olivia and headed for social studies.

Further distraction came when the guidance counselor, Ms. Wright, pulled Conor and Javier—along with Olivia and their classmates Marissa and Ifraho—out of social studies to talk to them about exam schools. The entrance tests were a good six months away, but she handed each of them a booklet of sample questions that would help them prepare. "It's never too soon to start getting ready," she said. "This is your future we're talking about."

Conor opened the booklet. The first thing he saw was a long word problem concluding, "Which equation, when solved for M, would give Matthew's speed in feet per minute?" He could blow that one big-time.

He slapped the booklet shut. "What if we get in and then decide not to go?"

"Why ever would you do an unacceptable thing like that?" Ms. Wright sent an evil glare in Javier's direction, clearly not recovered from Javier's declining his math and science school invitation the previous year.

"My mother's okay with me going now," Javier said. Ms. Wright gave a skeptical sniff.

"What if," Conor persisted, "I dunno . . . if you got sick or died or something?"

Ms. Wright eyed him fixedly. "I saw you wearing a bike helmet this morning, Conor. Is there something wrong with your head? Why have we not been informed?"

"I have a slight concussion. It's no big deal."

"Well, then, dying is unacceptable," Ms. Wright said. "Back to class now. And *study that book,* all of you."

When they got back to social studies, the bell was just ringing. Ricky Desmond sashayed out of the room in front of Conor, pinkies raised delicately in the air, proclaiming, "Ai'm going to Lah-tin Skewl."

"Shut up," Conor said. "It wasn't our idea."

"Yeah." Marissa was as red as her new plastic purse.

Conor stuck with Javier, who stuck with Olivia, Marissa, and Ifraho, all through special projects day in math class, which Conor couldn't blow because he'd take his whole team down with him.

He got a pass to go to the bathroom and, in defiance of school rules, sneaked a call to his mother at the clinic where she worked, to make sure she was all right. Then he called his father's cell. Then he called Grump.

"What's up, kiddo? I got glue drying."

"Are you okay?" Conor asked.

"I'm outta sight. Why?"

"Just asking. You're not igniting anything today, right?"

"Nope, ain't even finished the rocket yet. What's going on, Conor? The world scaring you again? And what was with the helmet, for cripes' sake?"

"I . . . gotta go, Grump. I'll see you."

"See ya, kid. Stop acting like a weirdo."

To make himself feel better, Conor located himself on his cell phone GPS. Sure enough, there he was at Barbara McMichael Middle School, one-point-seven miles from 36A Crumlin Street.

At lunchtime, Conor sneaked back into the boys' restroom and called everyone again. His grandfather, who had caller ID, picked up the phone and said, "I exploded the house. Quit bothering me." Then he hung up.

Javier bustled in as Conor shut his phone. "Andy Watson and Janet Morrow got caught making out in the janitor's closet."

Conor was momentarily distracted from his troubles. "Gross."

"Yeah. That place *stinks*."

"No. I meant . . ." Conor took a good hard look at Javier, who turned a shade redder. "Gross that they were kissing."

"Yeah," Javier said. "Gross." Avoiding Conor's eyes, he bared his teeth at the mirror and scrubbed one of them with his finger.

"Tell me if anybody comes in," Conor said. "I gotta call Glennie's school and see if she's okay."

Now Javier was the one taking a good hard look at *him*. "You're making a cell phone call during school hours? *You?*"

Conor retreated into a toilet stall, punching his speed dial.

Glennie was fine. But when Conor emerged from the stall, Javier was still doing the good hard look thing. "Dude, why you so strange today? I mean, jeez, calling your family during school hours, a helmet on the bus."

"I tried to tell you and you wouldn't believe me." Conor headed for the door.

"A *banshee*? That's your explanation?"

"Leave me alone, okay? I gotta get something to eat." He walked out, leaving Javier-silence—signifying data analysis—in the boys' room.

Everyone was outside for recess, but Conor sneaked to the cafeteria down in the basement, scoring a bag of popcorn and a fruit cocktail. He sat up on a table to eat, putting his feet on a chair in a burst of lawlessness. Munching, he eased his nerves by pondering whether the Land of Shanaya should include a northeast forest of carnivorous spruce trees.

A flash of color out the ground-level window caught his eye. He froze, then stood up on the chair to see better.

There, sitting on a sunny stoop across the street, was a red-cloaked figure with a long red braid.

Popcorn bag between his teeth, fruit cocktail syrup all over his hand, Conor raced upstairs to the side door. Opening that door was a rule violation beyond his wildest imagination. He took a deep breath and opened it anyway, keeping his feet firmly inside the threshold to make himself as law-abiding as possible. He beckoned furiously to Ashling. She skipped across the street, beaming.

"What are you doing here?" Conor whispered.

"Oooo, what is that?" Ashling leaned in the door and sniffed the remnants of the fruit cocktail. "Very pretty, but it smells like rot."

Conor was not to be distracted. "*What* are you *doing* here?"

"Is this school?" She peeked in at the worn linoleum and iron staircase, eyes shining. "I saw a picture of it in your sleeping place, so I could think myself here. Ooo, you are holding a little sack in your hand."

"I thought you were supposed to keep hidden."

"No one is paying me any heed. Open that sack. I want to see."

"You . . . this can't be what you're supposed to do."

Ashling smiled as if they shared a secret. "The Lady will never know. And if the Death comes near, I am sure it will call to me wherever I am. The Death might be you in any case, and then I'll be right here. Are you going to open that sack?"

I am Conor O'Neill and I am at McMichael Middle School, one-point-seven miles west of 36A Crumlin Street . . .

He opened the snack sack to show her. She poked the popcorn with a cautious finger, sniffed its aroma. "I like this better than the other thing. But mark you!" She fumbled at the leather bag pinned to her tunic and pulled out a small stack of cards. "See what I found in my sleeping place! These little skins offer many interesting facts about your world!"

They were ancient Trivial Pursuit cards. Ashling plucked one off the top and read, "'Vidal Sassoon was . . . the official . . . hairdresser of the 1984 . . . Olympics.' What are Olympics? What is 1984?"

"Banshees can read?"

Ashling shuffled through the cards. "Oh yes. Nergal taught me about these little marks, but with him it is all names and numbers and places. Nothing as interesting as . . . oh." She flipped a card over. "What is baseball? It causes eighteen thousand fack-ee-all injuries each year in U.S. kids aged five to fourteen."

"I think that's *facial* injuries."

Footsteps sounded behind him. "Conor O'Neill!" Fortunately, it was only his science teacher, Ms. Alexis, who took a broad view of rules. "Shut that door, on the double!"

"I have to go," Conor said.

"I will come with you." Ashling shuffled her cards. "I have many interesting facts to relate. This baseball one, or I saw one about killer whales."

"You can't come in. You have to go home now."

"But what if you are the Death?"

"Then . . ." Conor swallowed. "Then you can come back. Please. I have to go."

As he grabbed the door handle to close it, Ashling waved merrily and skipped back across the street, clearly with no intention of leaving.

"Who is that girl, Conor?" Ms. Alexis asked when he walked into the science lab.

"She's . . . my cousin."

Javier hiked himself up on his lab stool to peer out the window. "That's not any cousin I've seen."

"Another cousin." Conor sat down, wishing Javier would shut up.

"You don't have—"

"You don't know all my cousins, okay?"

Javier-silence. Big-time.

Ms. Alexis stood over him. Then she hunkered down to eye level, never a good sign. "Is everything all right at home, Pix . . . uh . . . Conor?" she asked beneath the classroom hubbub. "Do you want to go to the nurse? I understand you wore a helmet—"

"I have a slight concussion," Conor said, defiantly not looking at Javier. "But I'm fine."

That didn't convince Ms. Alexis, who immediately sent him to the nurse's office. The nurse determined that he didn't have a temperature and his pupils didn't look funny and he didn't have any bruises that seemed like he'd been hit—which he could have told her, but she always looked for them anyway. She made him sit for half an hour, then released him for his next class.

He'd had high hopes for language arts, because they were reading a book he really liked. But Ms. Clayborne was in a droning mood, a real book killer. Plus, he was sitting in the sun. The radiator was right behind him, pumping heat.

He smelled woodsmoke, heard a flute tune like a lullaby. It was sweet . . . lonely . . . distant . . .

The bonfires still scent the air, although they've been ash and rubble since daybreak. Cattle moan in pens nearby. Someone plays the flute, a lonely air.

The scent and music fade as he runs out of the king's enclosure, stolen sword at his belt, although the scabbard is his. Without a thought for spirits or raiders or beasts, he plunges into the woods. The footpath is a shortcut, the scouts have told him.

The moon dims any stars that could guide him. He keeps it to his back, hoping that will help.

An hour scuds by. Two. Moonlight dapples the woods, and he keeps losing the path. The spirits' fault: They brush against his face, howl behind him. Fear of them drives him to run without thought, without checking the moon. At last he stumbles into a clearing and stops, horrified. He's seen that boulder before. He's run in a circle.

Slumped on the ground, sword across his knees, he traces the engraving on the scabbard with one finger. He has been proud of this scabbard. But possessions mean nothing to him now. He has to find her before they do. He struggles to his feet, ready to run.

Shouts in the distance. He sets out toward them, grateful to have a direction. A girl screams, fearful yet enraged, over and over and over . . .

Except that wasn't a girl screaming. That was a bell.

The bell. Language arts was over, his classmates jabbering and laughing their way to the door. Conor tried to shake his head clear before anyone figured out he'd dozed off.

"I get it now." Javier stood there grinning. "You went outside with your grandfather last night, didn't you? So you didn't get any sleep and now you're all zombified."

Conor shook his head, still buzzing with moonlight and a girl's screams. He felt sick.

"Dude." Javier lowered his voice. "What the *heck* is going on with you?"

Conor got up without a word, collected his books, and abandoned a silent Javier for the third time in one day. Study hall was next. He went to the office for a library pass.

He still heard that girl screaming.

It was a dream. So why did he feel so awful?

The school library had a whole shelf of books about Ireland. Three from the end he found what he wanted: *Ancient Celts,* with spirals on the cover that reminded him of the scabbard in his dream. He sat at a table and flipped pages until a heading caught his eye: *Niall of the Nine Hostages, founder of the Uí Néill.*

The Uí Néill, pronounced *Ee Nay-ill,* eventually turned into the O'Neills. In the fifth century, they'd won land in Uladh (pronounced *Ull-oo*) from people called the Dál Fiatach—pronounced *Dahl Fyet'ugh*—who weren't happy about it. Uladh later became Ulster in northern Ireland.

Conor got out his notebook and copied a map of fifth-century northern Ireland with all its tribe names, the spellings so weird it felt like one of his fantasy maps.

Ashling must have lived—and died—around that time, speaking an early version of Irish. *How come we understand each other?* Conor wondered. *She must have a universal translator, like in StarQuest Galaxy.*

Somehow that wasn't comforting.

He wore his helmet on the way home, too. Javier sat three seats forward, talking loudly with James Johnson and Mohamed Ellis. Olivia was in the seat behind Javier and kept punching him in the shoulder.

Conor got stuck sitting with Andy Watson's best friend, Michael, who was so tall he had to keep his knees out in the aisle. But Andy had stayed after school and wasn't there to incite violence, so Michael left Conor alone.

Conor plastered himself to the window and watched South Boston slide by. Was this the last time he'd be on this smelly, noisy bus?

Javier laughed at something. *Maybe I'm imagining*

things because I have a brain tumor, Conor thought. He pictured himself having some kind of a fit and dying, right there on the bus. *They won't be laughing then,* he thought.

His blood went hot, and he was furious. Ashling had to know who was going to die—it made no sense that she didn't. She was holding out on him, not playing fair. *If somebody's going to croak, at least tell me who so we've got a fighting chance.*

He'd get it out of her. He didn't know how. But he had to do it, or he really was going to go nuts.

Chapter Five

Conor met his sister walking home. Her mouth was full of Fruity Foolers, a jelly bean she favored because it looked sweet and tasted so sour it almost sucked your cheeks down your throat. In response to the sugar ban at home, she kept a three-ounce pack of them in the waistband of her underpants at all times.

Maybe it's Glennie, Conor thought. *Then I'll be the one who's not laughing.* "I love you, Glennie," he said as they went up the front steps to their house.

"Mo-o-om." Glennie dropped her backpack inside the door. "Conor's freaking me o-o-out."

Their mother appeared at the top of the stairs, zipping up her jeans, still in the sweater she'd worn to the clinic. "Conor, stop freaking out your sister."

Conor took off his bicycle helmet and hung it on the banister. "I only told her that I love her." What if his mom was the one, and she died mad at him? "I love you, too."

"Pixie, are you feeling all right? Why did you wear your helmet to school?"

"Because he's a dweeb," Glennie said. "Do we have any cookies?" She asked this every day, even though she knew the answer.

"Have a banana," Mom said. "And don't call your brother a dweeb."

"When I grow up, I'm eating cookies for *breakfast*." Glennie stomped off to the kitchen, where she would dispose of her empty Fruity Foolers bag in the wastebasket, wrapped in a wet paper towel to escape detection.

Conor hauled his backpack up the stairs. He evaded his mother's attempt to feel his forehead and hesitated outside his bedroom door, waiting for her to go downstairs and gather up her stuff for nursing school. All was silent behind the door—maybe the banshee was gone. Maybe he'd imagined the whole thing. Maybe—

He opened the door. Ashling was ensconced on the beanbag chair, his windbreaker on her lap, Trivial Pursuit cards scattered all over the floor. She was brimming with news.

"Mark this!" She ran the windbreaker's zipper up and down, up and down. "It's the silliest thing I ever saw. And hear this!" She scooped up a handful of Trivial Pursuit cards and waved them at him. "Alexander the Great's hearse was pulled by sixty-four horses. Who was Alexander the Great?"

"Some Greek guy."

Ashling chose a card, flipped it over. "Anne Boleyn had eleven fingers. Who's she?"

Conor had to think. "Um. A queen. She got her head cut off."

Ashling beamed. "With an ax?"

"I don't know. Maybe." Conor remembered he was ticked off. "But listen, I can't sit around talking about axes and things. You have to tell me who's going to die and what we can do about it."

Ashling's face went stolid. "Who would be 'we'?"

"Me. My parents."

"What would they do about it? Your father doesn't even think I'm real. And anyway, as I *keep* telling you, even the Lady can do nothing to change this."

"And you don't know who the victim is. I don't believe that."

"Believe. There is no way for me to know. I can only accept and wait, and you must do the same."

"We're talking about somebody DYING!"

Ashling picked up a stack of Trivial Pursuit cards. "That's nothing new, Conor-boy. It happens every day, thousands upon thousands of times."

"Not in my family."

"Lucky you."

She flipped over a card and brightened. "President Gerald R. Ford survived two attempts on his life in seventeen days."

Conor stalked out of the room, slamming the door behind him. He racketed down the stairs, out his front door, and into 36B, his grandfather's side of the house.

"Don't dalk 'a me wor a sec," Grump said around the glue cap he was holding in his teeth. Hunched over the workbench that dominated his living room, he eased the nose cone onto a miniature Firehawk missile. Pulling his fingers away, he examined the set of the cone and let out his breath. "That'll do it." He stood up, half-glasses at the end of his nose, checkered shirt taut over his belly. "Hey there, kiddo. Got your Shanaya map?"

"Grump, we have a banshee."

Grump dropped into his easy chair. "So I hear. At least that explains the helmet. Your pop says it's all my fault for filling your head full of garbage."

"It's not your fault. The banshee's real. It's just that she disappeared when I tried to show her to Dad. And somebody's going to die. And"—might as well get it all out—"and I keep hearing a flute and I probably have a brain tumor."

Grump picked at the dried glue on his thumb. Removing the glue took all his concentration. Conor waited. Then Grump said, "I gotta say, kiddo, this is the first I've heard of a banshee hanging around socializing before the Death."

Something like a Firehawk missile exploded in Conor's head. "You . . . you don't believe me?"

"Oh, sure, kiddo, I believe you. At least . . . well, you know I believe in banshees, right? It's just . . . you been

66

under a lot of pressure lately, worrying about exam school and stuff, and—"

Without a sniff of warning, eighteen hours' worth of pent-up anxiety burst from the depths of Conor's inner being. He stood there, wailing, arms at his side, not even trying to keep the tears and snot from running down his face. He hated crying in front of Grump—impossible as it was, he wanted Grump to think he was brave, not a disgrace to the O'Neills, who used to be kings.

He'd figured Grump—with his Ireland birthmark, a red spot for Dublin—would believe him without question.

Grump didn't move, didn't bustle over to pat Conor on the back and tell him it was all right. That wasn't Grump's way. He sat in his easy chair picking glue off his skin until Conor ran out of tears, then beckoned him to a footstool and handed him a box of tissues.

"If y-you don't believe me, I don't know what to do." Conor blew his nose.

"The good thing," Grump said, "is that I seriously doubt you have a brain tumor. You're tying yourself up in knots about this Latin School baloney. If the idea of going there bothers you so much, kiddo, there's no reason you have to go. You got the O'Neill Spark—you'll do great wherever you are."

"Dad wants me to go to Latin School and then BC."

"Your pop wants a lot of things he ain't got. So does your mum. They're good people, hardworking. But"—

Grump leaned forward and gazed earnestly into Conor's face—"they ain't you." He sat back as if he'd said something monumental. He focused on the glue again.

"Dad says I need to get out there."

"Well, he's right about that. You gotta get out there and bend some rules."

"*You* think I need to get out there?" Double-crossed again.

Grump blew air out his nose. "Oh, cripes. 'Out there' don't necessarily mean Latin School. Anyways, you gotta stop listening to everybody else tell you what to do, including me." He ruffled Conor's hair. "Quit worrying, kiddo. It'll all work out. Out of curiosity, what's this flute you keep hearing?"

Conor gulped back his misery and told Grump about running into moon-dappled woods, fire and music behind him. About the sword scabbard. The girl screaming.

"Huh." Grump rolled the picked-off glue into a little ball between thumb and finger, concentrating on it, making it perfect. "And this scabbard, you say it had spirals and stuff on it? Did they look like anything in particular?"

Conor shut his eyes to recall it. "Not really. Some of them might have looked sort of, I dunno, like a duck or something. There's an eye and kind of a beak. It has a hat on."

"Here." Grump dug for his notebook and pencil, which he kept stuffed under his chair cushion in case of brilliant ideas. "See if you can draw it."

Conor leaned over the table next to Grump's chair and did his best. A thin line in a single spiral, thickening into something like a bird's head in the center, with an eye and an upward-curving beak, sort of a fat torpedo shape at the top of the head.

"Yep. That's a bird all right." Grump braced his skinny arms to heave his belly out of the chair. He shuffled to the bookcase and ruminated, selected a book, leafed through it. "Ha." He held the book out to Conor.

And there, in a color plate, was the scabbard from Conor's dream. The caption read, "Bronze Scabbard, Armagh, c. fifth century. Crested bird-head design."

"That's it! That's the scabbard!"

"You must've seen it in this book," Grump said.

"I've never looked at this book. Really, Grump. I swear."

"Kiddo, you could've come in here when I had it lying around. You could've been five or something, and it stuck with you."

Conor looked closer at the photo. It was the scabbard, no question. Maybe Grump was right and he'd seen this book before. "What's Armagh?"

"It's a city in Ulster, northern Ireland." Grump replaced the book on its shelf and plunked back down in his easy chair.

"Where the Uí Néill and the Dál Fiatach lived." He was careful to pronounce *Uí Néill* the way Ashling did, *Ee Nay-ill,* and to add the guttural sound at the end of *Dál Fiatach.*

Grump blinked. "Where'd you learn about them?"

"In a book at school. I looked it up today, because—"

"No, but how'd you learn how to say those names? They ain't pronounced the way they look."

"The banshee, Ashling. She said she's one of the Uí Néill. Or she was, when she was alive. She got killed by the Dál Fiatach. They put an ax in her head. And the Lady kept her as a servant."

Grump eyed Conor as if he were an unstable batch of rocket fuel. "The Lady. You didn't read that in any book at school. And I know I never told you about her, because your pop would have my hide."

"Grump, I told you. The banshee's real. She's in my room, playing with the zipper on my windbreaker."

"You sure she floats and goes invisible and all that? She's not some smart Irish girl who climbed in the window?"

"I saw the streetlight right through her."

"Huh." Grump furrowed his brow at the photographs on the mantelpiece: one of Conor's dad at age ten, face aglow, showing off his straight-A report card. One of Conor's gramma. And that other picture, the one of the little girl. Grump threw his ball of glue into the fireplace. "Cripes. Must be my time."

"What time? Whaddaya mean, Grump?"

Grump looked straight at him, and Conor realized what he'd been trying not to know, ever since last night. "No.

It's not you. It can't be you." To his shame, he started to snuffle all over again.

Grump held out the box of tissues. "Holy macaroni, kiddo—you'd rather it was Glennie? Or your mum or your pop?"

"I d-don't want it to be anybody."

"Me neither. But it's my time if it's anyone's, and there's no arguing with the Lady. I learned that good enough when Jeannie died."

No, no, no . . . I am Conor O'Neill, and I'm in 36B Crumlin Street . . .

The old man gripped Conor's shoulder. "Kiddo. I know we don't talk about her much, but I think I gotta tell you about when we lost our Jeannie. Think you can handle it?"

Conor nodded. He always felt braver with Grump's hand on his shoulder.

But Grump took his hand away. Leaning back, he gazed up at the faded picture of a black-haired five-year-old on the mantel. "We were at the playground, see, and my little Jeannie fell off the swings and hit her head. I had my back to her, talking to Kavanagh, so I didn't see her fall." He closed his eyes. "But I still see the blood and her just lying there, not even crying."

He rubbed a hand over his face and took a shaky breath. "O-o-okay. Somebody calls the ambulance, and your gramma gets there and I'm standing around because I don't know what to do. And there's this shriek, like nothing you ever heard. Everybody's thinking it's an owl or something that flies because it came from overhead. I look up and a wisp of something white disappears behind the trees."

Conor wished he had Grump's hand on his shoulder again.

"Your gramma goes off with my little Jeannie in the ambulance. I'm leaving the park with Brian—your pop, he was six then—and I see this redheaded girl standing outside the fence. She has on a green dress and a red cape, which she's using to wipe the tears off her face. She looks me right in the eye. And then she disappears, *poof.* Brian never even noticed her. I thought I'd gone nuts."

It sounded like Ashling. "Grump, this is supposed to be Ashling's first death."

"Maybe it wasn't her. But it was somebody. I couldn't think of nothing else for months after that. Your gramma wanted no part of it, but the first time I got the money together I went to Ireland to find out what I could. And of course I figured out the girl was a banshee. I spent my life waiting for one of 'em to show up again." He rubbed at the stubble on his chin, deep in thought. "Never heard one when your gramma died. Maybe because she only *married* an O'Neill."

"Do you think you can get Ashling to tell us who the Death is?" Conor felt a ridiculous surge of hope. "Maybe it was Gramma and the banshee's just late getting here."

Grump gave him a tired smile. "Nice try, kiddo. I don't think banshees fall behind like that. Anyways . . ." He swallowed. "See, I'm content to die—honest, I am—but I ain't quite ready to see the banshee's face."

"Maybe later."

Grump looked him straight in the eye. "Listen, kiddo: Banshees don't stick around long. The Death'll be soon. *My* death, with any luck."

"Grump." Conor ran out of words.

Silence fell on them like a blanket. As they sat and watched Crumlin Street darken outside the front windows, Conor lost track of how long he'd been there. Grump switched on the light next to his chair. Then the front door slammed at 36A, and Glennie whammed her hand on Grump's door. "Supper!" she yelled, then slammed back where she came from.

Grump gave Conor's shoulder a friendly slap and pushed out of the chair again. "I gotta wash up. I'll see you over there."

"I'm not letting you die," Conor said.

"It ain't your decision."

At supper, Conor got into a fight with Grump about how much butter he put on his bread. "What about me?" Dad said. "I got arteries, too, you know."

Conor couldn't think of what to say, but Grump rose to the occasion. "Conor's a weirdo," Grump said.

When Conor went upstairs after supper, Ashling had the

door open a crack, sniffing. "That smells very good. What is it?"

"Canned ravioli." *Don't get too friendly. She's here for Grump.*

Ashling returned to the beanbag chair and her Trivial Pursuit cards. To take his mind off his troubles, Conor settled into his homework—he had social studies, language arts, and pre-algebra. Usually, he and Javier texted a bit while they did homework, but tonight Javier probably hated him. He'd have to blow algebra all by himself. Still, he took his cell phone out of his backpack and turned it on, just in case.

When Conor thought about it, he had to admit he hadn't been a very good friend that day.

Something was humming in the silent room. Too early in the year for a mosquito. He almost thought it was that flute tune, but it was so faint he couldn't be sure.

Okay, this has got to be my imagination. He did his best to ignore it, and actually managed to do his algebra with six problems in such a tangle of x's and y's that his teacher would never unravel them. He closed his book with a sigh. Ashling laid down a fan of Trivial Pursuit cards at her side. "You are worried, Conor-boy," she said.

"It's my grandfather, isn't it?"

"Conor-boy, I don't know who it is. I keep telling you." She scooched closer, her face serious. "Anyway, death is a glorious thing, especially in battle. And it's not the end. Why would you fear it?"

The question was so surprising that it took him a minute to think up an answer. "For one thing, it hurts. Plus, you never see your family again. Also, what if you get reborn as a squid?"

"It's sickness that hurts, not death. And you may be happy as a squid."

"You're still a squid. And I don't care what part of it hurts, it still hurts."

"Maybe you'd be a bird. That would be a wonder."

"Okay, but what about missing my family?"

"You won't remember that you miss them. At least"— her gaze dropped to the Trivial Pursuit cards on the floor— "at least not if you're reborn. And even if you stay with the Lady, as I did, the memories fade." She got interested in rearranging the cards, head bent so Conor could only see her nose and the top of her red head.

"Huh," he said softly. "You *do* miss your family."

She bundled the cards into a stack on the floor to tidy them. "Miss them? I barely remember them."

Conor slid off his desk chair and hunkered down next to her. Something glistened on her cheek. "I didn't know banshees could just plain cry."

"Nor did I." She swiped at her cheek. "Potent Mother Maeve. Must be because I have a body again. I've not done this for centuries." A tear ran down the other cheek. She let it go. "I am almost enjoying it."

"How long since you saw anyone from your family?"

"I saw my father . . . oh, it must be many hundreds of years ago. I don't know the numbers." She flipped the top card off her Trivial Pursuit stack and made a show of studying it, although Conor doubted she even saw it. "I tell myself stories about my life—how I died, that I was betrothed to a man who stank, how I danced with . . . Well, never mind that. But I can't remember how it *felt*: the touch of my mother's hand, the sound of the children's voices. I know there was pain and sorrow, but it's all so distant from me now."

"That's good, isn't it?"

She smiled thinly. "Yes, I suppose. But the joys are distant, too."

There was that mosquito-flute sound again. Conor tried to shake it out of his head, but failed. "What *is* that music? It's driving me nuts."

"What music?" Ashling sounded subdued.

"Shh. Listen. Don't you hear it? And . . . and there it is, that sweet, smoky smell."

Ashling looked up. "I do smell smoke—is it not your own cooking fire?"

Conor shook his head. "You don't hear the music?"

"No, none at all."

"It's *constant*." Conor shut his eyes to catch the tune. Sure enough, it was the same one he'd been hearing all day. He whistled it.

She wrinkled her forehead. "I used to know that tune,

but I can't remember . . . Where did you hear it?"

"I told you. It's in my head and I can't get rid of it."

"Whistle it again."

He did.

She shook her head. "No. I cannot remember. Perhaps something I heard from my father . . . I don't know."

"What happened to your father, anyways?"

Ashling didn't answer, but whistled the flute tune under her breath.

"Hey." Conor jiggled her elbow. "I asked, what happened to your father?"

She gave her head a shake. "I don't know where he is. I am sure he's been sent back again and again. He could be you for all I know."

"Holy macaroni." He was just Conor . . . Could he be Maedoc, too? A big hairy guy in furs, who fought with a sword and had his eyebrows under control—how could that guy be him?

"Or maybe not." Ashling took his chin in her hand and gazed into his eyes—for a minute, the whole world was merry blue with wedges of gray. Her breath was on his cheek, smelling like woodsmoke but also the fresh air when you came out of the subway. His stomach gurgled.

Ashling let go of his chin.

"So?" Conor said.

She fumbled for her comb. "You may be somebody, but

I don't know who." She started unbraiding her hair. She wouldn't say anything more.

Conor changed into his pajamas in the bathroom, head spinning. Who *was* he? And who was Ashling—a monster threatening his family, or a girl who missed her dad?

It was too much; he couldn't figure it out; it was no fair that he was going through all this. No fair at all.

But one thing was almost certain: Whatever she was, monster or girl, Ashling had come for Grump.

She wasn't going to get him. He, Conor O'Neill—who used to be somebody else, maybe somebody brave—he would not allow it.

Chapter Six

There are drums behind the flutes. He moves closer, watching the dancers circle a bonfire, hand in hand. There is Ashling's red head—she's holding hands with a woman on one side, a brawny young man on the other. Radiant with firelight and happiness, Ashling smiles up at the young man, who smiles back.

She should stop dancing, leave that traitorous pig behind, come to stand safely at his side.

The drums thunder. The dancers circle. He stays where he is, watching, his blood beginning to burn.

"What did Sir Walter Raleigh lose in 1618?"

Conor sat bolt upright and tried to focus on Ashling's grin, her tousled head sticking out from the game cupboard.

"His head!" Ashling crowed. "What's the longest—"

"Ashling," Conor croaked. "Give it a rest, okay? I have to go to school."

"All right then. What were President John F. Kennedy's last words?"

"Do you think you might be a little obsessed with death?"

"He said, 'My God, I'm hit.'"

Reincarnated hairy guy or not, Conor left the house with his bike helmet on. Glennie pretended she wasn't with him as they walked to the corner. Which was fine with him—today's temporary tattoo was a large black widow spider on her cheek, to spite him.

Javier rode the bus with James and Mohamed again, so Conor didn't get a chance to apologize for being a bad friend until they were at their lockers.

"That's okay." Javier didn't take his head out of his locker. "Maybe there's something wrong with your brain after all." He walked off to homeroom without waiting.

It was a long morning, a stony-faced Javier two or three seats away in every class. At their usual lunch table of seventh-grade boys, he and Conor sat at opposite ends.

Before they were even halfway through their American chop suey, Andy walked by and snagged the chocolate cupcake off Javier's tray. The entire table froze. Javier just sat there, lips pursed, poking at his chop suey as if examining some insect habitat.

Conor got up, walked over to Andy's table. Andy grinned at him, his mouth full of cupcake. "That's attractive," Conor said, and grabbed Andy's own cupcake off his tray. He walked back to his table with body, honor, and cupcake intact.

It was a tricky moment, handing the cupcake to its rightful owner. Everybody knew that Javier should have been the one to take it from Andy. Conor thought for a second that Javier might refuse to accept it from him.

Andy now had had time to swallow. "Hey, Pixie-poop," he yelled, voice hoarse with frosting. "Where's your helmet?"

The rims of Conor's ears caught fire. Javier's mouth quirked up at one corner. "Ignore him."

"I am," Conor said.

Javier took the cupcake from Conor. "Not sure I want this thing," he announced in a loud voice. "It might have lice."

"Nah," Ifraho said. "Lice hate chocolate."

"Eat it," Conor said. "Chocolate feeds brain cells and I need help with pre-algebra." *Help blowing pre-algebra,* he thought. Javier, thinking the same thing, choked slightly on his first bite of cupcake.

They walked back to class together.

Conor didn't call home at all that day, although he kept wanting to. After school, instead of going to the lunchroom for Adventure Boys, he went back to the library. He did an Internet search for "how to get rid of a banshee."

He got a lot of video game answers at first, but after re-Googling a few times he found stories about old Irish guys shooting at banshees or otherwise driving them away from their loved ones. The loved ones always died anyway.

He got sidetracked into the Greek myth of Persephone,

who had to stay in Hades, the land of the dead, three months of every year because she ate three pomegranate seeds. He thought about buying a pomegranate to see if that would send Ashling back to her version of Hades, but came to the conclusion that eating food from a place probably meant you had to stay there. *Don't feed her. She'll be in the game cupboard forever.*

He read and read, searching for anything that would help. His nose was three inches from the screen, hand cramped on the mouse.

"Banshees again?" The shock of Javier's voice just about drove Conor's spine through the top of his head. "Is there some new game I don't know about?"

"Holy macaroni, creep up on somebody."

"I didn't creep." Javier pulled up a chair and sat down. "You're the one who's acting weird, remember?"

"I'm not acting *that* weird."

Javier picked up the bicycle helmet and presented it as Exhibit A.

Conor said, "There's something wrong with my brain, remember?"

"Yeah, right."

Javier-silence. Conor went back to surfing for banshees, but it was like trying to act normal with a black hole sitting next to you.

At last, Javier said, "Mr. Phillips wants to know how you're doing with American heritage."

"I got a book out. I'm working on it."

More Javier-silence. Then: "This is nuts. Conor, why are you freaking out about banshees?"

He didn't believe me before. He won't now. But then Conor had a brainstorm. "I'm making up a game about them."

The black hole closed with a snap. "You are? That's great, why didn't you say so?" Javier scooched his chair closer. "I could write the computer code. I got that book for my birthday."

"Yeah. Cool."

"This is awesome. It could be in the Land of Shanaya, right? I could help with the story line if you want."

It was getting late. Conor logged off the Internet, grabbed his backpack and helmet. "C'mon. Let's go home."

"Did you ever see *Darby O'Gill and the Little People*?" Javier asked as their bus lumbered away from the curb. "It's this old, old movie about this Irish guy, and a banshee comes for his daughter. He has a wish left over from a leprechaun and he wishes to die instead of her. Then the leprechaun rescues him from the death coach."

"I don't think I believe in leprechauns."

"Well, you don't believe in banshees either."

"No. Right." Conor leaned the front of his helmet against the window and watched a paper cup dance down the windy sidewalk. A kid caught up with it, stomped it flat, and left it there.

Javier-silence, a long one. Then: "You're not really making up a game, are you?"

"No."

The bus hit a pothole and the other passengers hooted at the driver, who was laughing. This was good, because the noise swallowed up the silence from the other half of the seat. But the silence was still there when everybody calmed down.

Then: "I don't see why you have to lie about it," Javier said.

"Hey, I didn't ask you to butt in." Conor closed his eyes, wished for a time machine to take him back to Tuesday. "Go . . . go talk to Olivia about her dance poster and leave me alone, okay?"

"Jerk."

They were silent the rest of the way home, a double black hole. They got off the bus without a word, parted with neither good-byes nor promises of texting.

Conor couldn't worry about Javier. Halfway home, he stopped dead (but not really) and thought about Darby O'Gill. It came to him what a brave O'Neill would do—like Darby, he would go to the Other Land in place of his loved one.

Maybe Ashling would find a way to make death not hurt.

If the loved one was Glennie, it made sense that her older brother would step up to protect her. If it was

Grump, though . . . Even Conor had to admit that there was something unnatural about a kid taking the place of an old man.

But wasn't that an excuse? Could he stand by and watch Grump die, knowing he could have prevented it? Wouldn't he hate himself the rest of his life?

Darby O'Gill stayed on his mind as he walked the rest of the way home.

When he entered his room, the world was upside down.

Or Ashling was, anyway. She was standing on the ceiling, braid dangling straight down, tunic skirt tucked between her knees. She was tossing Trivial Pursuit cards into the wastebasket, missing every third time because she was barely aiming.

"Kill something," she said as Conor closed the door. "I am going mad. I have read most of these little skins and even some of those things." She pointed at his bookcase.

"Why didn't you go out?"

"You didn't want me at your school." Her tone was sulky. "And I can't walk about attracting attention, and I can only wish myself where I've been before or if I've seen a picture. I went there"—she pointed to his Grand Canyon poster—"but people were everywhere and they screamed when I made myself visible. I am ready to keen and go home. Someone has to die *now*."

"Nobody's dying. At least . . . listen, Ashling. What if I

told you to take me instead of whoever it really is. Could you do that?"

"No." Ashling drifted down from the ceiling, righting herself slowly until her feet touched the rug. Her braid was coming apart. "No, I cannot do that."

"Why not? Darby O'Gill did it."

"Who is Darby O'Gill?"

"He's this guy from your country, Ireland."

"I don't know Ireland. My country was Uladh." As the library book said, she pronounced it *Ull-oo*.

"It's called Ulster now, and it's part of Ireland. Anyways, this guy's daughter was dying, and he had a wish from a leprechaun, so he wished he could take her place."

"Do you have a wish from a leprechaun?"

"No."

"There you are, then." She began to unbraid her hair. "Conor-boy, I cannot take the wrong person to the Lady. I don't make the decision, and anyway that is not the bargain I made to get my life back. Besides . . ." She bit her lip and got out her comb.

"Besides, it could be me, anyways, is that what you're thinking?"

She didn't answer, only combed. Conor watched her, too stupefied to work on his Land of Shanaya map or start his homework. As the comb moved through Ashling's hair, chaos became order. She redid her braid, the green ribbon woven just so.

He could see why she did it. It was calming.

Ashling gave her braid a final tug and tossed it over her shoulder. "It doesn't matter who it is, of course. Makes no difference to me. No difference at all. None."

Conor went downstairs for supper, then came back up to describe it for Ashling. For someone who didn't eat, Ashling was awfully interested in food, even when it was fish sticks. She went into her cupboard while he did homework—not all of it and none of it well. Finally he gave up, took out his map notebook, and started giving the Land of Shanaya its carnivorous spruce trees. He got so involved—trees with mouths turned out to be a hoot to draw—that he barely noticed when Ashling came out of the cupboard and stood by him, watching.

"What is that you're making?" she asked.

His pencil skipped, and the tree he was working on got an extra-wide maw. It looked amazing.

"This is a little like the pictures on your wall," Ashling said, "which you have never explained."

"They're maps. And I'm drawing one. With carnivorous—that's meat-eating—spruce trees."

"Maps?" She shook her head, baffled.

"A map shows you where you are." He pulled her over to his map of the United States. "See there? That red dot is South Boston; that's where we are right this minute. And see, if we went west—toward the sunset—we'd reach Albany and then Buffalo and Lake Erie."

She wrinkled up her face as if he were talking algebra.

"It's a . . . a picture, like what you'd see if you were a bird, high, high, high up in the air," he said desperately.

Her face cleared. "Ah. So what place are you making?" She dragged him back to his desk.

"It's a place I thought up in my head. It doesn't exist."

"You are making trees with mouths."

"Carnivorous spruce trees. They're not real either. I . . . thought they'd be fun."

She was silent, studying his work. "It is like the tales the bards told."

"It's not a tale. It's a place."

"Yes, but such a place! Danu, the mother goddess herself, would be honored to live in this land you have made."

Conor flushed with pleasure, even though he had no idea who this Danu was. "There's Twelve Mountains of the Skull and an antigravity vehicle port," he pointed out, in case she hadn't noticed. Ashling nodded solemnly.

But then she asked: "What is 'fun'?"

"Huh?"

"You said you put mouths on the trees for fun. I never heard that word."

He didn't know what to say. It was like describing how to breathe. "If something's fun, you like doing it. Fun is what you like to do best."

"I liked to slaughter hogs."

"That's disgusting."

"Better than slaughtering a cow. Cows are sweet."

"You danced. That seems more like fun to me."

"How do you know I danced?"

How *did* he know? *Oh right. That was a dream.* But also . . . "You talked about it."

"I never danced." She turned on her heel and crawled back into her cupboard, closing the door behind her.

"Sorry," he called to her, although he didn't know why.

"Sorry about what?" Glennie said through the door, on her way to the bathroom.

"Nothing. I—uh—I was talking on the phone."

"Da-ad, Conor's talking on the phone after eight thirty."

He could lose his cell phone for doing that. Conor scrambled out to the top of the stairs. "It was just a quick call," he yelled. "I'm not talking anymore."

His father appeared below. "Who was it, some girl?" He'd been asking questions like that ever since Conor turned twelve. They made Conor's stomach curl up..

"No. It was . . . it was Javier about pre-algebra."

"I saw Javier and he said he wasn't talking to you." Glennie emerged from the bathroom, half smirk in place.

"Shut up," Conor said.

"Don't tell your sister to shut up," Dad said. "Start getting ready for bed, both of you. If you're still up when your mom comes home, I wouldn't want to be any of us."

When Conor got back to his room, Ashling was in the beanbag chair, flipping through Trivial Pursuit cards. "I beg your pardon. I did say I danced, and I do remember it. I was in a ring of people."

"Who were the people?"

She shrugged. "It . . . I think it was at Beltine, after we ran the cattle through the fires. Many of us danced."

"You ran cattle through *fire*?"

"Between rows of fire, witless one. To protect the beasts for the grazing season."

His dream at school. He'd heard cattle lowing when it started.

"My father was not pleased that I danced, because I was betrothed to our neighbor." Ashling added a card to a stack of favorites at her feet, then added matter-of-factly, "The neighbor was old and bad-tempered, and his mouth smelled of rot and he never bathed. But he would have died in a few years, and I would have had his cattle to add to my own."

"*That's* disgusting."

She looked up from her cards. "This is the second time you've said that about my life. Mark this, boy—we slaughtered hogs to eat, and we married to improve our fortunes." She stood up, dignified. "I have no need of your approval."

"Yeah, but . . . you didn't even like this neighbor guy, did you?"

"I do not remember what I felt." Ashling marched back to her cupboard, crawled in, slammed the door behind her.

This time, Conor didn't make the mistake of saying he was sorry.

As he lay in bed later, the mosquito-like flute music came back with its whiff of woodsmoke. He closed his eyes and saw people silhouetted by flames, flickering . . . flickering . . .

Bellowing, drunken hulks of men grapple in the heat of the ceremonial fires, roaring insults, pushing apart so they have room to slash at one another with swords. Silhouetted against the dying flames, three brave souls play flutes, hoping to calm the fighters, although that has never worked before. In a pen nearby, cattle moan and snort.

He stands panting at the edge of light, the dark and the spirits at his back. He scans the shadows for Aengus, the pig, the traitor. His blood burns.

Why did they haul him away from the fight? He was winning. Aengus was on the ground, squirming like a pig to dodge his blade.

The fires are burning down, scenting the air with pitch and apple. Someone half his size is next to him. He smiles down at her.

The next morning, Conor awoke with woodsmoke in his nostrils. *Her hand on my heart,* he thought.

And then he thought, *Huh?*

He remembered most of the dream, still felt the anger that coursed through him. Who was Aengus and why was he a traitor? For that matter, who was *he,* the angry man in the shadows?

There was nothing in the dream about a hand on a heart.

He almost woke up Ashling to ask her about it, but he was late. He got dressed, gobbled breakfast, pelted for the door, grabbed his helmet . . . and was struck full-on by the futility of it all. He hung the helmet back up on its hook and ran after Glennie to the corner.

He regretted his decision the minute the bus door closed, and actually let out a shriek when the driver slammed on the brakes to avoid an aggressive Volkswagen on Dorchester Street.

"Jeez, Conor," said Sean Allen, who was sitting with him. "It was better when you had the helmet on."

Javier never even glanced back at him. He talked quietly with Mohamed, who also didn't look back. Conor was sure they were talking about him.

He did not, *did not,* call anyone in his family that morning. He was in social studies, trying not to think, when fate came to find him.

Mr. Rose was standing by the window when something outside caught his attention. "Conor, is that your cousin out there?" Obviously he'd been talking to Ms. Alexis. "Doesn't she go to school somewhere?"

"Uh, no. She's . . . she's visiting. From Ireland."

"Why didn't she come to school with you?"

"Uh . . . she . . . uh."

Mr. Rose marched to the classroom phone and punched in a number, then took the receiver out into the hall the way he always did when he might be talking about something tricky. He was beaming when he came back in.

"The principal says she can join us while she's here. You'll have to go to the office later and sign her in, but for now just bring her up so we can get back to work."

"Bring her *up*?" How did this happen? How in a million years could it be that Conor O'Neill was bringing a death-wielding banshee into his seventh-grade social studies class?

"Yes, Conor. Go now. Please."

When Mr. Rose said "Please," there was no hope left.

Ashling ran to him when he beckoned from the door. She was wearing her regular clothes—long green tunic, red cloak, rough leather shoes. But she'd added thick, bright pink lipstick—his mother's color—smearing some of it on her cheeks. She had on so much eye makeup she looked like somebody'd punched her twice. It was a misty day, and black streaks ran down her cheeks.

"I forgive you for saying I was disgusting," she said.

"What the heck is all that on your face?"

"I have seen this on the Dear Departed. It is the fashion amongst living women. I wish to fit in."

"It's melting all over you. Plus, what are you doing here again? I thought you were supposed to stay home."

"Yes, yes, I am. But the Lady will never find out. I know you don't want me here, and I will be very discreet. How can I sit there waiting when all this is out here?" Ashling gestured grandly at the ancient brick building and the row of wooden houses across the street. "I am quite able to pretend I am not what I am. I am the best liar of my family."

"Fine. I'm taking you inside. But stop in the girls' room and wipe that junk off your face."

As he waited outside the girls' restroom on the second-floor landing, he made a mental list of what she had to know before they got to his classroom. Cousin. From Ireland. Visiting. Not dead. Not here to make anyone else dead.

She probably shouldn't discuss being engaged to a man with bad breath, or slaughtering hogs.

Why am I so worried about people knowing what she is? Maybe he could tell everyone. Maybe Mr. Rose could suggest some way to prevent the Death.

Ashling emerged, the streaks gone from her cheeks but eyes still black-ringed and lips as pink as ever. "I must stay secret, you know, so the Lady does not hear of this." She was so cheery she might have been discussing hog slaughter. "If you tell your friends what I am, I will turn into a wraith and kill them all."

Stop thinking she's a girl, Conor thought. *She's a monster.* "You can't make yourself turn into a wraith when nobody's dying."

"I might be able to. I don't know. Do you want to find out?" She started up the next flight of stairs and tripped. She briefly became invisible.

"You disappeared for a second," Conor said.

"*Ach.* I must have been distracted."

Conor didn't want to follow her. He didn't want to take her into his class, spend the day wondering if she was going to disappear or kill everyone. He put one foot in front of the other and there he was, at the top of the stairs. "We'll say you're my cousin from Ireland."

"Cousin from *Uladh.*"

"It's called Ulster." And there was the classroom door.

Chapter Seven

"Ah yes," Mr. Rose said when the introductions were over. "Ulster, class, is in northern Ireland, and part of it still belongs to the United Kingdom." He pulled down a rolled-up map by the blackboard to show them.

"Ulster does not belong to any other kingdom," Ashling said. "Ulster is its own kingdom, the bravest and most beautiful of them all."

Mr. Rose grinned as if she'd made a joke. "A patriot! Makayla, perhaps you'd switch chairs so Ashling can sit next to her cousin."

In full data-collection mode, Javier was eyeing Ashling. "What is she, like, a hippie?" he whispered loudly to Katherine Foster as Conor sat down. Katherine giggled. "And what's all that on her face?"

Class that day was about Abraham Lincoln. Five minutes later, when Mr. Rose was talking about Lincoln being a lawyer in Springfield, Illinois, Ashling spoke up without raising her hand. "How many people were executed for Abraham Lincoln's assassination?"

Mr. Rose gaped at her, shifting gears. "Well, Ashling, I don't know that off the top of my head. I'll be happy to find out—"

"Four," Ashling said. "Executed means killed."

"Well, yes, it's a punishment for a particularly bad crime. In the past, criminals were hanged or—"

"Got an ax through the head. That is very painful."

"Well, yes, I suppose it must—"

"Assassination also means killing."

"Yes. It's killing an important person, a head of state or the like."

"With an ax through the head," Ashling said with authority.

"Not usually. You know, Ashling, on this side of the pond we raise our ha—"

"An ax through the head does not tickle."

"Thank you, Ashling. Now, in 1837, Springfield, Illinois, was—"

"What World War I battle saw sixty thousand troops killed on the first day?"

"The Battle of the Somme," Mr. Rose said, triumphant at last.

So it went all the way through social studies class, until Mr. Rose obviously was thinking dark thoughts about axes in relation to heads. When the bell rang for second period, Ashling screamed, "Banshee!" and dove under her desk. "How silly," she said, emerging. "As if I'm not one mysel—"

"Math class!" Conor yelled.

"Relax, Conor," said Mr. Rose.

Easy for him to say.

"Your cousin's cool," Ricky Desmond said as they left class. Ricky hadn't spoken to Conor since he'd done all that Latin School teasing the day before. Three other classmates smiled at him in the hallway. Perhaps there were advantages to impending mass destruction.

Nevertheless, Conor pulled Ashling into a corner by the fire doors. "This isn't fair," he whispered furiously. "You say you have to stay secret and then you go talking about axes and banshees and stuff."

"Relax, Conor." She mimicked Mr. Rose's exact tone. "None of that tells anyone what I am."

"It tells them you're a total freak. They'll start asking questions about you and what will I say?"

"That's your trouble, Conor-boy, not mine." Ashling set off after the tail end of the seventh grade, heading for math class. Conor caught up with her and whispered frantic instructions about the importance of raising her hand and not interrupting and, in general, shutting up.

"Shut up, yourself, Conor-boy." Ashling swept into Mrs. Namja's classroom as if she belonged there rather than on some fifth-century windswept bog.

Pre-algebra rendered Ashling incapable of speech. Conor had almost started to calm down when he and Javier got called to the board to do equations. Javier aced his. Conor was so distracted that he aced his, too.

"Well, good for you, Conor," Mrs. Namja said. "Glad to see you concentrating again. This stuff is bound to be on the high school exams next fall."

High school exams. Big deal. Hardly anyone ever died taking them.

"You did that task very well," Ashling commented as the class disbanded for lunch.

"Why should you care?" Probably he should be more polite to the death-wielding banshee, Conor reflected.

"What are exams?"

"Tests we have to take if we want to go to a special school."

"Tests of courage, strength, and agility?"

"No. We have to do math and reading and other things."

"Oh, that's all right then. You can do that." She clearly had no confidence in Conor's courage, strength, and agility. Which was fine, because neither did Conor.

They headed down the stairs to the lunchroom. "Will your school be for making maps?" Ashling asked.

The idea was so striking that Conor didn't answer right off.

"You should apprentice to a maker of maps," Ashling continued. "I knew an apprentice smith, and he was as good as his own father. Or at least he said he was."

"I don't think there are apprentice mapmakers."

"Oh, there must be. There are apprentices for everything." Ashling stopped in her tracks on the second-floor landing as Joey Mandrell sipped from the drinking fountain by the boys' room. "Potent Mother Maeve! There's a cunning thing." She had to take a drink of water before she'd move on. It went up her nose, which made her braid stand straight in the air. Conor grabbed it and held it down.

His arm buzzed. His own feet lifted off the floor.

He let go and his feet thumped back down right away, but not before Paula Reilly saw it happen and halted in her tracks.

"Did you . . . ?" Paula said.

"The science homework?" Conor said. "Yeah, but I bet it's all wrong."

Paula gave her head a shake and continued downstairs without another word.

"We can sit by ourselves for lunch," Conor said when Ashling had finished coughing and snorting and flickering out of sight.

"No." Ashling jutted out her jaw, Glennie-style. "I want to sit with others and see what school is really like. I've heard about it from so many dead mouths."

"Will you stop saying things like that?" Conor glanced around to see if anyone had overheard.

"Girls and boys our age, you know. They come before the Lady, and they say, 'But I have school tomorrow!' And the Lady tells them they're dead, and they'll be sent back as mere babes—or harts or hares, who knows. You should see their faces."

Conor wondered what would happen if he stuffed Ashling into a locker.

In the lunchroom, Javier was already at their regular table, ignoring him. Conor steered a reluctant Ashling to a table in the corner and left her there while he went through the line. He groaned out loud when he emerged to find Marissa Babcock and Olivia Kim sitting with her, eager to get to know the Irish girl who dressed like a hippie.

"Oooo." Ashling eyed Marissa's lunch tray. "What is that?"

"Macaroni and cheese," Marissa said.

"Holy macaroni," Ashling said.

"It's awesome." Olivia dug in to her own mac and cheese. "Aren't you eating?"

"*Awe*some." Ashling rolled the word around in her mouth like food.

Marissa held out a forkful of macaroni. Ashling sniffed it. "Awesome." She sneezed and disappeared from the waist down. None of the kids noticed, but one of the cooks dropped an entire tray of fruit cocktail.

Marissa inspected her forkful of macaroni, which might or might not have had Ashling's snot on it. "Want this?" she asked Ashling.

Ashling shook her head, holding her nose so she wouldn't sneeze again. "Thag you. Dot hu'gry."

"She ate a huge breakfast," Conor said.

Marissa unloaded the contaminated forkful on the edge of her plate and attacked the rest of her mac and cheese. Sinuses under control, Ashling watched every mouthful.

"Tell us about your home," Olivia said.

"Not much to tell," Conor said. "Right, Ashling?"

"It was beautiful." Ashling's eyes went misty. "Our house was round, on stilts in a pond. Any who wished to attack us needed a boat, so we were safe as eggs in a nest unless we went out with the cattle. No one lived better than we. No one."

"Attack you?" Olivia said. "Slightly emo, don't you think?"

"Eee-mo," Ashling said. "What is that?"

"It's when somebody's being too emotional," Olivia said. "I mean, *attack* is a pretty strong word for—"

"An ax in the head?"

"Oh, look," Conor said. "They have brownies for dessert."

He went to get one, which turned out to be a mistake: By the time he got back, Marissa had asked whether Ashling had a boyfriend.

"I was betrothed to our neighbor," Ashling said. "He stank, but he was very old and was always fighting, so he'd probably—"

"Ha-ha-ha, Ashling, stop joking around." Conor kicked her. Marissa and Olivia were wide-eyed.

"But he did stink," Ashling said. "His teeth were rotten."

"You . . . you were going to marry some old guy?" Marissa said. "No way."

"Yes, and when he died I would get his cattle," Ashling said.

"Ha-ha-ha-ha-ha," Conor said. "Quit it, Ashling. Jeez. What about the dancing guy, huh? What about him?"

"I danced with . . . Mother Maeve, I can't say his name. Oh, how could I forget his name?" Ashling slapped her hands to her cheeks. "He was part of my soul and now I can't . . . ah." Her face cleared. "Declan. His name was Declan. And I danced with another. Whose name was . . . Aengus, I think." She went silent, drawing something swirly on the table with her finger, then said, "Declan was to be a smith, like his father."

"How come you barely remember their names?" Olivia narrowed her eyes. "Do you do drugs?"

Brrrrriiiinnnng. Never had the end-of-lunch bell been so welcome. Olivia forgot about her question in the bustle of kids returning trays and lining up to leave. Upstairs after recess, prompted by a history display, Ashling imparted the information that World War II was waged by fifty-seven countries and, as an unrelated bonus, that the 1956 collision of the ocean liners *Stockholm* and *Andrea Doria* killed fifty-one people.

Science class was next. Conor was so exhausted that he forgot to avert his eyes when he walked past the poisonous spiders of the world poster by the door.

"Welcome, Ashling," Ms. Alexis said. "Take your seats, class. We have to chloroform our moths."

The moths fluttered about in a large bottle with a screen over the opening. Ms. Alexis dripped chloroform on a piece of cloth, pried up a corner of the screen, and dropped the cloth in. She reached for the screw-on cap that would block off the moths' air.

Conor, sitting next to the door, felt a chill breeze on his cheek. Startled, he glanced at Ashling, who showed him a face transformed in horror: mouth open, eyes wide and terrified, face pale and stretched out like Silly Putty.

"Oh, Conor-boy," Ashling whispered. "It is sad, so sad."

She was turning into a wraith in front of his entire class. Everybody would die.

He didn't stop to think. He grabbed Ashling's hand and bolted for the classroom door.

"Conor!" Ms. Alexis exclaimed. "What are you—?"

The door slammed behind them. The corridor was a blur—empty, thank heavens—then they reached the fire doors, and the stairs to the alley with the dumpsters. The outside door slammed behind them.

Ashling's hand was gone. He whipped around and saw the school's red bricks through a haze lifting skyward.

"Don't loo-oo-oo-oooook!" Ashling shrieked. Conor hunkered himself down as small as he could get, buried his face in his hands.

The keening began, and this time he thought there were words. *Gone, gone, gone, my love, my dove, ne'er again, ne'er again* . . . The sadness in the voice was wrenching, soul-tearing. Conor plugged his ears with his thumbs. What was the point of life if it ended like this?

He barely noticed when the sound stopped and the world went back to normal. A small hand shook his shoulder.

"Conor, Conor-boy, it is over. It's all over." He gazed into Ashling's eyes, blue as a summer sky. "I didn't mean to," she whispered. "Please believe me."

He almost did.

Almost. *She's a monster.*

The door banged open. Ms. Alexis. Mr. Rose. Dr. Dencill, the principal. "Conor," Ms. Alexis said. "What on *earth* . . . ?"

"I am very sorry." Ashling hauled Conor up by the arm. "It is my . . . my horrors. They come on me, you see."

"Claustrophobia?" Ms. Alexis said. "Or did it bother you that we were killing moths, dear?"

"Yes," Ashling said. "That."

"But why did Conor . . . ?"

Ashling gave a winning smile, brown tooth and all. "My horrors . . . they are well known in my family. Conor knew he had to get me outside."

"What was that shriek?" Mr. Rose asked. Dr. Dencill shuddered.

"That was a screech owl," Ms. Alexis said knowledge-ably.

"This time of day?" Dr. Dencill had been a science teacher once, too, and everybody knew she and Ms. Alexis didn't get along. "They're nocturnal."

"The *true* scientist," Ms. Alexis said, "knows that there are always exceptions."

Dr. Dencill's mouth went small. "Go back inside," she said.

"Yes, come along, Conor." Ms. Alexis held the door open for them all. "The moths are dead now. You and your cousin can sit by the window."

"Awesome," Ashling said.

By the time school ended, Ashling was an old hand at bells, intercoms, vinyl floor tiles, water fountains, pencil sharpeners, and shoelaces. Conor was worried about the bus, though. "It's big and sort of noisy," he whispered to Ashling as they made their way out of the school. "It has a motor, which means it moves without horses."

"Conor-boy, you forget that I sat outside two days ago. I saw many such vehicles."

But apparently she hadn't seen anything quite so big or quite so shiny and rumbly as a city bus. She stopped dead (in her case, really) on the sidewalk, blocking pedestrian traffic.

"Dude," James Johnson protested. Conor moved Ashling out of James's way, but couldn't do anything about her gaping mouth.

"Dude," she whispered. "It growls like a dragon."

"You had dragons?"

"No." She was trembling.

Conor lowered his voice. "It can't hurt you. You're, you know, dead."

"I don't *feel* dead."

"It's totally safe. Totally."

"Totally," Ashling whispered. She allowed Conor to lead her down the sidewalk and almost onto the bus before she halted again. "No way."

"Dude," James Johnson said out the window. "What's the holdup?"

"I am emo," Ashling whispered. "Dude."

"She doesn't think it looks safe," Conor said.

"Depends where you sit, Pixie-poop." Andy Watson shouldered past Ashling.

"Mr. O'Neill," said Mr. Quincy the bus driver. "We await your arrival."

Ashling whimpered as Conor took her hand and led her up the steps into the bus. He guided her to a seat in the back, shoving his way through thick silence and curious glances. Javier, sitting across the aisle with Mohamed, frowned slightly, analyzing.

It was only when the bus bounced out onto Dorchester Street that Conor recognized the next big hurdle. "My sister sometimes meets me at the bus stop," he whispered to Ashling. "I can't tell *her* you're our cousin. What'll I do?"

"Oh, see there!" Ashling pointed out the window. "A woman is attached to a tiny wolf by a string."

"Thanks for your help."

She gave him a Glennie-esque half smirk. But then her expression changed. "Oh no, that boy's swatting at something!"

"Hey!" Conor scrambled to his feet. "Leave it alone!"

"When did you go all Buddhist?" Javier muttered.

Several kids in the middle section of the bus were screaming and squirming as a maddened wasp dive-bombed people's heads. Jon Soucy, equally maddened, lunged after it, his skateboard magazine rolled up for the kill. Conor hauled himself forward seat by seat as the bus accelerated. Glancing back, he saw that, sure enough, Ashling's face was turning to Silly Putty.

He grabbed Jon's arm as it was sweeping down. It was a slow, silent struggle: Jon writhing to free his arm, Conor clinging to it with both hands. The wasp circled them once, then hurled itself against a window.

"Open the window!" Conor yelled to Marissa. "Let it out!"

The bus lurched to the curb. "What the heck's going on back there?" Mr. Quincy yelled.

Marissa slid her window open a crack. The wasp flew out. Jon got his arm free and started whacking Conor on the head with the skateboard magazine.

A meaty hand grabbed Jon by the collar, dragged him into the aisle. Another hand landed on Conor's shoulder, his knees almost buckling.

"Kids today," some guy said. Then the bus went silent.

"Mr. Soucy," Mr. Quincy said, "why are you beating Mr. O'Neill?"

Jon looked at Conor. Conor looked back. Everything was his fault, and they both knew it.

"There was a wasp," he said. "Jon was trying to kill it."

"Mr. O'Neill, I noticed you were wearing a helmet on my bus yesterday. Was that a comment on my driving?"

"No." Conor tried to think of something his helmet could have been commenting on, then remembered he already had a lie going. "I had a slight concussion."

"Mr. Soucy, is it a good idea to beat a person on the head when that person has had a slight concussion?"

"No."

"And if a wasp appears in this bus, what do we do about it?"

Jon, unable to move his head, rolled his eyes trying to see Mr. Quincy's face. "Kill it before it stings somebody?"

Mr. Quincy tightened his hand on Jon's collar. "No. We open a window and sit quietly until it goes away."

"An insect bite," said a voice from the back of the bus, "is nothing compared to an ax in the head."

"Very true." Mr. Quincy released Jon. "Everybody back in his seat."

Chapter Eight

As the bus trundled along, quiet and bug-free, Conor convinced himself that the wasp incident had delayed them enough so that Glennie would be safely home when he reached the bus stop. But as that stop drew near, there she was. Worse, she was standing with Tori Mullen, who'd ridden her bike home. Tori was telling Glennie something extremely interesting—it seemed to involve huge arm gestures and, at one point, pretending to run.

"Aw, cripes." There had to be a way to explain Ashling to Glennie, but all that came into Conor's head was a flute tune along with the smell of woodsmoke.

When he stepped onto the sidewalk, Glennie was waiting. Javier brushed past and headed to his house. Conor knew he should catch up and try to fix what was wrong between them. But there was Glennie, breathing hard through her nose.

"What's this about a claustrophobic cousin from Ireland?" Glennie looked Ashling up and down. "And she keeps talking about axes? *Northern* Ireland, Tori said." Her voice dropped. "Is she IRA?"

"What's—?" Ashling began.

"Hssshhht!" Conor's brain woke up. He plucked at his sister's sleeve. "Glennie," he whispered. "Nobody's supposed to know." Ashling narrowed her eyes at him. He winked at her, hoping winks meant the same thing sixteen hundred years ago.

"Listen, Glennie. Ashling—that's her name—she got smuggled in here. She landed at the docks." He waved his hand vaguely eastward, since he didn't know where Irish ships came in. Fortunately, Glennie didn't know either. "Her parents"—he locked Ashling's gaze with his, sending her a psychic "shut up" message—"were IRA. That's Irish Republican Army."

"I know what IRA means," Glennie said. "Why 'were'? Are they dead?"

"No . . . YES. Yes, they died. And even though there's no fighting over there anymore, there's still people mad at Ashling's family. So her relatives sent her over here, on the sly, see, to keep her out of harm's way."

He assessed Glennie's reaction so far. She gazed at Ashling with shining eyes. Glennie loved a rebel.

"And they asked Dad to take her in and he said no. They couldn't find another place for her, so they asked me if I'd sneak her in. And she's sleeping in the game cupboard, and she came to school with me today because . . .

because . . ." Why would anyone go to school if they didn't have to?

"Dude," Ashling said. "Because of my thirst for learning."

Conor held his breath. No one could believe all this.

But Glennie's eyes were soft. "And she's been locked in a container on a cargo ship for weeks and weeks, and her poor pale body . . ." Glennie blinked. Ashling was anything but poor and pale. "How come she's dressed like that?"

"It's what they're wearing in Ireland," Conor said. "So, listen, when we're home you have to pretend she doesn't exist. And don't talk about her at school, either, because we don't want anything getting home to Mom and Dad."

Glennie's mouth went pouty. "They know about her at *your* school."

"Well, they sort of have to, don't they, her being there and all? Because . . . of her thirst for learning." With a jolt, Conor realized that some of his teachers were on his father's mail route and would have a friendly chat with him at some point. And any one of his classmates could show up at his mother's clinic anytime. Plus, they'd talk at home. His parents had to hear something about Ashling eventually.

He wouldn't think about that now.

Glennie was doing enough thinking for both of them. "How will Ashling get upstairs? It's Friday. Mom doesn't have school until five."

"You go ahead," Conor said. "We'll figure it out."

"But I'm good at—"

"Off you go, girlie," Ashling said.

Glennie bristled at Ashling's tone, but then the romance of it all took hold and she did in fact go off.

"You go, too, Conor-boy," Ashling said. "I'll see myself in." She winked. "Totally."

Conor hoped a wink didn't mean anything fatal sixteen hundred years ago.

Ashling was already sitting in the beanbag chair by the time Conor had shed his jacket, given his mother a brief and fictitious account of what happened in school that day, and made his way upstairs. Glennie was sitting on his bed, gazing adoringly at the Irish rebel cousin and trying to get her to eat Fruity Foolers.

"I'm not hungry," Ashling said, but she watched carefully as Glennie popped an orange jelly bean into her mouth and scrunched up her face at the sourness. "Why do you eat it if it makes you do that?"

"She must have climbed up the fire escape," Glennie said. "She moves wicked fast."

"We have to do homework," Conor said, standing at the door.

"Ashling doesn't," Glennie said. "She's a guest. And anyways, it's Friday."

"I'm getting it over with now."

Glennie gaped at him—with good reason. Conor was

a past master of the Sunday evening homework panic. Conor held the door open for her in a significant fashion. She flounced out, leaving him alone with the monster who'd almost murdered the seventh grade.

"Why is there a rebellion in Uladh?" Ashling asked as soon as the door closed. "Has Uladh been captured?"

"You almost killed my whole class." This wasn't fair—he knew she hadn't meant to transform herself. *She shouldn't have been there in the first place,* he thought.

"You are being very emo. I told you I did not intend—"

"You almost KILLED them all."

She smiled at him. "But you saved them. You are a hero."

That was an interesting way to look at it.

Conor sank down on his bed, legs spaghettified. And in that moment he remembered the original Ashling-related problem: She probably was here for Grump.

Listen, kiddo, Grump had said. *Banshees don't stick around long. The Death'll be soon.*

Conor hid his face in his hands. He was not one bit closer to figuring out how to stop the Death from happening. And Ashling had been there, what, three days? It could be any minute now.

"Tell me, Conor-boy, what happened to my Uladh?"

He couldn't talk. His brain wasn't working.

She whacked his knee. "Uladh, Conor-boy."

"Uh." He pulled himself together. "It's . . . Letsee, it's the British, they invaded Ireland a few hundred years ago. The

114

IRA, the rebels, used to bomb people pretty often. I think it's better now."

"Bomb?"

"A bomb's a thing you explode."

"Explode?"

He handed her his copy of *A Child's Guide to Science.* He'd never liked that book, but he was glad he had it now. Ashling retreated into the cupboard with it.

Conor got his cell phone out of his backpack and switched it on. The only person who ever texted him was Javier, who wasn't speaking to him. But following routine gave him comfort. He was the calmest he'd been all day, despite Ashling's totally unrelenting attitude toward killing people.

He didn't know what to think about her. One minute she was crying about her family, the next she was contemplating mass destruction.

Ashling's head popped out of her cupboard. "Giant lizards walked the earth for a hundred and fifty million years!" she announced, and drew her head back in. Conor waited to see if any further information would be forthcoming. When it wasn't, he sat down at his desk and tried to dejangle himself enough to answer worksheet questions about the Civil War.

He didn't realize he was humming the flute tune until the cupboard door jolted open. "Stop that," Ashling said. "I do not wish to hear that old tune."

"What old tune? I thought you didn't know what it was."

"I have remembered it now. I wish to forget it." The cupboard door slammed shut. Conor lunged to open it. Ashling was in a fetal position on his regulation Adventure Boys sleeping bag, a stack of Trivial Pursuit cards in her hand.

"That tune . . . It's what you danced to, isn't it? With that guy Declan." No answer. "Listen, I was there. I mean, I was somebody else. Or me in another body. Whatever. I've been having these dreams, and I saw you dancing around a big bonfire. There were cows. Guys were fighting. *I* was fighting."

"The warriors fought all the time." Ashling's voice was dull. "They had to make good their boasts." Apparently, she didn't find it odd that he'd seen all this.

"What the heck is happening to me? I'm going nuts!" Conor backed away to let Ashling crawl out of the cupboard. He sat down at his desk. She took the beanbag chair and stared at her feet.

"So?" he said. "What about those fires?"

"Beltine, you must have seen. I told you about it. We light fires to celebrate the sun's return, then drive the cattle between the fires to bless them. Then we dance. The warriors drink and boast and belch and fart and fight." She wrinkled her nose.

"So . . . you danced," he prompted her.

"Did I?"

116

"You said so. At lunch. You said you danced with Declan. And Aengus."

"Oh. Yes. Declan."

"And . . . and was your father there?"

"He would have been, yes."

"He didn't like you dancing."

She smiled faintly. "He always said I was stubborn as a she-goat."

"Listen." Conor slid off his desk chair so they were face-to-face on the floor. "In these dreams . . . one time I ran away from the fires and got lost in the woods. Somebody was screaming. Another time I stood in the shadows and watched you dance. You had a woman on one side and a guy on the other, and I hated him but I don't know why."

That made her look up. "Who were you?"

"Oh, for *cripes'* sake." He pounded his fist into the carpet. "If I knew that, would I be asking all these dumb questions?"

Glennie opened his door without knocking and stuck her head in. "Supper, dweeb." Then she was gone and down the stairs.

Supper was corned beef hash again, but Conor barely noticed. His head was full of bonfires and cattle and fighting, belching warriors.

"You're awful quiet, Con," his dad said. "Girl trouble?"

Glennie snorted. "Oh, right. The pixie dweeb has *girl* trouble."

"Shut up," Conor said. It sort of was girl trouble, but not the way his father meant.

"Eat your vegetables," Dad said. "And don't say 'shut up.'"

"What're you doing tonight, kiddos?" Grump asked. "Wanna come over and watch a movie?" He was staring at Conor, obviously trying to send a signal.

Guess he's ready to meet the banshee. The thought made Conor's brain shut down again. "I'm doing homework."

The kitchen went silent as everyone tried to digest this.

"That . . . that's great, Con," Dad said at last. "Glad to see you're taking school seriously. Six months till exams!"

"Lay off about exams, Brian," Grump said. "Give the kid a break."

"I'm paying attention to my son when he needs it," Dad said.

Silence again, but this time it was like a western movie, when the sheriff and the gunslinger face off in the street and everybody hustles out of sight. Conor and Glennie shoveled in the last of their hash.

"I paid attention to you," Grump said. "But I also let you find your own way."

"In between ghost-hunting trips to the old country," Dad said bitterly.

"Oh, cripes, that again. That was years ago. Why can't you just relax about it, boy?"

Dad slammed his fork down on the table. "Relax? Oh, you mean instead of working like a dog and going to school now instead of when half my friends went, and all because my *attentive* pop spent my college fund on plane tickets to Ireland? Is that what you mean, Pop?"

"You coulda got that scholarship if you hit the books in high school."

"I thought I had a college fund. Turned out I didn't."

"How many times do I have to say I'm sorry? I'm sorry, okay?"

"*Sorry* doesn't turn back time."

"Oh, for cripes' sake, that fund wouldn't have paid for half a year of college." Grump gulped down the last of his hash. "And I found out a lot on that trip to Ireland. Anyways, all you're studying now is accounting. Don't need Boston College for that."

"I was going to study economics."

Grump snorted. "You never *heard* of economics till Jimmy came home from out west."

"I would've heard of it if I'd been in college," Dad said. "Anyways, quit trying to sell yourself to the kids as this big banshee scholar. I don't care what shape birthmark you got or where it is. You were on the run, Pop."

"May we be excused?" Glennie asked.

Grump went all quiet, even stopped chewing. "On the run? What's that supposed to mean?"

"It means"—Dad paused, and for a second Conor hoped

he would rethink what he was about to say—"it means, old man, that you didn't want to face facts. And the fact is, if you were paying attention to your daughter that day at the playground, she'd be sitting here right now. *That's* what it means."

Very quietly, Grump stood up. "Good night, kiddos." He headed for the front door. He still had his napkin tucked into his pants.

Dad stood up, too. "Dishes." He went out to the living room and turned on the evening news. Standing in the kitchen they heard him punch a sofa cushion—not too hard and only once.

"Another blissful night in the O'Neill household." Glennie squeezed dish liquid into the sink.

"Dad shouldn't've said that."

"Grump shouldn't've spent that money."

"How many times does he have to say he's sorry? Dad'll make the council—that's all he wants."

"Know what?" Glennie said. "When I grow up, I'm living alone."

They washed and wiped and put everything away in silence.

As she hung up the dish towel, Glennie whispered, "Are you taking food upstairs for you-know-who?"

"Uh, no. She . . . she smuggled something in for herself."

"I'm coming to your room so I can get to know her, too."

"No. Don't. Dad'll get suspicious." Which was true. Normally, Glennie would rather eat hash six meals in a row than spend time alone with Conor.

"Maybe I've started to appreciate your awesomeness."

"Yeah, right. Go watch a movie with Grump."

"Dweeb."

When he got back to his room, Ashling was sitting in the beanbag chair, reading the science book. "Humans have two million sweat glands," she said by way of greeting.

Conor didn't waste time. "Did you remember anything more? About that bonfire night, I mean."

She shrugged. "Declan was very important to me, I know that. But also . . ." She frowned into the science book. "He betrayed me in some way."

"How?"

"I don't know. I don't want to talk about this anymore. It makes me unhappy."

"But I'm going nuts over here! Why do I keep dreaming about these things?"

"*Ach,* can you not see? We must have known each other back then. As simple as that." She returned to her book. "Potent Mother Maeve. Did you know a brown bat can eat twelve hundred insects in a night?"

"You *are* as stubborn as a she-goat."

A corner of her mouth quirked up, but she kept reading.

Who was I? Somebody who hated the young man

Ashling danced with. Her father? Oh cripes, the old man with the rotten breath?

He couldn't do homework after that. Nor did he want to draw any more of Shanaya. Instead, he fled to the familiarity of his South Boston map, filling in more of the names he'd gotten from Grump's friend.

Ashling stayed on the beanbag chair, intent on the science book. They settled into silence, a surprisingly comfortable one, considering that she was a death-threatening monster.

Now and then she'd offer a news flash: "The blue whale is the largest mammal that ever lived!" or "The ostrich lays the world's biggest egg!"

He had to explain kangaroos, then algebra, as best he could, which wasn't that great. But it sort of made up for Javier not texting.

When he'd written all the names onto his map, he got into bed and Ashling lay in the cupboard doorway, flipping through Trivial Pursuit cards. And they talked.

He spent time like this with Grump, sure. And with Javier. But their lives were similar to his, once you got past Grump's age and Javier's love for fried plantains. Ashling, on the other hand, spoke longingly of empty hills and bogs, the large round mud-and-straw one-room house where the whole family and their servants slept and ate. Fetching water on a cold morning with a leaky wooden bucket, the damp eating into your bones. The colors of people's cloaks and the diseases they got and the dances they did to fend off death's humor.

She learned to fight with ax and sword, like her mother and father and their parents before them. She listened for hoofbeats and the shouts of attack, never knowing when they'd come or how they'd change her life—or end it.

Death was no stranger to her, even when she was alive.

To his astonishment, Conor found himself telling Ashling things he hadn't even admitted to Javier—notably, how much he wanted to stay in Southie, with everything just the way it was, safe and predictable.

"That's not a very interesting life," Ashling commented.

"I draw maps," Conor said defensively. "They're interesting. Maybe—like you said—maybe I could be a mapmaker's apprentice."

"I couldn't stand to be indoors. Too many people and too much smoke."

"I like fresh air, too. I go outside to measure stuff all the time."

"When the smelly old man died, I was going to have my own cattle. I thought I would take another husband and have brave and handsome children. Perhaps I still will. My older sister loved being a woman. I can't wait to experience womanhood. I . . ."

And then they both remembered why Ashling was there, flipping cards in the game cupboard, waiting to usher death into 36A or 36B Crumlin Street. This wasn't a sleepover. Ashling was preparing to trade Grump's life—or maybe Conor's, who knew?—for a new one of her own.

Anger washed over Conor like a rogue wave. "I'd like to experience manhood. If I don't *die* first, of course."

A smothering silence, except for the *flip flip flip* of the Trivial Pursuit cards.

Conor turned out his light. Outside the window, last fall's dry ivy leaves rattled like bones. Inside, the darkness was tangible, suffocating. *That is not a person in my game cupboard,* Conor reminded himself yet again. *That is death.*

He was being unfair—Ashling wasn't death. She simply came with it.

But nothing about this situation was fair.

Chapter Nine

Conor got up at seven the next morning, even though it was Saturday. He and Glennie spent Saturday mornings at Grump's, watching cartoons and eating sugar-coated cereal out of the box, a violation of at least three house rules. Saturday was their mother's one chance to sleep late, and they took full advantage.

A whiff of woodsmoke wafted past as Conor crept down the stairs. He stopped halfway, suddenly sure that he'd dreamed of Ashling again last night. He closed his eyes.

He is sitting next to her on a bench against a stone wall, the Beltine sun hot as a bonfire.

"I don't know how to describe it." She closes her eyes against the glare. "I feel calm in myself, and somehow I pass that along to the beast. I look into its eyes and put my hand on its chest and . . ." She opens her eyes, sees him watching her, and blushes. "I've never talked about this before."

"Why not? It's a gift."

"You're the first one to ask about it."

He can't help himself—he reaches out, touches her hair. She twists away from him, but also she smiles.

And then her smile dies. "There's something I must tell you."

The memory wavered, then faded; he couldn't keep it with him. "Dreams," he said out loud. "Cripes." He continued down the stairs.

Early as it was, Glennie was already at Grump's, pouring the last crumbs of Honey-Glazed Nutsos from the box into her mouth. Today's tattoo was a fluffy kitten on the back of her hand, but Conor wasn't fooled.

"Don't worry. I got more cereal." Grump grabbed his step stool.

Conor settled down for the opening credits of his favorite robot cartoon.

"Ju-u-ust up here," Grump said from the kitchen. "A-a-a-a-ah!"

Crash!

Conor and Glennie dashed into the kitchen, and there was Grump, on his side on the floor, the step stool overturned. Grump was out cold and had gone Arctic White, the exact color Conor had painted the kitchen for his Adventure Boys badge.

"GRUMP!" Conor flung himself down next to his grandfather. "Glennie, go get Mom!"

Glennie pelted out the door. Conor got a blanket for Grump and knelt beside him, patting the old man's shoulder like that would do anything. *If Javier ever speaks to me again, he's teaching me first aid. Or I'll ask Mom to do it.* Anything to stop feeling so helpless.

Grump's eyelids fluttered. "Still here," he whispered. One eye opened and regarded Conor. "Hear anything?"

Conor listened. A car drove by. Some kid yelled. But nobody keened. He shook his head.

"Early yet," Grump said. "Maybe later."

Mom and Dad came crashing through the front door in their bathrobes. Saturday morning, usually a cozy time of cartoons and Honey-Glazed Nutsos, turned into an ice field of sirens and whispers and scared eyes.

Dad got out his old beater of a car, and the whole family followed Grump's ambulance across the West Fourth Street Bridge. Conor watched the odometer and learned that the hospital was eight-tenths of a mile beyond the bridge, which meant it was two-point-nine-five miles from 36A Crumlin Street.

Two-point-nine-five, two-point-nine-five, he chanted to himself as he and Glennie found chairs in the waiting room. They'd been sitting there for an hour when he realized that if Ashling hadn't keened by now she probably wasn't going to.

Grump wasn't dying—not yet. But he would someday. The thought made Conor feel like he was drifting in uncharted space.

The despair must have shown on his face, because

when Dad came out to check on them he patted Conor heavily on the back and said, "Buck up, Con. This stuff happens to old guys."

"He'll be okay," Conor said. "But not forever."

His father pulled abruptly away and pointed to the wall television. "Great tie on that guy." It was a game show. The guy with the great tie had to phone a friend to find out who the vice president was.

"What a doofus," Glennie said. "People are smarter than that in cartoons."

Somebody prodded Conor in the back: an old man, but nowhere near as old as Grump, with brown hair and a deeply unhealthy grayness to his skin. Standing next to him were a three-legged cane and a rolling tank with a tube that ran to a pair of prongs in the guy's nose. "Is Davey gonna be okay?" the guy said, sounding breathless.

Conor went tongue-tied, but his dad jumped in. "We think so." He extended his hand. "Brian O'Neill. I've seen you around, right? But not for a while."

"I'm an O'Neill, too," the guy said. "Richard. I live a couple streets over from your dad's old store. You probably saw me around before I acquired this stuff." He jerked his head at the cane and oxygen tank. "Never smoke, kids."

"This is Conor, my son," Dad said. "And this is my daughter, Glennie."

"Are we related?" Glennie said.

Richard O'Neill gave a wheezy chuckle. "Oh, back in the mists of time, I guess. My dad was the one who knew all that stuff. I never paid much attention."

The guy looked like he could keel over then and there. Conor wondered if Ashling would keen for him, or if his part of the family had a banshee all its own.

"I used to love hanging around your dad's store . . . when I . . . was a teen . . ." Mr. O'Neill had to stop talking for a minute to catch his breath, his hand on his chest.

Her hand on my heart, Conor thought.

"He . . . your dad," Mr. O'Neill managed, "used . . . to tell me about banshees and the Other Land and stuff. He knew . . . an awful lot, especially about . . . death."

Dad scowled, but Mom came up behind him before he had a chance to change the subject.

"Mr. O'Neill," she said, and Conor realized she must have known the guy from the clinic. "Have you been doing your exercises?"

He grinned at her, breathing heavily. "Yes, ma'am. But they don't . . . do any good."

"They will if you keep at it." Mom gave Mr. O'Neill a stern look, then turned to her children. "Grump broke his arm and two ribs. They don't like his heart rhythm and they're not sure if he fell or blacked out. So they want to keep him, at least overnight. They're sending him to the ICU."

The intensive care unit smelled like disinfectant and

canned vegetable soup. Grump, Arctic White, had one arm in a brace and a tube in the other, wires stuck to his chest, and oxygen prongs in his bulbous nose. But when he opened his eyes, they had their usual mischievous sparkle. Conor's mom fussed around, adjusting pillows and making Grump drink water through a straw.

Swallowing looked like hard work.

"Pop," Conor's dad said, "I'm sorry I said that last night. About Jeannie."

Grump eyed him for a minute, then waved his hand in the air, dispelling the memory. "'S-okay. I've said worse to myself."

"It wasn't your fault, Pop. You can't watch a kid all the time."

"Yeah, I know." Grump's voice was like a wisp of fog. "I want to talk to Conor alone."

Dad looked down at his feet, feelings hurt. Conor hardened his heart. *He was mean to Grump last night.*

"You can't have any rocket parts in here, Davey," Mom said, "so don't even ask."

"I want to talk to Conor."

"Why?"

"Sometimes a kid needs to hear from his old grump, that's all."

Mom looked suspicious. Grump shot a conspiratorial wink at Glennie, who was always willing to undermine her parents even if she didn't understand why. "I didn't have enough breakfast," Glennie announced. "I want a boysen-berry smoothie."

"No sugar," her mother said.

"Mom," Glennie said, anything but sweet. "We're in a hospital. They probably don't even *have* sugar."

"I could use a cup of coffee," Dad said to his feet.

"Oh, all right." Mom gave Grump's pillow one more plump and stalked off. Glennie returned Grump's wink as she followed Dad out the door.

Conor moved to the head of the bed. "What is it, Grump?"

Grump took Conor's hand in his bony one. "Listen, kiddo, I want you to bring this Ashling in here. I need to talk to her."

It took Conor a second or two to see the problem with that idea. "Grump, I can't bring her to a big hospital. What if"— he swallowed hard—"somebody dies? She'll turn into a wraith."

Grump grinned under the oxygen prongs. "Oh yeah? Got any change?"

Conor fished in his pocket, held out a handful of quarters and nickels. "You want something from the machine? I don't know if they'll let you—"

"No, I don't want nothing from the machine. I want something small that a banshee could hold in her hand." Grump held up a quarter, waggled it significantly. "A little Worldcraft."

It was the Mississippi magnolia quarter, the one Ashling had said was beautiful but couldn't keep because . . . because . . .

Oh. "If she has Worldcraft on her she won't turn into a wraith," Conor said. "Will that stop the Death?"

"No, kiddo, of course not. Nothing stops death. But Worldcraft keeps a banshee solid so nobody else dies by mistake."

Conor wished he'd remembered that at school.

"I'll bring her."

When the rest of the family returned, Grump announced that he wanted to sleep and they should all leave him the heck alone. Conor's mom adjusted his pillow one last time and filled his water jug, then obeyed Grump's command.

"Bring me some Honey-Glazed Nutsos," he said as she headed for the door. "I want to eat 'em out of the box." She pretended she hadn't heard.

Mom took them all home and drove off to her Saturday study group. Glennie went next door to Grump's for some more Honey-Glazed Nutsos—it was still only ten thirty. Conor didn't feel like eating. He went upstairs, where Ashling was hanging upside down from the ceiling again.

"Dude, where have you been?" she said, righting herself. "Did you know that the killer whale totally is the fastest swimming marine mammal?" She was too jolly, as if they'd never had a fight and she wasn't death's best friend.

He handed her the Mississippi magnolia quarter. "Come on. Grump knows all about banshees and he wants to talk to you." He paused and added the obvious: "I told him you were here. Sorry."

Ashling furrowed her brow. "I can't walk around with this coin in my hand. It's not right. I have to be what I am. Which is the finest—"

"Grump's in the hospital and people die there sometimes. You only have to keep the coin on you while we're there."

"And what if this Grump is the Death? What if he begins to die whilst we're there? What then, Conor-boy, hey?"

"Easy. I'll rush you outside and take back the coin." He put his finger to his lips to silence her, and opened the door.

"Conor-boy, I need to say something."

"Shhhh!" He tiptoed out to the head of the stairs, listened, and whispered, "Nobody's around. Let's go."

"I'm around," Glennie said, coming up the stairs. "Where you going?"

Conor gave her a frantic hand waggle. "Shhh! I'm taking Ashling to see Grump."

"Why?"

"He wants to meet her. Because . . . because of the IRA." He didn't look at Glennie to see whether she bought that idea. Better not to know. "Where's Dad?"

"Right here." His father appeared in the downstairs hall. "What's up?"

133

Conor shut his bedroom door, brain frozen. "Uh."

Glennie smirked at him. "Hi, Dad. We want to go ride bikes."

"I dunno, kids. Grump's sort of a sick puppy right now. We probably should be on hand in case he needs—"

"We want to ride our bikes to the hospital," Glennie said. "To see him."

"Are you nuts?" Conor muttered out of the side of his mouth.

Dad looked stricken. "Aw, kids, I don't think your mom would like that."

"We'll take the bus then. We want to see Grump." *Smart,* Conor thought. Glennie had started with the really forbidden thing, then dropped back to something that seemed safe by comparison.

"It's across the bridge," Dad said. "Your mom won't want you going over there by yourselves."

"But . . . but I want to see Grump." Glennie's lower lip began to quiver. Conor leaned against the wall to watch her work.

"Your mom'll be home in a couple hours," Dad said. "We'll drive over then."

"I want to see him *now,*" Glennie wailed. She hiccupped— hiccups always preceded her sobbing routine. She hiccupped again. Then a third time. "Two hours might be too late." She buried her face in her hands. Her shoulders shook.

"Aw, honey." Dad hustled up the stairs and put his arms around Glennie. She kept her face in her hands—lately, she'd been having trouble summoning actual tears. (She blamed puberty.) "He's not *that* sick, Glennie."

"I want to see him *now*," Glennie fake-sobbed into her hands. Conor hoped Dad couldn't see her rubbing her thumbs into her eyes to make them red. He couldn't believe his father hadn't caught on to that trick, but he hadn't.

Dad was distraught, helpless as always when Glennie cried. "Honey, I got some guys coming over to talk about the council. Sort of important guys, you know? I can't tell them not to . . . Well, I don't think I could reach them now, anyways. Can't you wait for Mom to come home with the car?"

"I want to see him *now*," Glennie sobbed anew. Once she'd come up with a successful line, she liked to stick to it. But then, in a flash of foolhardy brilliance, she added, "Grump would've let you go when you were our age."

Conor held his breath. This could go either way: Dad might have good memories of Grump trusting him . . . or bad memories of Grump endangering his children.

Dad took in a long, deep breath. "You'll stay together, right?"

Conor barely restrained himself from giving a fist pump.

"Turn on your cell phone, Con, and keep it handy," Dad said. "Don't talk to anyone. And"—his gaze dropped to

Conor's feet—"we'll tell your mother you got a ride with somebody. Somebody she doesn't know."

"My teacher Mr. Rose," Conor said. "His father was a friend of Grump's."

Glennie emerged from behind her hands, wiping her face with her sleeves as if it were actually wet. "And we'll take Conor's new girlfriend."

"What?" Conor almost fainted.

"What?" Dad looked faint, too.

Conor's bedroom door creaked open. He groaned in spite of himself.

"Good day to you, Brian Uí Néill." Ashling smiled politely at Dad, who winced at her brown tooth.

But then a grin formed on Dad's face. "Good day to you, too. Who are you and what are you doing in my son's bedroom?" He winked at Conor, which somehow made the world a worse place.

"I am Ashling, daughter of Maedoc of the Uí Néill. I am from Uladh."

"Ulster," Conor said.

"Northern Ireland," Glennie piped up.

"I know, honey, thanks. Are you visiting someone around here?"

Ashling's smile broadened. "You."

"I mean, where are you sleeping?"

"Olivia Kim's," Conor said. "She just arrived." Conor felt this was the best he could do on the spur of the moment.

His parents didn't know Olivia. If he could keep everyone apart long enough . . .

Dad was puzzling it out, hands in pockets. "If she just arrived, how is she your girlfriend?"

Conor felt his eyebrows peak up.

"Pen pal," Glennie said. "From school."

"Is Olivia her pen pal, too? I mean, it seems odd that she'd fly all the way over from Ireland to stay with a Korean family she doesn't even—"

"I had to leave Uladh," Ashling said. "The IRS is after me."

"IRA," Conor said.

"Yes. That."

"The IRA is after you? What are you, thirteen? Fourteen?"

Conor's heart sank. His father had to stop believing this at some point.

"Because of my parents," Ashling said confidently. "Who are dead now, of course. I'm very emo about it."

Dad frowned. "So who put you on the plane?"

"Plane?"

"Dad," Conor broke in. "We gotta go see Grump. Can we talk about Ashling later?"

"Actually, son, I bet your mom's going to want to know who this girl is."

"I am Ashling, daughter of—"

"Thanks. I got that." Dad ruffled his thick black hair.

"Boy, it's one thing after another today." He scrutinized Ashling, then apparently decided she was all right and started down the stairs. "Okay, kids, head out. Stay with Grump until your mom or I get there."

"Let's go," Conor said, and they followed Dad down the stairs. Conor and Glennie grabbed jackets from the front hall closet.

"Do you need a jacket, Ashling?" Dad asked. "Or . . . I guess you're warm enough in that . . . that cape thing."

"A jacket? Oh, you mean those things, with the . . . the zippits? No, no. I'd better not. It would be too hard to get out of if I have to turn—"

"See ya, Dad." Conor grabbed Ashling's arm and hauled her out the door.

They headed down the sidewalk, Ashling flipping her Mississippi quarter from hand to hand and giggling. "What a thing this is. What a thing, indeed."

"They don't have coins in Ireland?" Glennie muttered.

"Metal shortage," Conor muttered back.

Glennie half smirked. Never a good sign.

Chapter Ten

They turned the corner on the way to the bus stop, then passed the convenience store that used to be Grump's.

"This is lovely." Ashling skipped over a sidewalk crack. "I've never taken a walk upon a surface such as this."

"Didn't you walk to school yesterday?" Glennie asked.

Ashling stooped to examine a root poking up through the pavement. "This tree is tearing up your hard surface."

"I mean," Glennie persisted, "how did you get there if you didn't walk on the sidewalk? Did somebody drive you?"

Ashling straightened. "I thought about it, and I went."

"But *how* did you—?"

"Look, Glennie!" Conor pointed, desperate. "The bakery has Easter cupcakes already!"

Glennie looked. "Big deal. They're the same as last year's. They weren't even all that good."

"I wonder why they put them in there so early. I mean it's two weeks away and"—Conor was babbling, couldn't stop—"by the time anybody wants them they'll be hard as a rock as if they weren't already, I've never liked this bakery all that much except for those sticky buns they make, remember when Mom got them for Christmas breakfast, I wonder why she doesn't get them every year—"

"Your eyebrows are peaking up," Ashling said.

"When we get to the hospital, I want to go up in the freight elevator," Glennie said. "I like freight elevators."

"I didn't know there was such a thing as a fright alligator," Ashling said. "The American alligator weighs eight hundred pounds." Conor grabbed her elbow and squeezed it so she'd shut up.

"I like the *idea* of a freight elevator," Glennie rambled on. "*Freight.* It's an awesome word."

The bus came. Ashling got on as if she'd been doing it all her life. As they jounced along she was mercifully silent, taking in the Saturday street scene of running kids, peeing dogs, chatting adults.

But then they came to the West Fourth Street Bridge, which took them over what was left of the channel. Ashling gave a sharp cry and pointed. "See how they built such a . . . a monstrous thing that crosses the river. Look at it! The craft! Will it hold if we . . . *Ach,* Mother Maeve, looks like we're going across."

The bus lumbered toward the bridge. Ashling gripped Conor's arm, stopping circulation.

"It's perfectly safe." He waited for Glennie to say, *They don't have bridges in Ireland?* But his sister was admiring the sequins on her sneakers, not even paying attention.

The bus crossed the channel and headed for the medical center. When they got there, the hospital's automatic doors rendered Ashling so speechless that she never got a chance to say anything stupid. Conor found an elevator that, while not for freight, was big and isolated enough to satisfy Glennie. He bundled her into it next to Ashling—who clung to the handrail, still bereft of words—and punched the button for the fifth floor, feeling that he was starting to get things under control. Even his eyebrows.

The elevator clanked upward. Ashling whimpered and pressed herself against the handrail. In the mirrorlike elevator door, Conor could see that Glennie was staring at Ashling as if she had grown bunny ears and a snout. He watched his eyebrows peak up.

When they got to intensive care, it turned out that Grump had been moved to a regular room. "He's doing great," a smiling nurse said, and gave them directions. As they wound through the corridors, Ashling took the coin from her leather bag and clenched it in her fist.

Grump was all alone in a double room, still draped in tubes and with oxygen prongs in his nose. "Other guy's in surgery for the day," he said to Conor. But his gaze was on Ashling. "Not the same one. Why not?"

"Same one what?" Glennie said.

"What is that sticking out of your arm?" Ashling peered at Grump. "And your nose! Awesome."

"Hey Glennie, kiddo," Grump said. "Wanna do your old grump a favor? I need a magazine or two to keep me from going nuts. Can you run downstairs and find me a couple? And get some sandwiches for you kids. Money's in my pants pocket in the closet there."

Glennie kicked at a leg on Grump's bed. "Why do I have to be the one to go get stuff?"

"'Cuz you're the smartest." Grump winked at Conor. "I trust your judgment."

Glennie blew out her cheeks and expressed her feelings by waddling like an ape to get the money. "I'm buying Fruity Foolers, too," she said in parting.

"Shut the door, Conor," Grump said.

Ashling hoisted herself up to sit on the shelf under the windows and studied Grump, who studied her right back. "I don't know who the Death is," she said. "So do not ask."

"How come you're not the one who came for my little girl? I thought it was one banshee to a family."

"Maeveen," Ashling said. "She would have been the one."

Grump waited for more. Didn't get it. "Well? Where is she now?"

"I can't say."

Why not? Conor thought. *Where'd she go?*

"Hmm." Grump narrowed his eyes. "And you don't know who the Death is."

"No."

"I want it to be me," Grump said. "How do I make that happen?"

"You cannot control death."

"I'm not asking to. But the Lady can."

"We don't cause death, Grump Uí Néill. The Lady sent me to keen when it arrives and accompany the Dear Departed to the Other Land. Even she doesn't choose who goes."

"The name's Davey O'Neill. Take me to see the Lady. I'll make my case to her."

Ashling rolled her eyes. "Dude. The Dear Departed stream into the Other Land in their thousands, with only us to keep track of them. The Lady does not have time to listen to an old man who wants to change fate."

Grump smiled the way he did when he was about to win a card game. "That so? How about if I ask to test the Birds?"

Silence, almost Javier-esque. Ashling drew a deep breath, let it out. "How do you know about the Birds, Davey O'Neill?"

"What birds?" Conor asked.

His grandfather's smile broadened—Conor realized Ashling had confirmed something Grump hadn't been sure he knew. "I've heard the tales, Miss Banshee Uí Néill. Tell me how to get to them Birds."

"Grump," Conor said. "What birds?"

Ashling pulled out her comb. "You think you know so much, Davey O'Neill." She undid her braid, fingers shaking.

"When a banshee combs her hair," Grump said, "you know you've upset her. If I ask to see the Birds, you can't refuse. That's right, ain't it?"

Ashling gave him an evil look, starting to comb.

Conor stamped his foot. "WHAT. BIRDS?"

"Keep your voice down, Conor," Grump said.

"The Lady's Birds," Ashling said, combing faster. "Three of them, big, black."

"Ravens," Grump said.

"They roost in a little room behind the Lady's throne," Ashling said. "Hardly anyone ever sees them— *Ach*." The comb caught in a knot. Blinking hard and fast—trying not to cry?—she struggled to disentangle it.

"If I outwit the Birds," Grump said, "they change fate at my command."

"How do you outwit them?" Conor asked.

"That's the question, isn't it?"

Ashling's shoulders drooped. She watched her finger trace the fancy carving on her comb. "The Birds," she said to herself. "No way."

"If you take Grump to see the Birds, you lose your new life, don't you?" Conor said.

She acted as if she didn't hear him.

"There's a bunch of tales," Grump said. "In some of

144

them the Birds give you the power of life and death. That's what I want."

"Don't be so sure what you want," Ashling said, head bowed. "The Lady is tricky."

"Holy macaroni, girl, this won't harm you," Grump said. "You'll get your Death all right."

"It has to be the right Death." Her voice was dull, defeated.

"I'm probably it anyways."

She looked up. Grump gave a short laugh. "You think so, too, I see."

Ashling put away her comb.

"It's fine if I'm your Death. I just want to make sure. Now . . ." Grump had a glint in his eye that Conor didn't like one bit. "How do I get there?"

Ashling straightened, pointy nose in the air, eyes glittery. "I don't know how a living man comes before the Lady."

Grump snorted. "You know, it's possible you're not a banshee at all. You could be some little trickster from the old country, out to snooker a boy and his grump. I got the map of Ireland on my leg, girlie, and I wasn't born yesterday."

"Conor knows what I am."

"Does he now."

Ashling smiled faintly. She plunked the Mississippi magnolia quarter on the window shelf, folded her arms, and lifted off until her head touched the ceiling. And there she stayed, bobbing in midair, staring down at the old man in the bed.

"I knew you weren't IRA." Glennie stood in the doorway, magazines, sandwiches, and three packs of jelly beans in hand.

Ashling groaned. "*Another* person finds out. Where will this end?"

Conor sat down on the end of the empty bed, feeling helpless. *I give up. I'll just see what happens.* It was a calming thought.

"Hey there, Glennie, kiddo," Grump said, as if nothing was unusual. "Come in and close the door."

For once, Glennie did what she was told without arguing. "Are you a ghost?"

"A banshee," Ashling said, still floating.

"*Our* banshee?"

Ashling nodded, descending a bit.

"Who's going to die?"

Ashling shrugged, which almost tipped her over in the air.

Glennie looked at Conor. "You're the oldest. Do something."

He almost said, *You're the brave one.* But he didn't, because Grump was listening. Ashling was floating there watching him. And Glennie was watching him, too, as if expecting him to act like the big brother. She'd never done that before.

"We're working on it," Grump said. "Miss Banshee here is going to take me to the lady who runs things to see if I can talk her around."

Glennie looked skeptical. "Talk her around to what? I mean, somebody has to die or we won't all fit on the earth."

"Exactly." Ashling drifted back down to her window shelf and settled there, one leg crossed over the other.

"Your hair's still floating," Glennie said in a helpful tone.

Ashling tried to gather her hair and braid it, but clumps kept escaping and wafting upward. She looked like an octopus.

"I know somebody has to die," Grump said. "I just want to make sure the Death comes from the right generation. The question remains: How do I get to the Lady?"

"I only know what to do with my Dear Departed. The living . . . nobody said anything about them."

"What would you do with the Dear Departed?" Conor asked.

"We would hold hands and I would think us to the Other Land. At least . . . so I'm told. I've never done it, as you know." She chewed her lip. "Here, Conor-boy. Come hold my hand."

He stayed right where he was. "I'm not, you know, dead."

Ashling jumped off the window shelf and held out her hand. "Dude, of course not. I will think us back to your home." Against his better judgment, he took the hand. She closed her eyes and went very quiet. Conor listened to Grump breathe, to his own heart beating. The pump clicked on Grump's intravenous drip.

Nothing happened.

Ashling released Conor's hand. "No, it will not work with the living."

"There's gotta be a way," Grump said. "There are tales of people facing the Birds and living to tell about it."

"So how do they get there?" Glennie asked.

"The tales never say." Grump watched Ashling try to get her floating hair under control. "Maybe you could float me there."

The thought came to Conor out of the blue. "Hey. You floated *me*."

Ashling's hair escaped. "I did?"

"At school. When you choked at the water fountain and your braid lifted. My feet went right up off the floor. Paula almost fainted."

"Hmm. Now that I think of it, Nergal has brought in the living sometimes, for what purpose I do not know."

"Who's Nergal?" Grump said.

"He's Babylonian," Conor said.

"He can't be." Grump sounded peevish. "The Other Land's Irish."

Ashling wasn't listening. "Such a journey would be difficult, old man. You are sick and weak."

"So? What's the worst that could happen . . . I die?"

"We would fly over the sea, find a small rock in the waves, walk through a long tunnel, pass the Kai-lyu'gh." Or that's what it sounded like. It ended with the same guttural sound as Dál Fiatach.

"Pass the what?" Glennie said.

"Kai-lyu'gh," Grump said. "Spelled *C-a-i-l-l-e-a-c-h.*"

"You can't do all that, Grump," Conor said.

"What's your suggestion, kiddo?" Grump said. "We wait and see? What if it's you that dies? What if it's Glennie?"

He keeps saying that. I don't want it to be anybody. Conor thought of Grump flying over an icy sea, dying, maybe, cold and alone. The thought was more than he could bear.

"Let's try it now, Davey O'Neill," Ashling said. "See if I can lift you up."

"I can't. I got all these tubes and things."

Ashling blew air out of her mouth. "Then how in the name of Mother Maeve do you expect to fly over the ocean with me, old man?"

"Good point. Help me get on my feet, kiddos. If we have to, we'll disconnect some stuff." He took out his oxygen prongs and swung his pale legs over the side of the bed. Conor tried to help him up by holding on to his good arm, but he couldn't get a grip because of the tube in it. He tried putting his arm around Grump's back, but that made Grump yelp because of the broken ribs.

149

Grump's feet didn't seem to function as feet anymore—it was like they weren't wide enough, or they were too soft or too sideways or something. He finally struggled upright, his hospital johnny open in the back. "Grump, your bum's showing," Glennie said, disgusted.

Grump fell back on the bed, swearing under his breath. The beeps on his heart monitor were twice as fast as before. "Shoot. That'll bring a nurse."

Sure enough, Conor had barely gotten him back up on his feet when a sturdy woman in blue flowered scrubs slammed through the door. Ashling captured the last of her floating clumps of hair and grabbed her Mississippi magnolia quarter.

"Mr. O'Neill! What *are* you doing?"

Grump sank down on the bed, panting. "Had to pee. Didn't want to bother nobody."

"Don't be silly. We're here to be bothered. Kids, wait outside, please."

Out in the hall, Ashling said, "Dude, this is crazy. I will drop him into the sea."

"But you'll make him light and floaty," Glennie said.

"Yes, but the wind will buffet us and he'll be freezing cold, and if we lose our grip for even a second he won't be light anymore."

The nurse came out. Her nametag said ANGELA TIMULTY, RN. "Don't you let him do that again, kids." She sounded friendly, but you could see she meant it. "He's getting better faster than I would have imagined, but he's had a rough day and we don't want to disturb that IV drip for another few hours."

Grump was back in bed and living up to his nickname. "Never in my whole life have I not been there when my family needed me."

"That's not true," Glennie said.

"Glennie!" Conor whacked her on the arm.

"Mom says he wasn't even at Dad's graduation."

"I was in Ireland," Grump protested. "Finding out stuff. Like about them Birds, which could save somebody's life if I wasn't such a weak-kneed old poop."

"Grump, you'll get better," Conor said. "You have to give it time."

"We don't *have* time. The Lady doesn't send a banshee weeks before the Death. It could happen any time now."

Grump's jaw was quivering. He was on the verge of crying. Grump, crying! Glennie, contrite, handed the old man a red jelly bean.

Somebody with a voice exactly like Conor's—using his tongue and vocal cords, in fact—took a deep breath and said something totally nuts. "Let *me* go."

Everybody stared at him. Nobody could believe he'd said that. Which was insulting, when you thought about it.

"*You* can't go." Glennie popped a green jelly bean into her mouth. "You'll get scared and mess up. I'll go."

Ashling scowled at Glennie. "How dare you say such a thing! He is a hero."

Glennie said in singsong, "*Conor* has a *girl*friend."

Conor's ears were burning but he ignored them. "I'm going," his vocal cords told Glennie, "because I'm older and I'm bigger and you'll think it's all a ginormous joke." That was true, but he didn't want to believe it. What he wanted was to be talked out of this.

"I'm better than you at puzzles," Glennie said. Which also was true. "And I lie better. You go dweebing along telling the truth all the time. What use is that?"

"She's got a point," Grump said.

Grump thinks I'm a dweeb? To his horror, Conor's eyes teared up.

"Conor, kiddo," Grump said, "you got more good qualities than anyone I know, up to and including the O'Neill Spark. I also think you need an adventure. But Glennie's as much of a con artist as I am." He pondered the sky outside his window. "Maybe we should all go."

"We have to *float* over the *sea*." Ashling finished her braid and flung it behind her back. "If I'm going to take anyone, I am quite sure I have to hold your hand or touch you or something. I cannot take three of you. I only have two hands."

Conor's pocket buzzed. He checked his phone and to his immense surprise found he had a text from Javier.

yr czin flots, it said.

huh? he texted back.

"There's that small computer," Ashling said. "And now you are reading it."

"Texting," Grump said. "A plague on modern society."

"Oooo. Let me see." Ashling reached for the phone. Conor evaded her, because Javier had texted: saw yr czin flot. u ok?

Spelling had never been Javier's strong suit, and text-speak didn't help.

He texted back: M ok. wut is flot?

He waited. Grump held forth on the many ways life had been better without electronics. Conor and Glennie each ate a chicken sandwich. At last, Javier texted: flowt. fly. u ok?

He meant *float*.

"Ashling," Conor said, "have you been outside floating around?"

Ashling drew herself up straight. "No, of course not!" They all eyed her, waiting. "Oh, all right, a little. This morning, when I awoke and was alone, I needed to think so I went to your roof for air. No one could see me."

"Javier saw you."

"*Ach.*"

Conor waved the cell phone at Grump. "What do I do now?"

Grump shrugged. "Hey, the more the merrier. We got a technical problem. Javier's got a technical brain. Tell him to get over here."

So Conor texted: At hsptl w grmp. rm 533. cn u cm ovr?

It seemed like forever before Javier texted back: b rite thr.

"Dude, I'm not taking *four* humans," Ashling said. "The Cailleach will eat you and then me."

"Javier will be our consultant," Grump said. "Now, what are our transportation options, Miss Banshee?"

"The Cailleach will eat us?" Conor said.

"Figure of speech, kiddo," Grump said.

Ashling gave a grim smile.

Chapter Eleven

"I bet you can fly with three people, Ashling," Glennie said. "What if two of us hold your hands and one holds on to your ankles?"

"I don't know if I can extend my lightness to so many." Ashling hopped off the window shelf. "Let's see." She held out a hand to Glennie.

Grump flung the covers off his legs. "Help me up."

"Grump," Conor said, "stay there. We'll test it with Glennie and me, and when Javier gets here he'll join us. We'll figure out if it's even possible." Grump lay back, Arctic White as ever.

Standing at the foot of Grump's bed, Conor and Glennie each took one of Ashling's hands. Ashling closed her eyes, took a deep breath, let it out.

Conor's arm felt funny. It buzzed like a bee in a bottle, then all the muscles relaxed. The feeling passed on to his shoulders, his neck, the other arm, his head. He might have been drifting in a pool. He closed his eyes. It felt wonderful.

His internal organs lifted—that sensation wasn't so pleasant, and he thought he might puke. He tried to recapture the good feeling, willing that chicken sandwich to stay in his stomach.

"Cool," Glennie said. "Cool, cool, cool." She burped.

Conor opened his eyes as the top of his head brushed the ceiling. His feet were dangling four feet above the floor. Grump watched him, grinning, monitor *beep-beep-beep*ing.

Glennie let out a long belch. "Coooooool." She reached out to touch the ceiling as if it might not be real.

Conor swallowed the rising contents of his stomach and closed his eyes again. "Don't let go of me."

"Dude, do you think I would?"

"No. But . . . don't."

"Open your eyes. You'll get used to it. Totally."

He didn't want to get used to it. But Ashling was the boss, so he opened his eyes.

"Whoa." Javier was standing in the doorway, bike helmet in hand.

"Hey," Glennie said, "Javier rode his bike all the way here. *His* parents are awesome." She did a scissor kick to see what happened. Her head dislodged a ceiling tile.

"In point of fact," Javier said in his precise way, "my mother would kill me. I'm not supposed to go over the West Fourth Street Bridge."

"Shut the door, boy," Grump said. "Oh, and arrivederci."

"That's good-bye," Javier said. "In Italian."

"Sorry. I get confused because it has *arrive* in it," Grump said. Conor was pretty sure he was kidding.

Ashling, Conor, and Glennie drifted down to the floor again.

"Javier," Glennie said, "we need you to grab Ashling's ankles to find out if she can carry three of us."

"I'm not grabbing anyone's ankles." Javier's mouth went firm and grim, the way it did when he hogged a video game.

"She can't get high enough in here to get an ankle-grabbing person off the floor anyways," Conor said. "But maybe it's like an electrical current—maybe it passes through one person to another. Let's see what happens if you hold Javier's hand, Glennie."

Glennie went beet red. So did Javier.

"You hold his hand, Conor-boy." Ashling tugged on her braid, which was floating. "The little girl is embarrassed."

"I'm not a little girl," Glennie said.

"Boys don't hold hands in this country," Javier said.

Ashling blinked. "Why not?"

"Unless they're gay," Javier added, seeking precision. "And I don't think I am."

"Oh, for cripes' sake," Grump said. "Grab the boy's hand, Conor."

"I'm not holding anybody's hand until I know how she goes up in the air like that." Javier sat down on Grump's roommate's bed.

They explained about Ashling being a banshee and what that meant, and how Grump wanted the Death to be him but nobody else did.

"That's very interesting," Javier said, "but it's not what I asked. *How* do you go up in the air like that?"

"I think it and it happens." Ashling frowned, concentrating. "If I want to take someone up with me, I have to think extra-hard, sort of push the . . . the lightness out to the other person."

"It feels fizzy," Glennie said.

"Like floating in a pool," Conor said.

Javier settled himself more comfortably on the bed. "So is there a gas involved? Or maybe—"

"Javier." Conor held out his hand. "Just come over here and we'll try this, okay?"

But it didn't work. Ashling, Glennie, and Conor rose into the air. Javier's feet stayed planted on the vinyl floor tiles. Conor was floating sideways, one hand in Ashling's, the other held down by Javier.

"Let go, boys," Ashling said. "Or I'll drop Conor." Javier, disappointed, released Conor's hand and went back to sit on the roommate's bed.

"Two is all I'll take." Ashling returned to her window shelf. "I'll not have anyone hanging from my ankles."

"You'll take me." Grump's jaw jutted out. "Glennie and Conor can flip a coin to see who the second person is."

"I can't let Glennie go without me. Mom'll kill me." But

in his heart, Conor knew, he was hoping Glennie would win the coin toss. Nobody would blame him for losing a coin toss, right?

"Why don't you want somebody hanging on to your ankles?" Javier asked Ashling.

"Because it will be cold flying across the ocean. The person's hands would freeze and wouldn't grip anymore."

"But the person would be lighter than air, right? We could lash the person's arms to your legs so they'd stay in contact." Javier jiggled his foot, excited. "I know how to do it from Adventure Boys. You use clove hitches."

Ashling shook her head. "I cannot have Worldcraft touching me, not if I wish to float or . . . or do anything a banshee would."

"You sure you can take us?" Conor asked. "We're from the World, aren't we?"

Ashling pondered. "All Nergal said was 'no Worldcraft,' and you are not craft. I think. Anyway, I floated you, so it must be all right."

"We could use your belt." Javier hesitated, licking his lips. "And we could . . . rip a strip or two from your cloak." Ashling folded her arms and floated with an attitude up to the ceiling.

"What if we fly all the way across the ocean and then we can't get in?" Conor said. *Somebody talk me out of this.*

"I told you it would be risky," Ashling said.

Conor had an even more horrifying thought. "What if the Death happens when we're over the ocean?"

"I'll turn into a wraith and you will fall." Ashling lost altitude and thumped back down on her shelf—an unnecessary demonstration, Conor thought.

Even Glennie blinked hard at that. But then she said, "What are the chances of that happening? Stop fretting, Pixie."

"Okay, fine, but we still don't know if she can lift three people."

"We'll find out tonight," Grump said. "When you spring me from this hellhole."

"When we what?" Conor didn't like the set of Grump's jaw, not one little bit.

"You heard me. You're getting me out of here. Ashling'll float you over, you'll bring me some warm clothes, and off we'll go."

"Grump, you can't even stand up. The nurse said you need that IV and stuff. Your ribs are broken. Your *arm's* broken."

"Baloney. Come over at ten o'clock. The nurses will think I'm asleep by then."

"How are we getting out of the house at ten o'clock on a Saturday night?" *It's movie night,* Conor thought.

"Hmm. Maybe later would work better. When your parents are in bed."

"But we're not allowed—"

Grump put his head back and laughed at the ceiling.

"Allowed?" He was getting some color back in his face. "Conor, kiddo, we're going up against death, the stubbornest rule in the universe. Time to stop worrying about what's 'allowed.'"

"But . . . visiting hours will be over."

"Conor," Grump said patiently. "What do you see out the window?"

"A roof."

"You land on the roof and knock on my window. I'll let you in."

The window was solid glass—the only way to let air in was to open narrow vents at either side, too small even for Glennie to slip through. *He's totally losing it.* "How're you gonna do that, Grump?"

"Kiddo, in a place like this, where there's a roof I promise you there's a door to get out on it. You knock, I'll go let you in."

"But you've got all these tubes and wires and things."

"You're going to leave soon, and I'll sleep all afternoon. That'll set me right up, I promise. I bet I can make 'em unhook all these things tonight."

"Won't they keep coming in and checking on you? They'll see you're gone and call Dad. And then they'll find out we're gone, too. Mom and Dad will freak."

"I thought about that already." Grump cocked an eyebrow at Javier.

Javier grinned. "I'll be you."

"Yep. We'll put you in this bed instead of me. And I'll tell my doc the hospital's making me nuts and I need a sleeping pill and a good night's sleep. He'll tell them to leave me alone tonight. I know he'll do it for me—his dad and I go way back."

"But . . . if you take a sleeping pill . . ." Conor was being stupid but he couldn't stop.

Glennie half smirked. "He won't really take it, dork."

The door to the roof turned out to be down a little side corridor around the corner from Grump's room. Finding it gave Conor time to think up one more argument against this insanity.

"We can't do this," he said, back in Grump's room. "Even if the real Death doesn't happen, what if somebody else dies when we come back to the hospital? Ashling can't keep the coin on her because she'll need to fly. She'll keen and kill us all."

He could see he'd finally stumped his grandfather. But then Grump gave him a doggylike grin, the kind that spelled trouble. "Well, kiddo, that's just a chance we'll have to take. So, midnight?"

Conor knew when he was beaten.

"Midnight," he said. "I guess."

Ashling thought herself back to the game cupboard. Javier hightailed it home before anyone saw him on the wrong side of the West Fourth Street Bridge.

Conor and Glennie went down to the lobby to head off their parents when they arrived. "Where's your girlfriend?" Dad elbowed Conor in the ribs.

"Stop it, Brian." Mom was trying to hold back a smile. "Don't tease him."

That afternoon, Javier taught Conor and Glennie how to do Adventure Boys round lashing with clove hitches. By suppertime, Conor could lash Glennie's arms to Ashling's legs in two minutes, using Ashling's belt. Equally important, he knew to leave a tail he could pull in order to undo the knots. "You never know," Javier said. "You might need to disconnect in a hurry."

Conor shuddered. Glennie tried to smirk and did not succeed. She downed a three-ounce pack of Fruity Foolers in two bites.

Ashling grudgingly allowed them to rip one strip from the bottom of her cloak, which they cut into two halves so Conor could lash himself and Grump to her arms. There still wasn't room to test whether Ashling could lift all three of them.

"We should have a real trial," Javier said, brow furrowed. "But it's still daylight out. Somebody will see."

"It'll be fine." Glennie danced a step or two. "Ooo, I can't wait." She looked at Conor and snorted. "Hey, Pixie, your eyebrows—"

"Shut up."

After Javier went home for supper, Conor got out a

topographical map of the Atlantic Ocean and tried to get Ashling to show him where the entrance to the Other Land was. "There's the Bermuda Rise," he said, pointing to a ridge off the east coast of the United States. "Think it could be there? Or over here, the Mid-Atlantic Ridge?"

He hoped not. The Mid-Atlantic Ridge was almost three thousand miles away—so far that Conor didn't have an exact distance, which he found unsettling.

"I don't see how there could be a rock poking up in the middle of the ocean," Glennie said.

"A bunch of islands are part of that ridge," Conor said. "See, there's the Azores, and here's St. Helena."

Ashling barely glanced at the map. "Conor-boy, I don't know where it is in that picture. The Other Land is where it is. That's all."

"I'm not going unless I see it on a map."

"Told you he'd wimp out," Glennie said.

"I told *you,* he is a hero. He will not wimp out." Ashling turned around so she could peer into Conor's eyes—into his brain, it felt like. "Conor-boy, I must talk with you. I . . . There is a thing I've remembered."

"Oooo." Glennie settled down on Conor's bed. "There's *always* a thing."

"It is not for you," Ashling said stiffly. "This is between Conor-boy and me."

"Is it about tonight? Something horrible we don't know

about?" *Maybe we can't go after all.* Conor's cowardly heart lifted.

Ashling shook her head. "It is about the dreams you've been having. I have had one, too."

A door slammed downstairs. "Hurry up, kids," Mom yelled up the stairs. "Pizza's here! Get it while it's hot."

"Can you tell me real quick?" Conor wanted to know what she'd remembered, but he also wanted an hour or two off—a normal Saturday night of pizza and a movie.

Ashling sank into the beanbag chair, woebegone. "I will have to tell you later."

The pizza was hot and the movie was funny. When the night was over, Conor and Glennie departed for bed without complaint.

"What, no late-night comedy show offensive?" Dad said. "Whatsamatter with you two?"

"We're tired because we're so worried about Grump," Glennie said, in a flash of brilliance.

"Aw," Mom said. "He'll be fine, kids. I just talked to him, and they took out the IV and everything."

Upstairs, Conor shoved a sad-faced Ashling into the game cupboard, put on his pajamas, and climbed into bed so he'd look normal when his mother came to kiss him good night. The minute she was gone, he leaped out of bed and layered on long underwear, corduroys, flannel shirts and two sweaters, finishing with his parka, hat, and scarf. Ashling emerged from the game cupboard and laughed in spite of herself at the care he took to organize his layers.

"What did you remember?" Conor whispered. "Can you tell me quick?"

The light went out of her eyes. "It's complicated. Last night, as I slept, I saw Declan as if I were standing with him, and so much came flooding back to me. I admired him, wanted to be with him—the feeling was strong. I watched him work, I loved his hands, his eye for beauty. But he boasted he would rescue me from the smelly old man, and that angered me. I said, 'I am a woman of the Uí Néill, not a thing to be carried off. I make this marriage for my family.' And I told my father and . . . and I told the smelly old man."

Conor fished his mittens out of his parka pocket and waited for more. She took her comb out and tidied up the end of her braid.

"Is that all?" he whispered. "Who was I?"

"I don't know. Declan was nothing like you. He was . . . big. Strong." She smiled, remembering. "Loud."

In other words, not a boy named Pixie with peaked-up eyebrows.

At eleven, Conor's parents came upstairs and turned on the television in their bedroom, which meant they'd be asleep in three minutes. Glennie tiptoed into Conor's room, mouth full of Fruity Foolers.

She had on corduroys, two sweaters, her winter jacket

and scarf, and a gray raccoon-face hat, complete with a stuffed nose and little ears. "It's the only one that ties under my chin," she said when she saw Conor's expression. Her mittens had frog faces on them and were tied to a string threaded through her sleeves.

"My sister, the walking zoo," Conor muttered.

"Take off that thing with the eyes." Ashling pointed at a frog mitten. "I must not touch Worldcraft, remember?"

Glennie took off one mitten and let it dangle. Then she helped Conor on with a backpack he'd stuffed with Grump's warmest clothes.

His cell phone vibrated, dancing across the top of his bureau. A text from Javier: Brng yr cel. "Oh, cripes," he muttered. "Why?" Typical Javier. No experience was complete without electronics.

"Dunno, but do what he says." Glennie handed Ashling her ravaged cloak. "Javier's smart."

At the open window, Ashling held out her hands to Conor and Glennie. "Shall we go?"

Glennie gave a soft squeal and danced over to take Ashling's hand. Conor did not follow. "We're going to fly now? Why not climb down the fire escape?"

Glennie made a *snerk* noise. "He's chickening out. I knew he would."

Ashling ignored her. "Come, Conor-boy. No sense putting it off."

Conor took off a mitten, stuck it in his pocket, and

grabbed Ashling's hand. His arm buzzed and went light, then the rest of him. He closed his eyes and concentrated on not puking. His foot knocked against something—the window frame? Cold air bathed his face, and he knew he was outside, floating.

It felt weird, like swimming without getting wet. And without the comforting presence of water, buoying him up.

"Wheeeee!" Glennie squealed.

"Shhh," Ashling said. "Conor-boy, where is Javier's house? You must open your eyes and show me. And you must help me kick, or we will float with the wind."

Conor opened his eyes a crack, saw lights under his feet. "Gohhhhh."

"Conor-boy."

He opened his eyes all the way. They were drifting over a deserted Crumlin Street, twice as high as any house. He pointed two streets over. "I think it might be that house there, with the gray chimneys."

"There's the cupcake store!" Glennie yelled. "And my school!"

"Dude, hush," Ashling said. "Time enough for shouting when we are over the sea. Kick now."

It was awkward, coordinating three sets of legs. Finally they figured out that they had to let themselves go horizontal, as if they really were swimming, and kick for all they were worth while Ashling pointed herself in the right direction. Their progress was slow.

"This is impossible," Conor panted as they herky-jerked along over the rooftops. "How are we supposed to cross an ocean like this?"

"Nergal said if I had to fly, I should rise above the clouds and the Other Land will draw me to it," Ashling said. "This part is harder because nothing is pulling us."

Javier was on the corner near his house, under a street-light. He pointed across the intersection, where there was a little park.

They met in the dim light under the trees. "We'd better go up pretty high," Javier said. "You were way too visible coming over the rooftops."

Great, Conor thought.

"Cool," Glennie said, smirking at him.

Ashling perched on the back of a bench. Under Javier's eye, Conor lashed Glennie's arms to Ashling's legs in best Adventure Boys fashion.

"Go up a little and see if it holds," Javier advised Ashling.

"See if it *holds*?" Conor and Glennie asked in unison.

"It will, it will," Javier reassured them. "But . . . you know . . . let's see."

"You'll be light, remember," Ashling said. "We must only be touching." She closed her eyes, breathed deep, and lifted off, Glennie dangling underneath.

"Ooo, I don't like it," Glennie said. "My arms feel weird sticking up like this."

Conor and Javier climbed up on the bench so Ashling could reach their hands. Conor felt himself go light again. He swallowed hard to keep his dinner down.

"*Guuuhhhh,*" Javier said. "Wish I hadn't eaten so much."

Ashling couldn't kick with Glennie tied to her legs, so Glennie did it for her. Conor and Javier kicked, too, and tried to stroke with their free arms as if they were in a pool. They could see the hospital in the distance, all lighted up, but for a long time it seemed they were making no progress toward it at all, just drifting on the east wind.

Conor was working up a sweat under his layers of clothing. *Can't believe I worried about being cold.*

After what seemed like hours, they reached the hospital and found the right roof. Grump was at his window, waving his good arm.

Ashling dropped Javier and Conor off first—literally, from about three feet over the asphalt roof, right by the door. Then she hovered while they untied Glennie. Conor prayed no one was looking out the window. They tapped on the door and it swung open, Grump grinning behind it. He was wearing his hospital gown and, oddly, a surgical cap.

Far away, a bell started pinging.

Excited voices. Footsteps, hurrying in their direction.

"Holy macaroni," Grump said. "There's an alarm on the door."

And the bell kept pinging.

Chapter Twelve

"Quick," Grump said. "Hide in that broom closet."

Conor and the others hustled into a large closet three steps down the hall. Grump stayed outside and shut them in. They were in pitch darkness, listening.

"Mr. O'Neill!" It was Angela Timulty, RN. How many hours did she work? "Did you open that roof door?"

"I needed some fresh air," Grump said. "I feel all closed in."

"Are you breathing all right? How are your ribs?"

"I'm fine. Here, take my pulse."

"You need to get back into bed, Mr. O'Neill. You'll make yourself sick and you won't be going home in the morning."

They walked down the hall, their voices retreating. "Dr. Murphy says we're to let you sleep tonight, but I don't see you sleeping," Angela Timulty said. "Didn't you have a sleeping pill?"

"Yeah, and it's kicking in. I'll definitely sleep now."

"Make sure you do."

And they were gone.

"How are we going to get to Grump's room now?" Glennie whispered. "She'll be watching it like a hawk."

"I wonder," Ashling said.

"Wonder what? Keep your voice down." Conor knew that nothing they'd planned was going to work. They were doomed.

"Take my hand," Ashling said. "Does this room have ee-let . . . ee-letra . . ."

"Electricity," Javier said. "Just a second . . . it must be here by the . . . yup." They all blinked in the blast of light.

Ashling grabbed Conor's hand, took a deep breath, closed her eyes, and vanished.

Conor felt cold air wash over him. He looked down at himself. He was gone, too—except for his outer sweater, floating in the air, and a pair of empty shoes on the floor.

"Whoa," Javier said. Conor had to admit, it was pretty cool. He danced his foot around to watch the shoe move by itself. Glennie giggled.

Ashling reappeared, beaming. "If I touch you, you disappear when I do!"

"Whoa," said Javier. "But . . . what's with the shoes and sweater? Some part of them must have to be touching Conor's skin."

"We'll take off our socks," Conor said.

"How will we all connect?" Glennie asked. "We can't tie me to Ashling's legs again."

"It's only down the hall," Javier said. "If we're each touching her hand with one finger it'll probably work."

They tiptoed out of the closet and down the little hall to the main corridor, Ashling keeping one arm out straight so Glennie and Javier could both touch it. Conor held her other hand, trying not to blush and grateful to be invisible. He carried his socks and cell phone, and pulled the sleeves of both his parka and outer sweater down over his hands to make sure they touched his skin.

They had to creep along, as they discovered right away when Javier kept losing contact and flickering into sight. It was weird once they made the turn onto the main corridor. Angela Timulty, RN, hurried past them without a glance, and they had to shuffle sideways to avoid a janitor with a big floor buffer. Glennie found it hard to keep touching Ashling's arm while shuffling, so she winked into view as the janitor passed. He stopped dead (not really) in his tracks and whirled around, but by then Glennie and Ashling had reestablished contact. The janitor shook his head and continued to the hallway leading to the roof door, where he stopped and plugged in his floor buffer.

Conor tried to avoid looking down—seeing only the floor tiles, with no feet on top of them, made him dizzy. Because he couldn't see his feet, he couldn't be sure where they were. He was afraid he'd step on himself and fall over.

When they reached Grump's door, a sneeze erupted

out of thin air. Javier. They all froze. A guy standing at the nurses' station down the hall glanced up. He stared straight at them just about forever, then shook his head and returned his attention to a chart he was reading.

Grump was sitting on his bed, disgruntled, but he cheered up when he saw them all materialize inside the door. "That's a neat trick. Can we all do that?"

"My left foot is still invisible," Glennie said. "It kind of tingles."

"Shhh." Conor glanced at Grump's roommate, a tiny little guy with a huge snore.

"Oh, he's out like a light," Grump said. "I would be, too, if I'd taken that pill they gave me." He handed Javier his surgical cap. "Smart, huh? So you can pretend to be me. I said my head got cold. This way they won't notice you got all that nice black hair."

"I plan to snore if anyone comes in," Javier said. "That'll keep them away."

"A nice loud fart would do it better, *amigo*," Grump said. Javier was so horrified he didn't even roll his eyes about the *"amigo."*

Glennie tiptoed to the door and listened. "Cripes. That janitor's working right by the door to the roof."

I knew it, Conor thought. *We're doomed.* His brain went into overdrive. "Okay. Okay. So . . . we'll go out the front door. We'll go invisible. But"—he considered Grump's pallid face—"we need a wheelchair."

"I don't need a wheelchair," Grump said.

"Yes, you do." Glennie jutted out her jaw. "All you did was walk down the hall and back, and you sound like a walrus."

Grump jutted his jaw precisely the same way as Glennie. "I. Don't. Need. A. Wheelchair."

Conor's heart sank. His eyebrows peaked up.

Grump got a load of Conor's eyebrows and the set of Glennie's jaw, and grunted exactly like a walrus. "Oh, for cripes' sake. Okay, okay. Curb the eyebrows and find me a friggin' wheelchair."

While Grump and Javier changed their clothes, Glennie stood watch at the door. Conor and Ashling, holding hands, tiptoed out into the hall invisible. There was a wheelchair about thirty feet away—pretty close, but also within a couple yards of the nurses' station. No chance the staff wouldn't notice it making off by itself down the hallway.

The only hope was to empty the nurses' station. "Can you think yourself to the elevator and create a disturbance?" Conor whispered to Ashling.

She nodded. Conor's hand went empty—and became visible. He ducked into Grump's doorway. Thirty seconds later, a blood-freezing scream echoed down the hallway on the other side of the nurses' station. "Ahhhh!" Ashling yelled. "The fright alligator! It has me! Ahhhhh!"

Which made no sense, but it didn't seem to matter. The

nurses exchanged a panicked glance and rushed off in the direction of the noise. Conor scuttled down the hall, nabbed the wheelchair, and hustled back to the room, arriving just as Ashling rematerialized.

"It's *elevator,* not *alligator,*" Glennie informed Ashling.

"I wondered," Ashling said. "The American alligator lives fifty years in captivity, thirty-five in the wild."

Grump was all dressed, and Javier had on the hospital gown and surgical cap. He stuffed his clothes in Grump's closet, first taking out a wide belt of sturdy white canvas. He lunged at Grump and, without asking, snaked the belt around the old man's waist, outside his winter jacket.

"What in the Sam Hill is this?" Grump picked at it with his good hand.

"It's called a gait belt." Javier cinched it tight. "It belonged to my grandmother. Conor and Glennie can grab it if you start to fall."

Without waiting to catch the look on Grump's face—which would have terrified a soul-sucking demon warrior—Javier climbed into bed and pulled the covers up until only the top of his head was showing. They stuffed a pillow in at the foot of the bed to make him seem taller.

"Conor." Javier's voice was muffled by blankets. "Got your cell?"

"Yeah." Conor patted his jacket's inside pocket. "Don't see what good it'll do me."

"I'll text you if anything happens that you should know."

"*Text* me? Javier, we'll be in the afterlife."

"You never know. Maybe they get a signal."

"If you could text dead people, I think it would have been on the news by now."

"Just keep your phone on, okay? And zip it in before you take off . . . You don't want it to fall in the ocean." Conor envisioned the cell phone falling down, down, down into the water. It hit him that he was about to fly over the Atlantic Ocean holding hands with a banshee, to a place he'd never seen on a map.

His stomach gurgled. He sat down on the end of Grump's bed, spaghetti-legged.

"C'mon, kiddo." Grump got into the wheelchair. "Let's get this show on the road."

The wheelchair had to stay visible—there were too many separate parts, and no way somebody's skin could be touching all of them. "Is there anyone at the nurses' station?" Conor asked.

Ashling went invisible. The door opened all by itself, and closed. They waited. Then the door opened again and Ashling reappeared. "There's a man sitting there talking to himself. I'm scared of him."

"Does he have one of these?" Conor fished his cell phone out of his pocket.

"I don't know. I didn't stay long enough to notice."

Conor looked at Glennie, who shrugged. "We have to try it," she said.

Javier's voice rose from the mass of blankets on the bed. "If someone sees you, stop and hope they think the chair rolled by itself. If you stay by the wall, maybe they'll leave it there."

Conor sighed. *This will never work.* "Okay. Let's go."

He and Glennie took hold of the two handles on the back of the wheelchair, Ashling between them with her right hand on Grump's neck. Glennie grabbed Ashling's right wrist. Ashling put her left hand on Conor's wrist. Again, he felt that wash of cold air, and where his feet used to be, there was nothing but floor tile.

He'd forgotten his cell phone, which was hanging in midair. He took it out of his pocket and gave it to Grump, who was already holding everybody's socks.

The corridor was empty as they pushed the wheelchair out of Grump's room. They hugged the wall all the way to the nurses' station, where a guy in scrubs talked on his cell phone. He had his back to them, and the long, curving counter would have kept him from seeing the chair anyway, but they had to inch along for the wheels to stay as quiet as possible.

The counter curved around to another corridor, the one that led to the elevators. Conor, who was on the outside, pushed his half of the wheelchair a little harder to make the turn. He couldn't consult with Glennie, though, and instinctively—competitively—she pushed harder, too. The chair wobbled in its course, squeaking, and then—

disaster!—bumped against the counter, probably grazing Glennie's knuckles.

Glennie let out the teeniest, tiniest *huff*.

"Hang on," the man in scrubs said. "I heard something weird."

The man heaved himself up onto the counter on his belly so he could see over it. "Huh," he said to the wheelchair. "Look at you. You weren't there before, were you?"

Conor tried not to breathe, concentrating on absolute stillness. Grump's walrus breathing quieted, too.

The man slid off the counter and got back on his phone. "Nothing. Just a wheelchair. Must have rolled from someplace." He listened to whoever was on the phone, staring straight at Conor, who felt an almost overwhelming urge to duck down and hide.

He can't see me, he can't see me, he can't see me . . .

Minutes ticked by, and still the man stood there and talked. But then Angela Timulty, RN, hustled up the corridor from the elevators. The man stuffed his cell phone into his pocket.

"What's this wheelchair doing here?" Angela Timulty paused in mid-hustle.

"I think it rolled here," the man said.

"Well, roll it back. This is a terrible place for it."

"Yeah, I was going to. You find the screamer?"

"No, and security didn't either. I'm going down to check on Mr. O'Neill. He's a bit of a happy wanderer."

Angela Timulty hurried down the hall. The man in scrubs craned his neck to watch her go, then hauled out his cell phone. His back was to them now, as he kept his eye out for the nurse's return. "I gotta go, babe," he told the cell phone. "Hatchet Face is back. She's working a double shift, so she's even more . . . Huh? Yeah, I guess."

It was now or never. Conor reached around Ashling to poke Glennie, and they pushed the chair slowly down the corridor to the elevator.

The man kept talking on his phone. Conor kept waiting for pandemonium to erupt in Grump's room. But nothing happened. They reached the elevator. Conor pushed the call button. They waited. And waited.

The man said good-bye to whoever was on the phone. He rustled around behind the desk. Any minute, *any* minute, he'd come out to deal with the wheelchair and find that it had rolled all the way to the elevator.

The elevator bell rang. "Hurry," Conor whispered. "Oh, hurry, hurry."

They didn't wait for the door to open all the way, just shoved the wheelchair in. Conor flung himself at the CLOSE DOOR button.

"Hey," they heard the man in scrubs say. "Where'd that wheelchair go?"

Conor pushed LOBBY, although he wondered if that was a good idea. Would the empty wheelchair roll out of the elevator into a whole troop of security guys?

"Sorry I made noise," Glennie said out of thin air as they turned the wheelchair around to face the door.

"Wasn't your fault," Grump said. It was like the wheelchair was talking.

"In 1998, forty-eight people lost their lives in roller-coaster accidents." Ashling's voice quavered. "This thing we're in, is it like a roller coaster?"

"Why would that worry you?" Glennie's voice again. "You're already dead."

"Don't be rude to the banshee, kiddo," the wheelchair said.

The elevator stopped moving.

Conor braced himself for the worst.

The door opened.

It was the worst.

Three security guys stood there, staring into an elevator that looked empty except for a wheelchair. "What is this, a joke?" the tall one said.

"Any idea which floor it's from?" the short one asked.

The third security guard, who was medium size, reached for the wheelchair's arm. He missed, stumbled a little, and braced himself on the elevator door. The other guys cracked up.

If he jerked the chair out of the elevator, could Ashling stay in contact with them all so they'd still be invisible? Conor doubted it.

Glennie, however, had her own ideas. She poked him

and breathed, "Push it out." Without waiting for him to reply—as if he could—she made a whirring noise and pushed.

Conor pushed, too.

He also prayed.

Ahead of them, three jaws dropped. The tall, medium, and short security guards backed hastily away as the empty wheelchair rolled out of the elevator and headed for the front door. Glennie kept up the whirring noise.

From the general vicinity of Grump came a crackling sound, like a walkie-talkie. "ER to cardiac ward," Grump said in a high-pitched, muffled voice. "Repeat: Please send electric self-guiding wheelchair to the ER. Inside doors blocked, use the front. Over."

Grump made the crackling sound again, then said in a deeper voice, "Already on the way. Over and out."

"Will ya look at that?" the tall security guard said. "Did you know they had electric self-guiding wheelchairs?"

"You didn't know that?" the medium-size guard said. "Where you been?"

"I never seen one," the short guard said. "But I heard about 'em. You gotta stay on top of things, Louie."

The sliding doors opened. They were outside.

"ER's to the right," Conor whispered. All he could hear was his heart pounding. They turned, conscious of the three guards watching them through the lobby's huge windows. "You guys are nuts. I can't believe that worked."

"Quiet, kiddo," Grump said. "We ain't out of this yet."

"I don't understand why they let us pass," Ashling whispered. "What is a self-chiding wheelchair?"

"We'll explain later," Glennie said.

They scuttled past the emergency room and around a corner, seeking a private spot. In a dark alley, everyone disconnected. Grump was visible by the gleam of his wheelchair. Glennie was a shadow with white raccoon eyes.

"Rats," Conor said. "We didn't bring a flashlight." How was he going to tie knots in the dark?

Glennie pressed something plastic into his hand: a mini-flashlight, part of the stocking haul from last Christmas. "Glad I came?" she said.

He didn't have to see her face to know it was half smirking. Grump's voice came into his head: *Glennie's as much of a con artist as I am.* Exactly what had Conor contributed to this effort so far? Glennie should have gone alone.

Conor's cell phone vibrated.

U get out? Javier texted.

Yup. How u?

Nrse km, no prob. Snored. Dint fart.

K.

Set yr fone 2 ring.

Y?

So u here it, dork.

K. By.

Gd luk.

Gd luk.

Conor hesitated, then reset his phone ringer. "This is stupid. It'll never ring anyways."

They put their socks back on—nobody'd notice floating shoes in the dark. They pulled their scarves up and their hat brims down, so all that showed were their eyes. Ashling took Grump's hand. Conor lashed them together with a strip from Ashling's cloak, while Glennie held the flashlight. Then Grump stood up and Ashling floated them high enough for Conor to lash Glennie to her legs. Last of all, he stood on the wheelchair seat to do a sloppy, one-handed job of lashing his hand to Ashling's.

The invisibility chill washed over him. Everything fizzed and lightened. He shut his eyes, grateful that six hours had passed since dessert.

"Good-bye, wheelchair," Glennie said.

"We must kick straight up," Ashling cried. "Kick, kick, kick!"

"Grump can't kick," Conor yelled.

"Then you and the girl must kick harder!"

Conor got his legs moving. Below him, Glennie made an *oof* sound—she was kicking, too. Cold air rushed past his face—heading straight up turned out to be much faster than bumbling along horizontally.

"Whooooooo-hooooo!" Grump yelled. "Yeeeee-haw!"

"There's South Station!" Glennie hollered. "And the John Hancock building! This is sooooo cooool!"

Conor had never hated her so much in his life.

He opened his eyes a crack. Boston was a spiderweb of lights, just like a satellite map image and maybe the last familiar thing he would ever see. The city got smaller and smaller. He shut his eyes again. And kept kicking.

Up, up, up . . . and they were soaking wet. Cold wisps drifted across Conor's eyelids. His eyes flew open and he saw . . . nothing, at first, then a faint grayness. Even under the scarf, his nose was so cold he thought it might fall off. He shut his eyes again so his eyeballs wouldn't freeze. It got harder to kick—he was almost too cold to move.

"I'm letting us go visible," Ashling shouted. "It's too much work to keep us invisible and floating." It hadn't occurred to Conor that keeping them in the air was an effort. His stomach clenched in terror.

"It's freezing," Glennie yelled below. "I hate this." He wanted to ask her if she was glad she came, but he didn't think he could unfreeze his jaw. Grump hadn't said a word for several minutes. Was he all right? If he wasn't, there was nothing Conor could do about it now.

The cold hurt. He couldn't feel his hand or his eyelids. He almost wanted Ashling to let him drop and be done with it.

But then they burst out of the mist into a moonlit cloud-scape, the air still freezing cold but clear and dry. The moon was behind them, so bright that they cast a shadow on the dead-white plain of cloud. Here and there, the flat surface swept up in bright, moon-washed peaks.

It was so beautiful Conor almost forgot to be cold.

Almost.

"Stop kicking now," Ashling said. "We must wait to be pulled."

They bobbed in the frigid air, still rising gently. Nothing happened.

"Remember when Grump used to hold us up to touch the moon?" Glennie shouted.

Conor craned his neck to see how Grump was doing. The old man's head was sunk on his chest. Ice had formed on his scarf and the sling holding his arm. As if he sensed Conor's concern, he lifted his head and gave his grandson a stiff nod.

"How's the arm?" Conor yelled.

"Hurts like a son of a gun." Grump's voice seemed to float away on the wind. "But cold air helps."

"You okay?"

"Sure, kiddo. Why not?"

Conor knew he was lying.

"Ah!" Ashling said. "Aha!" They jerked forward, then stopped.

Something forced them backward, then sideways. Conor hoped his lashing held.

And then they moved forward, slowly at first, then faster,

much faster. A cloud peak slid by underfoot, then another. Their speed made Conor's eyes water.

"Here we go-o-o-o!" Ashling yelled.

They must be over the ocean now. Conor imagined freezing cold whitecaps. Sharks. The fairy horse that drowned and ate you. He'd almost prefer spiders.

Almost.

Chapter Thirteen

The night dragged on. The cloud peaks no longer amazed. Conor half dozed, cold, scared, tired, aching. He couldn't imagine how Grump felt, or even Glennie, dangling below.

His eyelids drooped. There was a sharp, cold spot on his neck where his scarf needed adjusting, but the rest of him went warm. Which made sense . . . because his blood was burning.

He stands there in the shadows, angry and panting, looking for Aengus so he can continue killing him. But she distracts him, puts her hand on his chest. "Calm yourself," she murmurs. "Breathe." The firelight catches her strange eyes, blue with a wedge of gray.

He's seen her do this to a panicked young bull six times her size. He wonders if he should be insulted. But he does breathe, just as she said. His heart slows. "You are good with cattle," he tells her, covering her hand with his. "I am the best of all," she says. But then she slips her hand away, suddenly shy, her uncanny gaze on the ground.

"You had something to tell me," he says. She keeps her gaze stubbornly down.

He jolted awake, shivering, sorry to be back in reality. *This is nuts. I'm dreaming this stuff because of what she's told me. It's not real.*

Ashling rolled her head around on her neck, as if getting the kinks out. *That was you, for sure,* he thought. *Who was I?*

"Are you getting tired?" he asked, whitecaps and sharks on his mind.

"What will you do about it if I am?"

Good point.

Ahead, the horizon had a halo of gray. As they rushed forward, it acquired a rosy hue. Without meaning to, Conor let out a moan. Surely they must be almost there.

Wherever *"there"* was.

"Patience, Conor-boy," Ashling said.

As it turned out, "there" arrived with absolutely no warning. One minute they were scudding along, the next . . .

"*Ach!* Here we go!" Ashling yelled. Conor had time to say "Whu . . . ?" and then they were spiraling down, plunging through the clouds, hurtling toward the exact whitecaps that had been haunting his thoughts.

He closed his eyes. Glennie was shrieking. He tried to think about Grump, his parents, even Javier. *Good-bye,* he thought.

"I didn't think of this!" Ashling hollered.

"Think of what?" Conor yelled back.

"We're falling too fast. We will all land on top of the little girl."

"Slow down!"

"I'm trying! Help me—spread your arms out wide!"

Conor spread-eagled facedown like a skydiver, his cheeks rippling, his teeth so cold he was afraid they'd shatter. Below him, Glennie was doing her best to spread out, too, but was hampered by having her hands tethered. Not much Grump could do, with his arm in a sling.

Below, the whitecaps broke on a pile of rock in the middle of the Atlantic. It was getting closer by the second, drawing them to it.

"Conor-boy," Ashling hollered, "untie your sister!"

"Are you KIDDING?"

"DO IT! NOW!"

Every instinct screamed that untying Glennie would kill her. Conor imagined his sister smashed on the rocks or drowning in the waves. He couldn't do it—he wouldn't. He tried to stretch his arms out beyond the capacity of blood and muscle, anything to slow them down.

They didn't slow down.

"CONOR!" Ashling screamed. "We will crush her!"

"Okay! Okay!" Conor pulled his mitten off with his teeth, and it flapped away on the wind. Ashling bent over, lowering him so he could pull the tail of belt leather that

190

would release Glennie's arms. He swung back and forth, stretching, and just missed the flapping tail.

It seemed to him they were slowing down—was that wishful thinking? The pile of rock—a small island now—loomed closer. Its surface was in motion, but he had no time to puzzle about that.

The tail hit his hand. His fingers were too cold to grasp it.

"CONNNNNORRRR!" Glennie shrieked. Below her was nothing but rock, still coming on too fast.

He swung again, desperate . . . and caught the tail in his hand, clutched it, tried to pull. It was stuck, frozen. He used his legs to swing himself, then pulled, pulled, pulled.

And it worked. The lashing unraveled on one arm.

Then the other.

Glennie fell, screaming.

Grump shouted.

Conor shut his eyes, not wanting to see. They were slowing down now, he was sure of it—if he'd waited, kept Glennie with them, could he have saved her after all?

But then his feet glanced off something soft and landed on something hard. Ashling crashed into his side, almost wrenching his arm out of its socket. He slipped and slithered, then thumped down on his butt in what felt like a puddle. The air smelled of seaweed, salt air, and something disgusting—poop, lots of it, and wet animals. He opened his eyes.

He was on a rocky shore. A wave smashed into smith-
ereens a couple of yards from his feet. He was in fact sitting in a puddle, Ashling beside him, Grump beside her,
lying there panting.

Conor's butt was soaking wet. But his most immediate
concern was his nose.

Which was less than an inch from the much larger nose
of a giant red grizzly bear.

Its tawny eyes gazed deep into his. It bared its teeth.
Something changed in its eyes, promising disaster.

But then the bear put out its tongue and slurped him
once, from chin to forehead. It turned away and snuffled at
a crab near Conor's hand, but didn't eat that, either.

"That creature's dead," Ashling said. "It's not hungry
anymore. Everybody and everything here is newly dead."

"Where's Glennie?" Grump struggled to sit up.

"Glennie!" Conor yelled. What if she'd fallen in the
ocean? What if she landed too hard and broke everything?
What if something ate her?

"I'm here!" Glennie hollered, her voice far away and
muffled.

Conor's spine turned to jelly, and he slumped with his
head on his knees.

"Conor," Grump gasped, "can you get us untied?"

Conor undid all the knots, then struggled to his feet.
Water from the puddle ran down the backs of his legs. He
was on a giant rock, barely big enough to be called an

island. It should have been freezing, stuck up in the middle of the ocean like that, but it was comfortably warm.

It also was crowded: dogs, cats, cows, sheep, chickens, people in funny clothes, llamas, people in regular clothes, several parrots, lizards, a dozen orangutans, some lions, an alligator, a bunch of animals he couldn't name.

Glennie appeared in the distance, raccoon hat untied, frog mittens dangling, leaning on a tiger.

"I landed on him," she yelled. "All he did was lick me. It's SO COOL."

Conor took a step and his foot almost slithered out from under him. He looked down. The rock was slimy with white bird dung and a greasy brown substance. "If they don't eat," he asked Ashling, "why do they still poop?"

"One of Death's great mysteries," Ashling said. "Are you all right, old man?"

"Yeah," Grump said, "but I feel like heck. The painkillers wore off over Bermuda."

Glennie left her tiger and wandered over. She cocked her head at Conor's soaked corduroys. "What did you do, wet your pants?"

Conor took off his parka and one sweater and tied them around his waist. They were too warm anyway.

"We must hurry," Ashling said. "Careful you don't slip on your way to the portal." She pointed. Next to a cluster of men in long colorful robes was a jagged cave entrance, about the size of 36A and 36B Crumlin Street combined.

Ashling set off, pushing and shoving, manhandling and lionhandling her way forward. Glennie followed, supporting Grump by his good arm, with Conor in back, holding him up by the gait belt. Conor wasn't sure he and Glennie were accomplishing much—if Grump started to fall, they'd all go down in a poop-smeared heap.

"This stinks," Glennie yelled to Ashling. "It must be gross inside."

"The animals do not relieve themselves in there," Ashling yelled back.

"Why not?"

"Another of the great mysteries."

Every time Conor felt himself falling he grabbed an animal that would normally be on TV or far away in a field. But even the lion didn't object when Conor clutched at a handful of mane—it regarded him sadly, with just a hint of reproach.

"No wonder everyone hates this portal." Ashling tugged at her cloak, which was trapped under a moose's foot. "I hardly ever come here."

"Why isn't everybody going in?" Conor asked.

"You'll see soon enough. Move, blast you, you great big whatever!" Ashling shoved the moose repeatedly in the back of the knee. At last, the hoof released her cloak.

One of the men in the long robes came up to them. "Excuse me. Where are we supposed to go?"

"You speak English!" Conor said.

"We are speaking Urdu."

"No, no, we're . . ." Conor's brain engaged. *Sweet. I have a universal translator.* "Um. I think you're supposed to follow the animals through that entrance."

"Guh." The man returned to his companions.

"What's the problem?" Conor yelled, but got no answer. He and Glennie maneuvered Grump around a cow and a giraffe, slithered past a Shetland pony.

They arrived at the portal. And they saw the problem.

About ten feet inside the huge cave entrance was a rock wall with a slit at the base, barely wide enough to accommodate the polar bear that squeezed itself in as they watched. When the bear was gone, a llama sniffed at the entrance and tried to back away from it. The crowd of beasts behind the llama growled and pressed forward until it reluctantly slipped inside. Its place was taken by a leopard, who also stopped and sniffed.

"Cripes. This'll take a while," Glennie said.

Grump groaned and clutched at his broken arm, leaning back against Conor so hard they both almost fell down. Glennie shooed six penguins off a rock so Grump could sit for a minute.

Grump was panting. "Holy macaroni," he kept saying.

"Stop complaining, old man," Ashling said. "You wanted to come."

"He's trying to save his family," Conor protested.

"He's a hindrance."

Conor wanted to hit her.

The island was getting more and more crowded. Humans and animals kept appearing out of thin air, dazed and nervous, clearly with no idea where they were. Conor supposed some of them might have died so suddenly that they didn't even know what was happening. He could see the advantage of having a banshee guide. He wondered if the Irish were the only ones to come up with that idea.

He had his answer when a tall black woman in a colorful robe and headdress strode past the moose and shoved a warthog out of her way. She hauled behind her a skinny old woman in a pink T-shirt and a long orange-print wraparound skirt, her face contorted in a silent shriek.

"What a mess," the tall woman said. "I hate this portal." She paused, assessing Grump. "What's wrong with that old man? He looks as if he's in pain."

"He is in pain," Conor said. "Can you help him?"

The woman pierced him with a look. "Pain? How is that possible?"

"He's not dead. Me neither."

"What is this?" The woman wheeled to face Ashling. "You have brought the *living* to the *Underworld*?"

Ashling flicked Conor a long-suffering eye roll. "This is my affair, not yours."

"That old man is in *pain,* the boy says."

"Dude, he does not know real pain. He should try an ax in the head."

"Why do you call me 'dude'? Is this a rude epithet?"

"We have business with the Lady. If you don't like the old man's pain, take it away from him."

"Only the Lady can do that. Or Nergal."

"Then you'd better stop being emo and let us go find them."

The old woman in the pink T-shirt whimpered. The tall woman pulled her aside and talked to her in a soothing voice.

"Who is that?" Grump eyed the tall woman as if she'd broken his other arm. "What's this 'Underworld'?"

"That's Oya," Ashling said, not fondly. "She guides the Yoruba dead. Their Underworld is the same thing as our Other Land. It's right here."

"Yoruba?" Grump sputtered. "This place is Irish!"

"The Yoruba are from West Africa," Conor said, doing Mr. Rose proud.

"I know where they're from. My point is—"

"My tiger's not from Ireland," Glennie said. "Neither are moose."

"*My* point," Ashling said, "is that Oya has no right to scold me. Only the Lady has that right. And sometimes Nergal."

"He's Babylonian," Conor said. A flock of pigeons and an armadillo slipped through the narrow cave entrance. He stared past them, hoping he'd see light flickering down there somewhere.

He didn't. The armadillo took three steps, and then Conor couldn't see it anymore. *It's like stepping into nowhere.*

"What . . . what's in there?" He hated how his voice sounded, an octave higher than usual. "Does it go underground?"

"Wimp-out alert," Glennie said.

"He's not wimping out." Ashling turned to Conor. "Yes, it goes underground—down to the Lady."

Tons of rock. Tons of ocean water, too. Pressing, pressing down, down, down.

He couldn't do it.

Oya was back, blocking the path to the cave entrance. She glared at Ashling. "The living cannot enter the Underworld. You know the rules." Conor wanted to kiss her.

"They have asked to test the Birds," Ashling said coldly. "If you will step aside, we will be on our way."

"The Cailleach will never let them pass."

"We will try our luck."

Glennie held a package of jelly beans out to Oya. "Fruity Fooler?"

Oya eyed the garish yellow and orange package with deep suspicion. "Is that food? We may not eat."

"Why not?"

"A mystery of death." Oya selected a red jelly bean, sniffed it. "I do not know what would happen to me if I ate Worldcraft." She sniffed again, then returned the candy to the package. "They smell nice."

Glennie rustled the package enticingly. "You could keep one. Just to sniff."

A smile flickered on Oya's face, then went out. "It will not last more than a few minutes. Food decays quickly in the Underworld." But she took back the jelly bean and held it to her nose. "I will enjoy the scent while I can. Thank you, child." She drew herself up so she could glare at Ashling from her full height. "Go, then. Pray I do not tell the Lady you called me 'dude.'"

"Follow me." Ashling slithered over to the narrow doorway, waited for an orangutan to waddle through, then slipped in herself. The darkness took her.

I can't do this, Conor thought.

"You're a brave kid, Conor," Grump said. Taking Grump's arm, Glennie eased sideways into the narrow doorway, pulling him after her.

Conor latched on to Grump's belt before it got away from him. Ahead was darkness and depth and next to nothing—behind him, everything he'd ever been. He stumbled forward. *I am Conor O'Neill, 36A Crumlin Street, South Boston, Massachusetts, thirty-two hundred feet from Boston Harbor. I do not go into dark places under rock.* But then, he also didn't fly across the Atlantic Ocean with a banshee.

The passageway air was dead with dust, the walls inches away. The darkness felt solid, brushing against Conor's face.

Something snorted and followed him into the passageway. He closed his eyes so the dark made sense. Grump
was breathing like three walruses.

"This is sorta fun." Glennie's voice echoed ahead. "It's
like blindman's bluff."

He hated her so much.

Chapter Fourteen

Footfall after footfall, down, down, down. Darkness and more darkness. Conor wanted to curl up in a ball on the floor, go to sleep until it was over. But he kept walking.

Think of something else. A map. "Mid-Atlantic Ridge," he muttered. "Gotta be." He envisioned his topographical map of the Atlantic Ocean and drew an imaginary circle where he thought he was. For a second or two he breathed easier.

Average ocean depth at sea floor, three miles, his mind supplied before he could stop it. His breathing went raggedy.

The tunnel widened, then narrowed again. *Good thing I'm smaller now,* he thought.

Huh? Smaller than what?

Behind his dark eyelids, something like a memory formed.

He's no longer young, but slavery has kept him muscular. He knows now that he's dead—nothing left to fear. Still, he seems to have a body and this tunnel is too narrow for it. He turns sideways, fighting a panic that shames him.

The animal ahead stops short, snorting. He shoves at it, but it won't budge. From behind, another animal presses against him.

The panic almost overwhelms him. He breathes deep and thinks of her, as he always does when he needs to escape from pain. Her red hair. Her uncanny eyes. She's been dead for years . . . Will he see her now? Probably not. But hope descends on him, quiets his breathing.

The animal ahead bellows and writhes, squeezes itself through the tight spot. The line struggles forward again.

Conor's eyes popped open.

He gasped, because the world was gray, no longer black. Dimly, he could see Grump's gait belt, his own hands gripping it.

"Ooo," Glennie said. "Torches."

They rounded a corner. The tunnel widened and turned into steps leading downward, flickering under torchlight.

The animals spread out in the extra space, leopard and llama amicably side by side. Far below, a figure dressed in white labored up the steps, weaving through the murmuring, bleating crowd.

"Grump," Conor said, "can you do these steps okay?"

"Of course I can. Quit asking stupid questions."

As they got closer, the figure in white turned out to be

a bald man in a toga. "Hello, Charon." Ashling moved to one side so the old man could pass.

"Charon?" Grump burst out. "He's a Greek myth, for cripes' sake. First some African lady, now this. What the heck is going on around here?"

"One person's myth is another's religion," Glennie said, prim under her raccoon-faced hat.

"If I want your opinion I'll ask for it." Grump leaned back against the wall to catch his breath.

Charon stopped several steps below them. He and Grump were performing a walrus-breathing duet. "You . . . think . . . Keltoi . . . the only people on earth?" Charon panted.

"Keltoi?" Glennie said.

"Celts." Grump glared at Charon. "That's us. In Greek, though."

Charon bent over, catching his breath and watching a stream of beetles and crickets flow around and past him. "Glad to see . . . they're moving. I was so worried . . . things would get . . . backed up."

"They did," Ashling said. "I don't see why you don't widen this entrance."

"Pure theater, dear." Charon straightened, joints creaking. "The Dear Departed like a last challenge, you know. Although I do need to go up and move things along."

"Oya's up there now," Ashling said.

Charon groaned. "Ohhhhh, lordy . . . Mistress High and

Mighty will have one or two words to say, I'm sure. She's always after me about the portals."

"Dude, she's right."

"'Dude,' did you say?" Charon's eyes lit up. "You've been in the World. I went there a few times." His eyes went unfocused, a soft smile playing around his lips. "Watched a joust. Three people died. I brought them home with me. Very pleasant they were. So pleasant."

"We'll be going now," Ashling said. "Is the Cailleach at the second gate?"

Conor hoped Charon would say no.

He didn't. "Ill-tempered as ever, the old bat. But you'll get through fast enough." Charon beamed at Glennie. "My goodness, you're a healthy-looking one. If I didn't know better, I'd almost say you were al—"

"Thank you, Charon," Ashling interjected. "We must move along now."

"Me too." Charon took a deep breath, trudged up two steps, then stopped in mid-trudge. "You don't have coins in your mouths, I suppose?"

Conor shook his head.

"Didn't think so." Charon sighed. "Greek thing, mostly, although the Keltoi sometimes did it in ages past. Used to be a rule—no Dear Departed would dream of coming to the Underworld without a coin for me. Even the Greeks don't always do it now. I've no use for the coins, you understand. But it's a lovely custom."

Charon seemed very knowledgeable.

"Um, sir?" Conor said. "Can you tell us where we are? I mean, is this the Mid-Atlantic Ridge, or—"

"You're dead, son. Relax. There's no going back."

"But, no, you don't understand . . ."

A horse rounded the corner up above, then a cow. Charon waved pleasantly and headed up again, hugging the tunnel wall to get past the animals. The tiger arrived and butted his head against Charon in playful fashion.

"Isn't Charon going to get squished?" Glennie asked.

"He's a demigod," Ashling said. "They don't squish. Hurry, we must move."

Grump took a step forward, tottered, and slumped back against the wall. "Grump!" Conor tried to hold him up by the gait belt, but the old man was too heavy and too tired. Conor had no choice but to let him slide his back down the tunnel wall and sit.

"Give me . . . a minute," Grump panted. "I'll be fine."

"You have to get up, old man," Ashling said. "We do not have time for this."

The horse and cow were upon them. Conor huddled over Grump, face to the wall, trying to shield his panting grandfather. Hooves clopped past, missing Grump's foot by a hairsbreadth.

"Aw," Glennie said. "Look, he remembers me." The tiger was leaning against her, purring, gazing into her face. "I guess he likes people dropping on him."

"Old man," Ashling said. "We must move."

"Help me up, kiddos." Grump put his good hand up for Glennie. Conor grabbed the belt from the front, and they both heaved. Grump gritted his teeth but let out only one gasp when he stumbled back against the wall, jostling his broken arm.

Glennie clutching his good arm and Conor holding on to the belt, Grump took a tentative step down the tunnel. "Stupid old fool," he muttered. "Useless."

Something nudged the back of Conor's knee. He looked down to see the tiger's huge head butting into Grump's legs. "Hey! Cut that out!"

Grump staggered. The tiger squatted, thrust his head forward and through Grump's legs. Grump tipped over backward, landing square on the tiger's shoulders, Glennie and Conor desperate to hang on and keep him from sliding off sideways.

The tiger shrugged Grump into a more comfortable seat on his back. Then the beast walked calmly forward. Conor and Glennie had to scurry to stay on either side of Grump, who was openmouthed speechless for the first time in Conor's memory.

"He's giving Grump a ride." Glennie was awestruck. "Good boy." The tiger rumbled in acknowledgment and kept walking.

"At least someone has some sense," Ashling said. "Come. Hurry."

They could move faster now. "It's not as slimy down here," Conor commented to Ashling's back. "This must be where they stop pooping."

"I told you."

They rounded another corner, then another. Conor lost all sense of direction—they could have been heading back west to Boston for all he knew. The steps got less steep, then steeper, then evened out again. At last they reached a place where the tunnel sloped gently downward, without any stairs at all. "Almost there, I think," Ashling said.

It was colder. Conor put his sweater and jacket back on. Glennie's nose was red, her breath coming out in clouds.

And then the growling began—or rather, Conor finally noticed the growling and realized it had been an undercurrent in the air ever since the tunnel went flatter.

"What's that noise?" Glennie was not smirking.

"Probably Dormath," Ashling said.

"Doormat?" Glennie tried to snicker, but managed only a tiny bleat.

Ashling shot a blue-eyed stare over her shoulder. "I wouldn't jest right now if I were you."

"What's Dormath?" Conor was proud that his voice didn't shake.

"He is a dog. The Cailleach's dog."

"Is he friendly?"

"Not very."

Conor had never been afraid of dogs. But he was open to changing his mind.

The growling was so loud that it bounced around on the rock walls. Conor kept whirling to look behind him, thinking the dog was there. The tiger remained placid, perhaps feeling that nothing could threaten a dead tiger.

"If Dormath doesn't bother the animals, he won't bother us," Conor ventured to Ashling.

"They're not alive. You are."

Conor halted, aghast. "Will he even let us in?"

"I don't know." Ashling kept walking.

"Why did you bring us here, then?" To make her stop, he raised his voice. It quavered among the echoes.

She did stop. "I thought you wanted to save your family."

"I thought we'd talk to the Lady. I didn't think we'd get torn apart by a dog."

"Look at your eyebrows, peaking up like that. Have you no pride?" Ashling started walking again. "I'll do what I can to save you."

"Just because you're dead doesn't mean the rest of us want to die, too," he flung at her retreating back. She ignored him and disappeared around the corner.

"I don't like dogs that much," Glennie said.

"You're not afraid of anything," Grump said from the tiger's back.

"Okay, I don't like big huge dogs who want to eat me."

She stroked the tiger's shoulder. "But our friend here will protect us."

"I don't know," Conor said. "He doesn't seem all that riled up to me."

His legs carried him down the tunnel, then around the corner. Where they froze. Along with every other part of him.

"Irish wolfhound," Grump said. "What a beauty. I hear they're very protective of their masters."

To Conor, Dormath was a shaggy, skinny goblin on four impossibly tall legs. His bottomless black eyes were level with Conor's, about a foot away. Yellowish gray and rangy, the dog's face reminded him of Grump. Even the raggedy eyebrows looked like an old man's.

Dormath opened his mouth and panted, drool streaming from his lower fangs. His breath smelled like cinnamon and something dead. The low growl they'd been hearing came from deep in his throat.

There was space to walk around the dog, but that didn't seem like a good idea. Beyond Dormath, Ashling waited with a tall figure veiled in black. They stood before a high archway, also black-veiled.

The veiled figure had a battered beige laptop computer, supported by a strap around what seemed to be its neck. Its bony fingers *tap-tap-tap*ped incessantly on the keyboard as llamas and leopards and beetles and grasshoppers swarmed past.

In one flowing move, the tiger sat down and Grump slid gently to the floor. The tiger touched Glennie's nose with his and shouldered past Dormath. He paused before the black-veiled figure, which typed something into its computer and nodded. The tiger pushed through the black-veiled archway and was gone.

Dormath grinned, his drool now a puddle on the stone floor.

"Do something, Conor," Glennie whispered.

"Help me get Grump up." A bit stronger after the ride on the tiger, Grump could stay on his feet unaided.

Dormath yawned, closing his mouth with an ominous snap.

"Hello," Conor tried to say, but really he sort of squeaked.

Dormath gazed into his eyes, drooling. *"Wow-whoa."* His voice was a croak.

"Can . . . can you talk?"

"Wow-whoa," Dormath croaked again.

"Hel . . . hello. My name is Conor."

"Wow-whoa."

"I guess we'll walk around you now." Conor shuffled to the left.

Dormath took Conor's sleeve in his teeth and rumbled like distant thunder.

Chapter Fifteen

"This dog won't let us get by," Glennie whispered, clutching Grump's arm.

Conor tried to tug his sleeve out of Dormath's teeth, but the giant dog wouldn't let go. "Ashling. Some help here?"

Ashling confronted the tall figure in black, who continued to type. "Madam Cailleach, these humans would petition the Lady for their family's safety. May they pass?"

"They live." It was a ragged, frosty voice, the kind you'd hear behind you on a moonless winter night, and when you whipped around there'd be no one there. *Tap-tap-tap* went the Cailleach's fingers.

"Yes, madam. They would challenge the Three, as is anyone's right."

"The living are not permitted here." The voice froze into Conor's bones. Glennie, shivering, snuggled close to Grump for what little warmth an old man might generate.

"Nergal brings the living sometimes," Ashling said.

"You are not Nergal."

"They are heroes. Heroes are permitted anywhere."

"Heroes?" Glennie whispered. "Us?"

It was a ludicrous thought, but Conor straightened his shoulders anyway. It wasn't like they could go back up the tunnel and huddle on the rocks, waiting to be rescued. The only way was forward.

Behind him, something clopped around the corner and came to a halt. Something else snorted. "We have to get out of here or we'll get squished," Glennie said.

"Come to me, boy," the Cailleach's frosty voice said. She didn't stop typing.

"Will the dog let me?" Conor asked. Dormath had dropped his sleeve, but didn't look any friendlier.

"Try, and find out," the Cailleach said.

Conor tried to sidle past the dog, who moved to block his path.

"Madam Cailleach," Ashling said. "Can you not control your dog?"

"No," the Cailleach said, typing.

"How is this boy to approach if Master Dormath won't let him?"

"Come to me, boy."

"Oh, this is stupid." Glennie pulled Grump closer to the giant dog. "Listen, that lady wants us to go see her, so you LET US PAST, you big, hairy . . . soul-sucking demon warrior." Fists on hips, she launched the Glennie scowl, terror of the playground.

Dormath loomed over Glennie, a rumbling deep in his

throat. He opened his mouth slightly and drooled on her foot. Glennie kept the scowl going, but she also whimpered.

The tunnel went quiet except for the tapping of the Cailleach's fingers and an occasional snort or snuffle from the annoyed animals backing up behind them.

The Cailleach's chill voice broke the silence. "What is a soul-sucking demon warrior?"

"Perhaps it is the daemonosaurus," Ashling said. "The daemonosaurus was a small, meat-eating dinosaur active 205 million years ago."

"I know about dinosaurs," the Cailleach said. "Messy creatures." The veiled head turned toward Conor and Glennie. "I see no resemblance in Dormath."

Dormath's dreadful breath stirred the hair at Conor's temple.

Conor's jacket pocket played the *Star Wars* movie theme: *Da DAH da da da DAH dah*. "You gotta be kidding me," he muttered.

Dormath growled.

"Is that your phone?" Glennie whispered.

Dormath sniffed at Conor's pocket. He growled again.

"Um." Conor looked deep into Dormath's eyes. "I'm going to unzip my pocket and get something out." Dormath looked deep into Conor's eyes and rumbled. "Okay?" Dormath rumbled some more.

"Here I go, then." Moving like a glacier, Conor eased

the zipper down, pulled out his phone, flipped it open.

Dormath jumped backward.

Howzt goin? U OK?

"Wow." Glennie peeked around his shoulder. "You got a signal all the way down here?"

Dormath found his courage and advanced, licking his chops.

Conor texted: OK but bad dog here. Wut do?

Dormath sniffed at the cell phone.

Dn't lok in eyz. Scrtch chin.

"You gotta be kidding me." *I already looked into his eyes. What now?*

"Scratch his chin or yours?" Glennie whispered.

Dormath sniffed at his mouth. "Oh my god." Conor tried not to move his lips. "What's he doing? What's he doing?"

"He has not smelled living breath," the Cailleach said, "for many eons."

Not meaning to, Conor gazed right into Dormath's unblinking black eyes. He could see his reflection. The dog showed his teeth and rumbled.

Nothing to lose, Conor thought. Slowly—horribly, painfully, glacially slowly—he raised his hand to the dog's chin. He gave it a little scratch.

Dormath growled, right in his face.

"Nice doggy," Glennie said. Conor scratched a little harder.

Dormath lowered his head and butted it gently against Conor's chest. Conor raised his other hand and scratched the monster's ear. Dormath heaved a great doggy sigh.

"Aw," Glennie said. "He's kinda cute."

"Boy," the Cailleach said, still typing. "Come to me."

Dormath put his chin on Conor's shoulder and snuffled in his ear while Conor texted: All gd. Thx. When he started toward the Cailleach, the dog followed, chin still on his shoulder, drool running down his neck.

"Um," Conor said to the Cailleach.

"Be off, Dormath," the Cailleach said. Instantly, the dog lifted his chin and trotted off to a wall niche filled with straw, where he circled three times and lay down.

"You could control Dormath the whole time!" Ashling said to the Cailleach. "You said you couldn't."

"Cleanse that tone from your voice, girl," the Cailleach said. *Tap-tap-tap.*

"Was that some kind of test?"

"It is not your place to ask, girl."

"Stop calling me 'girl.' I'm at least sixteen hundred years old."

"I formed with the earth. I count my years in millions."

"Excuse me," Conor said. "Aren't we supposed to be hurrying?"

Ashling pulled the veil back from the archway, revealing a massive cavern of flickering lights and moving shapes. "Come in," she said.

"Hold." The Cailleach made a sharp gesture toward Ashling with what Conor could only figure was her arm under her black draperies. The veil in the archway glowed briefly. Ashling gave a cry and dropped it as if it burned her. The archway went pitch black. "I told you, the living are not permitted."

"And I told you, they would challenge the Three."

The Cailleach wasn't typing anymore. Her black-draped head inclined toward Conor. He strained for a hint of human features behind the veil. There was a bump, which he assumed must be her nose.

"What will you give me, boy, to achieve your goal?" the frosty voice said.

"I . . ." Conor felt in his jacket pocket. A stick of gum. A stubby pencil. Javier's plastic Iron Man action figure. The spare house key, which he should have hung back on the hook.

His cell phone. But he might need that. "I don't have anything you'd like. Tell me what you want and I'll try to get it."

"Fruity Fooler?" Glennie whispered.

"They won't exist anymore," Ashling said.

Sure enough, Glennie shoved her hand into her pocket and brought out an empty package. "Rats," she said.

"You have what I want," the Cailleach said, unhooking the strap from around her neck and passing her laptop to Ashling. "See how steam comes from your face. You breathe. You are warm. I never experience warmth."

She held out an arm. The draperies fell away, revealing what probably was a hand. It was more like a chicken foot Grump had tried to make Conor eat at Mulcahey's China Café.

The Cailleach held it out to Conor, unmoving.

"What am I supposed to do?" He hated the way his voice piped, like a scared little kid.

The Cailleach gave an annoyed *huff,* making her veil poof out. "Take my hand, boy." The fingers made a grasping motion, crablike, too spidery for Conor's taste.

"What will happen to me if I touch you?"

"Try, and find out," the Cailleach said.

"Let me do it." Grump shuffled forward, Glennie at his side.

"Not you, old man," the Cailleach said. "You are nearly as cold as I."

The hand was waiting.

Conor glanced at Ashling, who shook her head. "I don't know what will happen, Conor-boy."

Conor shut his eyes and reached out. He felt the chicken hand grip his.

It wasn't too bad at first. But as the crone's grip tightened, a chill seeped into Conor's bones and up his arm, across his shoulders, down his back.

But it wasn't cold seeping in . . . It was warmth seeping out. Conor felt he was being drained of heat as a vampire drains blood, leaving him exposed to the cold of the tunnel, of the world, of the universe.

"Oh!" Glennie cried. "He's turning blue!"

"Let him go!" Grump was pulling at Conor's shoulders. "Conor! Let go!"

He couldn't let go. He couldn't move anything, couldn't even open his eyes. His feet had frozen to the tunnel floor. He imagined thick frost spreading all over his body, chilling him into an ice boy, a statue, a former person now dead and gone.

"Ahhhhh." The Cailleach sighed. "Ahhhh, like the beginning of me. Ah, the bliss, the life, the light, the warmth."

"Stop it!" Ashling said. "This is not right!" He could feel her tugging on his arm, trying to break the connection between him and the crone. He wanted to tell her it was too late. This connection was permanent; he was here forever, feeding the Cailleach with his human warmth until the universe folded in on itself and died.

"Cailleach." A new voice, a deeper one. "You must let this boy go. His life is not for you."

"No," the Cailleach said. "I have earned this." The cold intensified—how was that possible? Conor imagined himself bursting into shards of sparkling ice.

"Cailleach," the voice said. "Obey, or I will fetch the Lady."

"You are not my master."

"I am if I choose to be."

"Try, and find out!" the Cailleach shrieked.

"Large animals are here. And dead humans. You must return to your task."

"I have done nothing but my task for millennium after millennium. I deserve a time of warmth."

"You wouldn't like warmth. It's not in your nature."

"I'll be the judge of that." The Cailleach's voice wavered. Conor's toes felt warmer. Was it his imagination?

"You chose your fate," the deep voice said. "Honor your choices."

The Cailleach gave a little sob. Her hand slightly loosened its grip on Conor's.

"Besides, the warmth is making you smell funny," the deep voice added.

That was true. It was like something had rotted in the back of the refrigerator.

"I suspect," the deep voice said, "that you will melt into a greasy spot on the floor if you keep this up."

His hand was free. Conor collapsed onto the floor of the tunnel. Warmth seeped through him, starting at his feet. Its return made him shiver and shudder. Glennie brushed aside a newly arrived tribe of cockroaches and knelt to put her arms around him, which helped a lot.

He looked up, hoping to see the owner of the deep voice, but he was too late. Whoever it was had exited through the veil over the archway. It was still swinging.

"Who was that?" he asked Ashling.

"Nergal. Babylonian lord of the dead."

"Babylonian," Grump said. "For cripes' sake."

The Cailleach had her laptop strap back around her neck, her veiled head bent over her keyboard. "I don't know how to register you," she said peevishly. "There is no line for live humans."

Ashling craned her neck to look at the screen. "There's a blank space right here." She pointed. "You can make your own line—" But then she twitched and leaned in closer. "Holy macaroni. Move the screen down." She read, lips moving, then looked up at Conor, eyes round and horrified.

What's the problem? he thought, but then it hit him. *She saw who the Death is.*

"Allowing them in is very irregular," the Cailleach said. "Nergal will not know where to file my report."

"Yes, yes he will." But Ashling wasn't paying attention. She was fumbling for her comb.

"He'll print this page out and pin it up on his wall until he finds a place for it. It's no system, no system at all. It will break down completely one of these years." She tapped some keys. "Names and ancestry?"

Grump took over. He told the Cailleach their names and ages, then settled into a recitation of their forebears, on his side, anyway. He'd gone back six generations when the Cailleach raised her hand. "Enough. We shall trace you from here."

During Grump's recitation a camel arrived, along with the men in long robes who'd been huddling outside the narrow portal. The Cailleach resumed her incessant *tap-tap-tap*. The cockroaches headed for the curtain.

"We'd better go in now," Ashling said.

"Not my affair what happens to you next," the Cailleach said, typing. "Good riddance."

Ashling stepped through the curtain and held it open for Conor, Glennie, and Grump.

"Welcome to the Other Land," she said.

Chapter Sixteen

The noise of the crowd was an assault after the quiet tunnel. Donkeys brayed, dogs barked, tigers roared, people jabbered at one another. Weaving through it all were tendrils of faint music, sometimes harp, sometimes flute—somebody's attempt at keeping everyone calm.

Conor glanced up and almost forgot how to breathe: Rough stone walls ascended to a roof so high it was lost in shadow. Looming out of the rock, carved in sapphire blue, were gigantic stone faces—ancient, expressionless, eternal. He felt very small and very temporary.

In desperation, he got out his cell phone and turned on the GPS. It said: *Your current location is temporarily unavailable.*

"Keep moving." Ashling wasn't meeting anyone's eye.

Who's the Death? Conor wondered. But he didn't know how to ask without Grump and Glennie hearing, too.

Maybe it's me.

They pushed through the throng of people and animals. The human Dear Departed wore earth-colored robes, bright-colored dresses, jeans and cowboy hats, leather jackets, high heels, boots, slippers, sandals. Some had bare chests with cloth wrapped around their waists or rough cotton trousers. There was hair of every color Conor had ever seen, and some he'd never considered. Eyes of every shape, bodies of every size.

"What will happen to us?" a woman in a red dress said to the man next to her. "Will we stay together?"

"I don't know, beloved. We'll have to see." He took her hand in both of his and hugged it to his chest.

Glennie watched them as if they were in a movie. "That's what happens when there's no guide, right, Ashling?" She bounced on her toes with excitement. "Good thing we have you, right?"

Ashling didn't respond. Conor wanted to pull her aside. But he still was shivering so hard he could barely walk. He was no use at all to Grump. Glennie had to pull both of them out of the way of a large farm horse with a cat on its back. Conor stepped on the foot of the woman in the red dress, but she didn't notice.

"They don't feel anything," Ashling said. "Come on."

At first the crowd seemed to be milling around aimlessly. But here and there Conor noticed overworked authority figures with laptops like the Cailleach's—odd-looking figures, some human-looking, some not. One had horns; another had a head like a dog's. They shoved people here, animals there, with no ceremony and little conversation.

The animals headed for a large archway to the left—Glennie caught sight of her tiger and waved excitedly. The tiger nodded to her and Grump, then padded majestically through the archway.

Conor took advantage of the distraction and leaned close to Ashling's ear. "Who's the Death?"

She jumped as if he'd sneaked up on her. "Don't . . . don't ask."

He shook her arm to make the words fall out of her mouth. "Come on. I have to know."

"Stop that."

"Tell me!"

"Fine. *Fine!* It's your sister." Ashling turned from him, but not before he saw the misery on her face.

He lunged for her ear and whispered, "Don't tell Grump."

"I shouldn't have told *you*. Why do I keep telling you things?" She freed herself and resumed pushing through the crowd.

Conor wanted to sit down somewhere and think this through. But they had to keep moving, if only to prevent Grump from getting trampled. *If he had any idea Glennie was the Death, he'd let himself get trampled.*

"Do all these people get to meet the Lady?" Grump sidled past a cluster of shouting, gesturing women in business suits. "There's not enough time in the universe."

Ashling waited for them, pale of face. "She only talks

to one in a thousand. A hundred and fifty thousand pass through here every day, Nergal says. And they keep track of each one."

"Why?" Glennie asked.

Again, Ashling didn't answer.

Something had been vying for Conor's attention, and now it beckoned harder. The Dear Departed around him exchanged panicky glances as it beckoned at them, too.

Somewhere, someone was shrieking. And shrieking and shrieking. The noise was muffled, but also it echoed.

"Is this Hell?" quavered a little old lady in white athletic shoes.

"What *is* that?" Glennie said.

Ashling's mouth was a grim line. She took Conor's elbow and shoved through the crowd in an entirely different direction from the way they'd been going.

"Hey, wait for us." Glennie followed, hauling Grump behind her.

The crowd thinned as they got closer to the source of the shrieks, a small archway in the rock wall. None of the Dear Departed wanted to be near it, and those who couldn't get away fast enough had their hands over their ears.

The archway was barred, beyond the bars a comfortable room with a pillow-strewn bed and carpets on the floor, colorful hangings softening the rock walls.

There was even an easy chair. In it sat a redheaded girl, wearing a tattered green tunic and red cloak. Her face was streaked with dirt and tears; her hair was unbraided and wild. She clutched the arms of her chair as if she were afraid she'd fall off otherwise. She was shrieking, shrieking, shrieking . . . but then she saw Conor, Grump, and Glennie and went silent, her mouth open.

"Hello, Maeveen," Ashling said.

Maeveen flung herself at the bars. "No, no, no!" She reached for Ashling, who evaded her. "No live ones. No. No."

"It's all right." Ashling caught Maeveen's flailing hand and held it. "I will fulfill my Death. I promise."

"Li-i-ive ones," Maeveen moaned. "No-o-o."

"That's her," Grump said. "She's a mess now. But that's her, the one who took Jeannie."

"LI-I-I-IVE ones!" Maeveen shrieked.

"Move away from here," Ashling said. "You upset her."

Conor and the others stepped to the side, out of Maeveen's sight, and listened to her mutter and moan. What could have happened to her?

Ashling murmured steadily, raising her voice once to say, "Someday you will be well. This cannot last."

"La-a-ast," Maeveen moaned.

Ashling joined them, even paler than before. "What happened to her?" Conor asked. Maeveen's shrieks began again.

"She abandoned her Death," Ashling said shortly. "She found a way to prevent her keen from starting. This is the result—she keens now without relief, feeling the horror of death but not its blessing."

"Why did she abandon her Death?" Glennie asked.

"Is it not clear?" Ashling snapped. "She tired of her task, that's all. She told herself if she did not keen, the child she'd been sent for would not die." Grump sucked in his breath. "Not your child, Davey O'Neill. Another." She shuddered as Maeveen's shrieks amplified. "And the child died anyway."

"Will that happen to you?" Glennie was white-faced.

"No," Ashling said. "I will get my Death. It may not be the one I was sent for, but it will be a Death, that I promise you." She launched herself into the crowd of Dear Departed.

"Come on." Conor ignored the chill in his heart. "We have to keep up."

They pushed and shoved and slipped and slid through the crowd, following Ashling's back, Maeveen's despair fading behind them. The figures with laptops were directing the mass of Dear Departed toward a huge archway in a far corner of the cavern.

Next to the archway was a massive stage, gleaming in the torchlight, an intricately carved throne set against the wall. The stage and throne were made of smooth rock, black as the inside of your eyelids on a moonless midnight. To one side of the stage, waving regally at the dead passing through the archway, stood a hooded figure all in white.

"This way." Ashling headed for the steps to the platform.

"Are we allowed up there?" Conor said. The shiny black rock was chiseled on the sides but its surface was smooth as glass, the size of a school gym. It was empty except for that solitary white-draped figure, standing with its back to them.

"I am allowed." Ashling ran up the steps and, turning, extended a hand to Grump. Conor and Glennie got behind him and pushed. But then . . .

Woodsmoke. Conor stepped backward, dizzy, as a memory washed over him—not his, someone else's. But maybe his, too.

Ashling pulled Grump up the last step. She looked harried. "Hurry, Conor-boy."

But he was drowning in the past. "I saw you up there— you were with her on that platform," he heard himself say. "I was old but you were as young as the day I met you. I waved and you looked right at me and you didn't know who I was."

She stood rooted there, staring back down at him. Grump bumped against her, trying to keep his balance.

The moment passed. The memory faded and was gone.

Conor shook his head. What was happening to him? Cripes if he knew. He scuttled up the steps to the platform, aware that Ashling was trying to read his face.

"Hey! How come they get to go up there?" shouted a

man in a gray suit, rushing for the steps. But when he reached the first step, his foot went right through it, as if the step were vapor. He tried the second step. Same result.

"What is this?" the man yelled at Ashling.

Ashling gave herself a shake. "One of Death's great mysteries," she called to the man. "Come on," she said to Conor. "Time is passing."

"Why did we get up here and that man didn't?" Glennie asked as they walked across the smooth rock.

"Seriously—it's a mystery. I don't think even Nergal knows. The Lady doesn't care, as long as the steps keep letting her up. And me, of course." Ashling raised her hand to stop them and advanced the last few paces alone. "My lady. I am back."

It occurred to Conor that he had no idea what the Lady would look like. She was in charge of death, after all. Would she be a skeleton? A hag with flaming eyes? Something so horrible he'd never even imagined it?

The white figure turned, head bowed so her hood covered her face.

Glennie huddled in close to Conor. Grump squeezed Conor's shoulder so hard he thought he heard it crack.

Conor wanted to close his eyes, but he couldn't.

The figure pushed the hood from her face. Conor held his breath. And there before his eyes, taking his breath away once and for all, was . . .

The sunniest, rosiest face in the universe. The Lady's

cheeks were like apples, her blue eyes bright as winter sky, her snowy white hair set in a fluffy permanent wave. She should have had an apron with bunnies on it.

"Hello, Ashling dear. My goodness, what a sad face. Oh, but here's our little . . . my goodness, *three*. How on earth did that hap— Oh." The Lady's blue eyes hardened. "Ashling. Pet. They're alive."

"Yes, Lady. They wish to test the Birds."

The hard eyes acquired a wicked twinkle. "Ooo, how thrilling. All of them wish this?"

"I don't know. I suppose."

"I want to be the Death," Grump said. "I'm probably who it is anyways."

Ashling didn't look at Conor. Nor did Conor look at her.

The Lady smiled at Grump, and it was not the smile of a cookie baker. "And you are?"

"Davey O'Neill. Crumlin Street, South Boston, Massachusetts. You took my daughter when she was—"

"I can't be expected to remember every death, dear," the Lady said. "If you seek your daughter, I have no doubt she's moved on to another life. She may be quite near you, but I'm afraid we can't let you know that."

"I'm not looking for her, Lady. I want—"

"You want to be Ashling's Death. I understand. I'm afraid I don't control who dies when. We merely keep track of who goes where."

"It's my right to test the Birds."

Conor wasn't sure it was a good idea to go talking about "rights." But the Lady didn't seem to mind. "Yes, yes, indeed, it is your right," she said. "And, of course, my very great pleasure. I don't think anyone's tested them in, oh, it must be at least a century—a long, tedious century, I might add. What do you hope to accomplish, Davey O'Neill?"

"I want the power over life and death," Grump said. The Lady raised her eyebrows, and he added: "This once. Not forever."

"Well, *that's* a relief." With no warning, the Lady swooped in nose to nose with Conor. Up close, her face was plump and rosy but hard as ice. "And you, boy, what do you want?"

Gazing into the heartless blue eyes, Conor said the first thing that came to mind. "I don't want anyone to die."

The Lady gave a high-pitched titter that only a dog should have been able to hear—and right in Conor's face, which almost made him fall over backward. "But how *silly,* dear. Somebody has to die. Otherwise where would they put you all?"

"That's what I thought." Glennie had on her playground scowl. "But now we know it's just the same souls recycling over and over. Why not let us be the same people forever?"

The Lady threw back her head and laughed. "Oh, what a novel idea! Little one, this system was set up long before

I existed. It's not for me to change it. I don't even understand how it works."

"And anyway," Ashling told Glennie, "you don't know what boredom is until you've been the same person for a few centuries."

"Very true. It makes one quite mad sometimes." Again that high-pitched titter. "So, Ashling dear, isn't it a shame you didn't do what I asked?" The voice was as hard as the face now.

Ashling mirrored Glennie's playground scowl.

The Lady didn't seem to care. "I kept you by me, hoping for a little entertainment in my dreary, endless existence. But, century after century, always the same moan from you: 'I want a new life, I need a new life.' So at last I can't stand it anymore and I *try* to accommodate you, and look what happens. You do realize, pet—if they defeat the Birds, you most likely will not get the Death you were sent for."

"But there will be a Death," Ashling pleaded. "Won't that count?"

"Pet, you were told to come back with the correct soul, not three live ones on a quest."

Ashling opened her mouth to argue, then snapped it shut, looking as if she'd seen the end of the world.

The Lady tittered. "Oh, pet, if you could see your expression." She stuck out her bottom lip in a pout that anyone could see was fake. "Ashling, dear, choosing my companions is one of the few things I can control. Is it really so bad, living here by my side? And now, serving your people as a banshee—you'll see the World that way—isn't that enough?"

Ashling didn't soften. She shook her head.

"Ah, well," the Lady said airily, "it is what it is. La la la." She turned her attention to Conor, Grump, and Glennie, eyeing them almost fondly. "Now, what shall we do with all of you? I only have to let one of you test the Three, you know, since you're all here about the same Death. You're so adorable—I don't know how I'll choose just one."

"That's fine," Grump said. "I'm the one who wants to do it."

The Lady's gaze met Conor's. "And you, dear? Are you going to let this old man die for you?"

"That ain't the way to put it," Grump said.

"Scrumptious!" The Lady clapped her hands with delight. "You *are* interesting. How would you put it, Davey dear?"

"I'm standing up for what's right. We had one kid die young in our family already and that's enough."

"Do you agree, little man?" The Lady was practically dancing.

"No," Conor said. "I don't think it's time for Grump to die."

"Is it time for your sister to die? Theoretically, of course."

"No."

"Was it time for all of *them*?" The Lady fluttered a hand

at the Dear Departed, filing past the platform and into the archway.

Probably not. "But we were brave enough to come here. That must count for something."

It sounded lame even to him.

"Come here, dear boy." The Lady beckoned, and Conor obeyed without thinking. She grasped his chin between thumb and forefinger and lifted it so she could stare into his eyes. She smiled into them.

"Well, hello there," she said softly. Her wicked gaze cut away to Ashling. "Pet, you do know who he is, don't you?"

"I thought he might be someone. He's not my father, I know that."

The Lady gazed into Conor's eyes again, and he smelled woodsmoke. The flute tune was playing in his head, pretty loud this time. She blew gently on his eyes. He shut them.

The fire roars . . .

Chapter Seventeen

They are in the smithy, the fire built up and ready to serve. "Don't talk to me about the accepted way," he hears himself say. "I do this *to the accepted way." He holds up a twig of bronze, snaps it, hurls it away from him.*

"She's betrothed to her neighbor," his father says. "She's not for you."

"I can rescue her from him anytime I want."

"You have said too much to too many. You fought Aengus last night because he danced with her, and Aengus is your friend. You were too loud, standing by the fires, talking to her of love and rescue. Her father has heard of your boasts. He is angry, but he wishes to avoid trouble."

"Hah! And how will he do that? I know what I want. More than that, I know what she *wants, and it's not that old man."*

"You are a skilled craftsman, becoming better by the day. I will find you a worthy wife. Be patient."

"I have found my wife."

Conor opened his eyes. "I don't understand."

The Lady blew on his eyes again.

"They've left for home." With his thumb, his father tests the edge of a sword, then sets it down on the workbench. "I watched them leave three hours ago, with all their cattle. They will travel by moonlight, be home tomorrow."

"NOOOO!" he roars, louder than the cattle in the pens, on his feet before he knows what he plans to do. He snatches up the sword his father just set down, shoves it into the scabbard he himself made, the one with the bird heads she admired—symbol of a life about to change for the better.

"Sit down, boy. There are rules for these things."

"Don't talk to me of rules." He runs out of the smithy, past the cattle pens and the ruins of the Beltine fires, toward the side gate.

A troop of scouts is at the gate, dirty and weary from travel. One of them grabs his arm. "Where are you going, boy?"

"Out."

"Well, don't go far. There are raiders out there. Dál Fiatach. They'll have you for a slave before you can draw your sword."

Even more reason to go. He must warn her.

Conor wanted to open his eyes, find out what was happening to him. But then . . .

The spirits have delayed him, confusing him in the

woods. He's too late to deliver a warning—the raiders are there with ax and sword and horse, rounding up the cattle. Ashling's brother is dead on the ground, clearly visible in moonlight bright as midday.

Her back to the wagon, Ashling swings a sword with her two hands. It's a disgraceful, dull sword, and he curses as he pelts toward her. He would have made her a better one than that. But Ashling herself is sharp enough for two swords, dodging left, slashing at the legs of the raider who's trying to catch her, dodging right. Behind her, from the dark under the wagon, three small faces peer out, white with terror.

"Ashling!" he shouts. "I'm here!" He's running hard, covering ground. "Craven pig," he howls at the raider, who turns to sneer at him. "Half your size, yet she holds you off!"

The raider's wild eyes meet his, and in a rush of horror he knows his mistake. The raider never wanted to kill her—they're here for cattle and slaves. But the man is stupid with battle lust, and the insult was a challenge.

"Noooo!" But the raider turns on Ashling—oh, she's so sturdy and brave, with her bright red hair, her uncanny eyes. Her way with beasts.

Her hand on his heart.

The raider lifts his ax . . .

Conor stumbled backward. Someone tall and strong caught him from behind, lowered him until he was sitting on the floor. He opened his eyes—Ashling was staring into them. Blue eyes. Wedges of gray.

His heart filled with joy—Declan's joy. But also heaviness, a feeling of guilt. "I was Declan. He—I made them kill you."

"*Ach*. I almost remember."

"I—he got lost in the woods, in the dark. He got there too late and then he insulted this guy and the guy killed you."

She closed her eyes, brows drawn together, trying to remember. "I fought. They killed my brother."

"He wanted to warn you, to save you. He—I got lost."

"And I died."

Conor reached out to her, then let his hand drop. It was so confusing—he was Conor O'Neill, age twelve, who had never even danced with a girl. And yet he also was Declan, old enough to steal a sword and chase the love of his life into the wild.

Ashling settled back on her heels, eyes narrowed, peering into the past. "I do remember now. I was glad to see you—him—and then . . ." She shook her head. "There was pain, and then nothing."

"I'm sorry you died. I should have kept my big mouth shut."

She smiled into his eyes. "I forgive you. Anyway, it wasn't really your fault."

The heaviness lifted. He felt better than he'd ever felt in his life.

A high-pitched titter. The Lady was standing over them. "How *sweet*. But whatever will you do, Ashling? Is he your Death? If so, you'll bring him back here and then you can return to life together. Assuming that is what you want, of course. You were rather annoyed with him when you first came to me, all those centuries ago."

Ashling stood up, close to the Lady's ear. "He's not the Death," she whispered, loud enough for Conor to hear her. "You know he's not."

"What are you whispering?" Glennie was several yards away, propping up Grump.

The Lady said, loud enough for everyone, "And if he's not, you have two choices. Let the Death take place as fated, complete your bargain with me, and hope you return to the World near him as an infant. You may even remember something of who you are, having spent so much time here." The Lady simpered. Then her face went hard and icy. "But if they win the Birds' favor and the Death does not occur as fated, I am afraid you must stay with me until I choose to let you go."

The tall person behind Conor cleared his throat. "My lady." It was the low rumble of a voice that had beaten down the Cailleach. "If I might say a word."

"Oh, go ahead." The Lady sounded petulant.

Conor just about twisted his neck into a pretzel to see the voice's owner.

From his vantage point sitting on the floor, the man was

tall as a Boston Celtics center, seven feet at least. He had a broad ivory-colored face, wild golden hair and beard. His mouth looked a little like a cat's, with a strong cleft in the upper lip.

But the most important thing about him—especially when you were sitting right next to him on the floor—had to be his legs, which were those of a lion. His long, tawny tail had a lion's tuft at the end. He leaned on a stick carved with a lion's head on the top.

He gave off a strong, musty odor.

"Nergal," the Lady said. "Don't you have filing to do?"

"Welcome home, Ashling," Nergal said.

"Dude. This is not my home."

Nergal's catlike mouth went up at the corners. "I agree. I was rooting for you to win a new life. As you know."

The Lady shot him a peevish look. "Oh, yes, yes, she's a young soul and should be back in the Great Cycle. Blah, blah, blah."

"The Lady visited the World fairly recently," Nergal said to Grump and Glennie. "*Blah, blah, blah* was the latest slang then. Early twentieth century, I believe."

"Awesome," Glennie said weakly, blown away by the lion-man with the deep voice.

"*Awesome,*" Nergal said. "I like that one. Not so sure about *dude*."

"Time's a-wasting," Grump said to the Lady. "Do I get a shot at these Birds or not?"

"Not, I think. Nergal, would you get this gentleman a chair? He and the little girl will stay here while the boy—should I call you Conor or Declan?—faces the Three." She beamed down at Conor.

"No dice," Grump said. "I'm doing it."

"My dear Davey," the Lady said, "you can hardly stand up. And no one may help the one who faces the Birds."

"I'm not a little girl," Glennie said. "I'm ten. Who's Declan?"

"I can stand up perfectly well," Grump said, swaying.

"No, you can't, Grump," Conor said. "I'll be fine."

Ashling fumbled at her leather bag but couldn't seem to get it open. "What if he dies?" she asked the Lady, giving up on the bag.

Is she talking about me? "What do you mean, *dies?*" Conor asked.

"Conor-boy. People often die facing the Birds."

"You never said that before!"

"I thought you knew. Davey O'Neill knew."

"You bet I knew," Grump said, "and that's why I'm going to be the one to go in there. Conor, you will do what you're told."

Yessir, Conor thought. *Anything you say.* But his body let him down again—he shook his head, not even looking at Grump to see how he took it.

"Who. Is. Declan?" Glennie's playground scowl reached a new level of fury.

241

"Me," Conor said. "In another life."

Glennie opened her mouth but no words came out.

The Lady beamed. "This is *so* much more entertaining than I expected. Although it is a bit upsetting, isn't it, Ashling, dear? If the boy tests the Three and wins, you don't get your Death and you have to stay with me." She lowered her voice so Glennie and Grump couldn't hear. "If he loses, dear, he'll most likely be dead on the spot. Later on his sister will die, and you will have your new life. Perhaps you'll be sent back near him, perhaps not. He might return as a parrot. In any case, can you let him die? Oh, it's just delicious!"

"You did this on purpose," Ashling said. "All that rushing around at the last minute, turning me into a banshee— you'd found out who he was and that he would be caught up in a death."

"I could hardly predict that they'd want to test the Birds, now could I?" The Lady touched Ashling lightly on the cheek. "But I have to admit, I did expect that *something* would go wrong for you, considering who he was. Especially if he started to remember, and your own recollections grew stronger. It's not unusual for bits of memory to return when a person's near someone he or she loved."

She smiled at Conor. "You loved her, and you made her die. That's a very strong combination of circumstances. No wonder you remember so much."

"I was trying to save her."

Ashling grabbed his hand in both of hers, squeezing it so hard he almost yelped.

"I ain't sending my grandson in there all by himself." Grump hobbled toward the Lady in as threatening a manner as possible, considering that he was leaning on a ten-year-old in a raccoon hat.

"Nergal," the Lady said. "A chair."

Nergal thumped his staff on the floor. An ornate, throne-like wooden chair appeared next to the Lady, with a smaller one for Glennie. The Lady gestured to them graciously, but neither Grump nor Glennie paid any attention.

"I'm doing the Bird thing," Grump said. "Not Conor."

"Or I'll do it," Glennie said. "Conor'll mess up. I don't care who he was a bazillion years ago."

"He will not mess up," Ashling said.

"You've known him for four days," Glennie said. "Trust me."

"I have known him for sixteen hundred years."

Conor gave his head a shake, because his brain kept going back in time. He couldn't stop thinking about those moon-dappled woods, his panic when he realized he was lost, his despair when the raider lifted his ax.

The universe was huge and cold and unfeeling. People sometimes died too young. Anything could happen.

I am Conor O'Neill, 36A Crumlin Street, South Boston, Massachusetts, son of Brian and Moira. My house is nine-

teen blocks from school and I know every street in South Boston. My best friend is Javier Ramirez. My sister has raccoon ears.

I think I am somewhere under the Mid-Atlantic Ridge. Current location temporarily unavailable.

Ashling clung to his hand. He saw her through two sets of eyes: those of Declan, who rushed to save her, and those of Conor, who would sacrifice her for his sister.

"I always let you down," he whispered.

She shook her head.

"I have to try to beat the Birds. I can't let Glennie die. And I . . . I don't want to be dead right now, either."

She nodded.

"I wish I could make it all right for you."

She dropped his hand and looked him in the eye. "Do what you must. I will do the same."

What does that mean? He scrutinized her—the girl who calmed his heart, the monster who almost killed the seventh grade. It was possible she wanted him dead today.

"Dude," she whispered, uncanny eyes filling with tears. "I loved you. I don't want to watch you die."

He hardened his heart. "I'm not going to."

Nergal was ushering Grump and Glennie to their chairs. "She's made up her mind about the Birds," he said to Grump. "You may not like it. I may not like it. But there it is." Nergal's broad face was expressionless.

"Thank you, Nergal." The Lady stretched her arms over her head. "That will be all."

"I believe I will stay," Nergal said.

On the floor of the cavern, the Yoruba guide, Oya, ushered her Dear Departed into a roped enclosure beside the platform. Oya tugged at the Lady's robe. The Lady rolled her eyes in annoyance, but turned around.

"This one wishes to speak with you, my lady," Oya said. The woman glanced up at the Lady and cried out, clinging to Oya's arm. Conor crept forward to see what was happening.

He almost swallowed his tongue. The Lady's apple cheeks had darkened, and her blue eyes had gone brown, changing shape. Her nose lengthened. Her white hair shortened. She was still dressed in white, but now she was a beaming African grandmother.

Nergal nudged him with his staff. "You wish to face the Birds? Follow me."

The Lady kept her gaze on Oya's Dear Departed. "I'll be right along. Don't start without me."

"I'm coming, too," Ashling announced.

"I thought you didn't want to watch me die." Conor sounded sulky even to his own ears.

"Knowing is better than not knowing."

"You may not help him," Nergal said.

"Why would I help him?" Ashling gave a short, brittle laugh. "If he wins, I lose."

"Awesome." Nergal patted her shoulder and paced off on his lion feet, heading for a small, curtained doorway at the back of the platform. Ashling followed.

Grump huddled in his fancy chair, Glennie holding his good hand. Conor went to them. "I'll be okay." He handed Grump his outer clothing and a couple of sweaters. Taking his cell phone out of his jacket, he put it in the back pocket of his jeans.

"I can't believe you're doing this," Glennie said.

Grump's eyes were watery. "Don't be a hero, kiddo. It's my time to go, not yours."

"It's nobody's time," Conor said. "You got rockets to build."

Grump gave a tiny *huff,* the closest he could get to a laugh. "I built enough of 'em."

Oya's old African woman burst into tears. Oya's arm was around her as they rejoined the crowd. The Lady moved toward Conor, changing back into the pink-cheeked granny as she came.

"What did you do to that woman?" Glennie asked.

"Tut-tut, dear. I didn't do a thing. She wanted to wait and be reborn with her husband. But that's so *silly,* of course I can't control that. He's not far behind her, so they'll be together anyway. They just won't know it. Come along, Declan dear. Time to meet the Birds."

Conor hugged Grump—carefully, because of the arm and the ribs. He also hugged Glennie. She even hugged back.

"Do the right thing, kiddo," Grump said.

"Don't wimp out," said Glennie.

Conor and the Lady walked across the smooth black stone together. "Why do I get to know?" Conor asked.

"Know what, dear?"

"Who I used to be. That I used to be *any*one."

"Because you asked to face the Three. That puts you in a whole new category."

"What category?"

"Heroes, dear. Didn't you know?"

"Are we under the Mid-Atlantic Ridge?"

She pushed aside the curtain on the door. Behind it was a smaller cave, lighted by a single energy-efficient bulb hanging from the ceiling.

The Lady saw Conor looking at it. "Torches are *so* much more dramatic, but in a small space like this they're too smoky. The Birds kept getting the croup."

There they were, the three Birds perched on a roost thirty feet away. They were huge, almost as tall as Conor, plump and glossy, with cruelly curved bills. The bird on the left had a purple bill, the one on the right was white-billed. On the center perch was a bird with a golden bill, which glistened in the faint electric light.

The Birds' eyes glittered at him as he approached, making him feel he wasn't dressed properly or had a booger hanging out of his nose. But they had no right to be superior—the floor under the roost was slimy white with droppings. As Conor watched, the bird on the left added to the pile.

"I thought creatures didn't poop in here," Conor said.

"The dead ones don't," the Lady said. "These are alive."

Ashling and Nergal stood off to one side, Ashling furiously combing her hair. Opposite them, against the wall, were three huge bowls carved out of the rock, their contents squirming. Conor averted his gaze, hoping they wouldn't be involved in whatever was about to happen to him.

He had a bad feeling they would be.

Glennie was yelling outside. Something made a swishing noise behind him. He whirled around to see a Burmese python the length of a city bus oozing through the door, a small snowy white rabbit on its back.

"Oh drat," the Lady said. "Anubis got distracted again." A porcupine waddled in and started snuffling around the edge of the cave. "Ignore them, dear. They're dead and won't hurt you."

She pushed him toward the Birds, who shuffled on their perch, leaning forward, intent.

"Allow me to introduce you," the Lady said. "This fellow on the left with the purple bill is Crakk, who sings the dead back to life. On the right is kindly white-billed Graw, whose song lulls the living into the sleep of death. And this beauty with the golden bill—ah, she is the one you want to please. She is Kawla, who conveys the power over life and death." The Lady bowed to Kawla, who inclined her head majestically.

"Uh, hullo," Conor said. "Pleased to meet you."

Crakk opened and shut his bill with a snap, then made a noise like a rusty hinge. The Birds eyed Conor expectantly.

"I . . . I don't understand you." He appealed to the Lady. "What am I supposed to do?"

"You feed them, silly." And, sure enough, the Lady led him to the three bowls with writhing creatures.

One had moths in it, their wings folded, walking all over one another. The second had earthworms, twisting like snakes but for some reason not scary at all.

The third was a different story. Conor had watched enough Saturday morning cartoons to predict what that one had to be. *You always have to face your worst fears.*

And he was right.

It was, of course, spiders.

Chapter Eighteen

"Those spiders are really dead, of course," Conor said.

"Oh dear no," the Lady said. "I can't feed dead food to live birds, now can I?"

Conor swallowed and raised himself on tiptoe so he could peek into the stone bowl without getting any closer. All kinds of spiders were in there—Conor was pretty sure he saw black widows. Certainly tarantulas.

The Lady was talking. "There are tarantulas, of course. Black widows, and those smaller black and red ones that aren't black widows—I forget what they're called, but they're every bit as poisonous. There's an Australian funnel-web spider, nasty little cuss. Oh, and that biggish one, the hairy brown one there, that's a Brazilian wandering spider—you'd be dead in two hours." She tittered.

Conor backed up three steps. It was all he could do not to run out of the cave and get Grump.

"Now," the Lady continued, "all you have to do is pick the right food for our dear Kawla and her lovely golden bill, and she will grant you her power. Temporarily, of course."

"I just guess?" It didn't seem fair.

"An *educated* guess, dear. Think about what each bird would want to eat, considering its powers."

"What if I choose wrong?"

"Well, dear, the bird who wants the food you offer will take it. And that bird will use its power—sing something to life, for example, or sing it to death." She patted his shoulder. "The creature being sung to death would be you, of course."

Conor swallowed hard and told himself that being sung to death wouldn't be so horrible.

Think. What would please a bird with the power of life and death? He so wanted the right food to be the earthworms or the moths. He tried to remember biology class. What did he know about moths?

Start as a caterpillar, end as a moth. First one thing, then the other. Like being dead first, then alive? Alive, then dead? Has to be one of the other two birds then. So not the moth.

And earthworms? *They eat organic matter in the soil and expel dirt. They convert one thing to another? So that's one of the other birds, too.*

I knew it. I have to face my worst fear. Like seven out of ten episodes of *Robot Destiny.*

He couldn't think of a reason why a spider would appeal to a bird with the power of life and death. Still, he knew what he had to do. The question was, how to survive it?

If only Javier were here. He had badges in insect observation, first aid, and bird study. Surely one of them would have provided the answers.

"You don't have forever, dear," the Lady said. "Unlike the rest of us."

A tarantula draped a leg out of the bowl, started to pull itself up. The Lady flicked it back down. Conor imagined thrusting his hand into that bowl, with all those horrible, unpredictable wiggly legs and bodies. Getting bitten to death was almost beside the point.

He heard himself say, "Can I phone a friend?"

"Can you do what to a friend, dear?"

"Phone him. Can I phone a friend?"

The Lady wrinkled her brow. "Phone?"

Conor was surprised someone surrounded by laptop computers didn't know about phones. He plucked his cell phone out of his back pocket to show her. "See? I can type a message or I can talk to somebody. I may not get a signal underground, though."

"We're not underground in the strictest sense." Nergal's deep voice, right behind him. "The term *Underworld* is misleading. Technically, we're beside your world, not under it."

Beside it? What the heck did that mean? "Where would I be on a map?" Conor's own voice sounded far away to him.

"You wouldn't be."

252

"Wouldn't be . . . ?"

"On a map."

I'm off the map. Conor's knees buckled. Nergal's strong arm kept him from falling on the floor.

"Where did you think you were, boy? Dude, I mean." Nergal peered into Conor's face. "Do you want to back out of this? Shall I get your grandfather?"

Conor shook his head. *Okay. Okay. I'm off the map. At least I have a cell phone.* "So can I call?" he asked the Lady. He wanted to hear Javier's voice, know he was talking to someone in Boston, Massachusetts, even if that person was on the wrong side of the West Fourth Street Bridge.

"I don't know. Nergal, can he?"

"I'm sure he can. We even get wireless sometimes."

"We get what?" The Lady looked stunned.

Nergal gave a brief smile. "There's a thing called the Internet. You wouldn't like it."

Conor's phone had three bars . . . good enough.

"Is that a cell phone? I've heard of them," Nergal said. "Never seen one, though."

"I thought he wasn't supposed to get help from anyone," Ashling piped up from the background. *Guess she's changed her mind about wanting to watch me die,* Conor thought bitterly.

Nergal hesitated, eyeing the cell phone as if it were an emerald. "My lady, I think in this one instance . . ."

"Oh, let him do it," the Lady said. "I want to see what happens."

There wasn't time to text back and forth. Conor texted, Call me. Then he waited.

And waited.

The tarantula tried to get out of the stone bowl again, along with a Brazilian wandering spider. The Brazilian spider actually made it to the floor before Conor whimpered and pointed. The Lady put it back, but not before stroking it with her finger.

Conor's phone intoned "I-EX-IST-TO-SERVE" like the robot in his favorite cartoon. "Hello?"

"Where are you?" Javier whispered.

"The Other Land, which I guess is also the Underworld. Sort of. Where are you?"

"In the hospital bed. It's been an hour."

"You're kidding." Conor looked at Nergal. "Is there something weird about the time in this place?"

"Of course there is. Sometimes it's slower. But other times it speeds up or goes backward. Don't count on it one way or the other."

Conor got back on the phone. "I guess time's weird here. It feels to me like I've been away for days."

"So what's it like?"

"Uh . . . cool. Really cool. But I can't talk right now. I'm phoning a friend, and you're the friend."

Javier-silence, then: "You're kidding, right?"

"No, really. I need help."

"Hang on. Someone's coming."

Conor heard a woman talking, but he couldn't understand what she was saying. Javier snored. The visitor talked on and on and on. Conor heard what had to be a loud fart. Somebody giggled, and then the background chatter died.

"I'm back," Javier whispered.

"Was that Angela Timulty? Was she talking to you?"

"Guy in the other bed. They're having trouble waking him up, so she keeps coming in and talking to him. She actually seems pretty nice."

"You farted, didn't you."

Javier-silence.

Conor pressed on. "Listen, Javier, you know all about spiders, right? Like, if I had to pick one up."

"Pick one up? YOU?"

"I don't have time to explain. There's a bowl full of them. There's tarantulas, black widows, and some other black and red ones, and Australian funnel something-or-others. Plus some Brazilian thing."

"Brazilian wandering spider," the Lady said.

"If it's a Brazilian wandering spider," Javier said, "don't go near that one, especially if it stands up on its hind legs. That means it's going to attack. You're best off with a tarantula. Their bite hurts but they aren't as poisonous as the others. People have them as pets."

Conor felt like something was crawling down his back, even though he knew there was nothing there. Most likely.

"Let it crawl onto the back of your hand," Javier said. "Move slowly and carefully, and it may not even care. No sudden movements. Like, don't shudder."

Conor shuddered.

"Want me to stay on the phone?" Javier asked.

"No, thanks. I can concentrate better alone." He went to flip his phone shut, then put it back on his ear. "Hey, Javier? Javier. Listen. Thanks."

"No problem. Call if you need something else. I'll be here."

When Conor flipped the phone shut, the Lady put out her hand for it. "I want to see that. You were talking to someone back in the World? Tell me, how is that possible?"

Conor hesitated, then gave her the phone. "I think I'm going to do this spider thing right now."

"Of course." The Lady poked a button on the phone's number pad. Then she poked some more. *Dah-DAH-da-da-da-DAH-dah.* "Ooooo!" she squealed.

"Good luck," Nergal said to Conor, and ushered the Lady back to where Ashling stood, comb tangled in hair.

Conor approached the bowl, keeping a safe distance. The tarantula had two legs dangling over the top now. As he waited for it to get farther out, a Brazilian spider and several of the black ones toppled over the edge and onto the floor. Conor kept an eye on them, ready to dart away if they came near him. The black spiders headed for the wall, but the Brazilian spider scuttled into the shadow of its bowl and sat there, blending in with the surroundings.

Conor tried to memorize where it was.

Crakk made another rusty-hinge noise. "Don't waste time, Conor-boy." Ashling's voice was shaking.

"Hush," Nergal said. "You promised not to interfere."

"Wha-a-at?" Ashling sounded incensed. "But you just let him ask his friend—"

"Hush."

What does she care anyways? Conor thought.

The tarantula positioned the front of its body on the rim of the bowl. Conor tried to pull his sleeve all the way over his hand, but it wouldn't reach far enough.

He took one step forward.

The Brazilian wandering spider stood up on its hind legs.

Conor decided to see if he could reach the tarantula from where he was.

The tarantula waggled its front legs, deciding where to go next. Conor took a deep breath, bent over practically double, and thrust the back of his hand toward those questing legs. He felt he could topple any second.

What would the Brazilian spider do if he fell over? Right now it was swaying from side to side, waving its front legs in a threatening manner. Not good.

The tarantula's legs found Conor's hand, poked at it, exploring.

Conor did not scream. He also did not breathe.

The tarantula moved forward, feeling its way. Two legs. Four. Six.

Eight. The spider was on his hand, surprisingly heavy.

Conor straightened, took a step back, arm outstretched. He couldn't see the Brazilian spider anymore—was it moving? *Don't think about it. Keep walking.*

He pivoted on one foot, trying to stay smooth. The tarantula shivered. Was it scared? Would it bite? One foot forward, then the other foot, first foot, second foot, first foot . . . He made his way to the ravens' roost.

"Gah!" the Lady exclaimed. The theme song for the Silly Mustache Brothers game blasted out of Conor's cell phone. *Boop-boop-boop-da-da-da-da-doodly-doot-doot . . .*

Conor froze. But the spider wasn't bothered by the distraction. In fact, it wanted to explore: Its front legs felt around Conor's wrist, his cuff. It started walking. It got confident and moved up to his elbow. Then his shoulder. Something sharp and hairy prodded his neck. Several sharp somethings, very hairy.

Oh god it's going down my shirt I know it is I know it is . . .

It didn't. It climbed up his neck, tickled his ear. Perched on his forehead.

"Keep walking, boy," Nergal said.

"What are these little men *doing*?" said the Lady. *Boop-boop-boop* . . .

One foot, other foot, first foot, second foot . . . The Birds leaned forward, watching him. Conor stepped close to the roost so the golden-billed bird could reach the tarantula on his forehead. He hoped she grabbed it quickly.

He shut his eyes. He waited.

Something hit him on the forehead. The tarantula's weight was gone.

He opened his eyes. Kawla, the golden-billed raven, stared down at him, unmoving.

Crakk, however, had a tarantula's leg hanging out of his purple beak. He tilted his head back and swallowed what was left of the spider.

"Wrong choice, boy," Nergal said. "Many spiders die to continue their species, creating life from death just like Crakk. Now he will make something dead come back to life."

The Lady said nothing, intent on Conor's cell phone. *Boop-boop-boop* . . .

Crakk's eyes glittered at Conor. He opened his purple beak, and . . . well, Conor wasn't sure he'd classify what came out as a song. It was a series of croaks and cat-mews, rising into a screech, then lowering into a whine. It lasted about a minute. Conor could see how it might wake the dead.

"Conor-boy! The snake!" Ashling sounded terrified. He whirled around in time to see the python flip the rabbit off its back and thump on top of it, trying to squeeze it to death but not succeeding because the rabbit was already dead.

"S-so . . . the snake's alive now?" Conor said. "And, like, hungry?"

"Interesting." Nergal watched the snake's head rise from the floor, weaving back and forth in a wide semi-circle. "It's looking for something alive to eat now. Which would be you, boy."

"Stop that! Stop it!" the Lady cried.

Oh good, Conor thought. *She'll save me.*

The Lady shook the cell phone. "Why does this little man keep walking into the wall?"

The snake's weaving head narrowed its radius. It was honing in.

"Boy," Nergal said, "since her ladyship is otherwise occupied, I think I'll give you another chance. But you need to feed the right bird so the Lady can send you out of here. That snake will smell you soon."

"You keep helping," Ashling said. "Why can't I help?"

"You are not me," Nergal said. "Besides, why do you care?"

"I care, all right?"

Conor couldn't move. The snake's tongue flickered, looking for a scent.

His heart was racing. He. Couldn't. Move.

"Ashling!" Nergal snapped. "Get back here!"

But Ashling stood before Conor. Her eyes—uncanny, blue with gray wedges—gazed deep into his. She put her hand on his chest. "Breathe," she said. "Calm yourself."

Warmth suffused him. He breathed deeply—once, twice, three times. His heart slowed. The tension left his shoulders.

He could do this.

"Hurry, boy," Nergal said.

Not even stopping to thank her, Conor shoved past Ashling to the stone bowls. The Brazilian spider was nowhere to be seen, but he didn't even care.

Worms.

Moths.

Which?

Okay. The bird has the power of life and death. Opposites. Beginning and end . . . and then back to the beginning again, in that Great Cycle the Lady mentioned earlier.

He'd have to call Javier. Could he get his phone back from the Lady?

Boop-boop-boopboopboop . . .

"Conor-boy," Ashling whispered. "The snake."

It was contemplating the porcupine, which shivered against the wall with its quills up. Slowly, lazily, the snake eased toward the little creature until it was inches away.

Then it halted, indecisive—because of the quills? Because the porcupine was already dead?

"I need my phone," Conor said.

"You don't have time, boy." That was Nergal. "Anyway, good luck getting it away from her."

"What if I choose wrong this time?"

"The white-billed bird will sing you to death," Nergal said.

"Breathe," Ashling said.

This was a problem like any other, right? *Except it could kill me.* He thought back to math class.

1. Understand the problem.

2. Translate the problem into an equation.

3. Solve the problem . . .

Okay. Okay. Breathe.

1. X = something that the golden-billed bird wants to eat.

2. So X is something that feeds the power of life and death. What does that mean?

3. Life and death are opposite sides of a cycle, right? Right?

He peeked into the bowl of moths, looking for answers. *A moth changes from one thing to another. Does a moth turn back into a chrysalis?* No. It does not. So, not a cycle.

Earthworms. *They poke holes in the soil.* Great. So what?

Both male and female organs. Opposites, right? Yeah, but how was that a cycle?

They eat their way through the dirt, pooping out more dirt as they go. Recycling, right?

Right?

The snake decided against the porcupine. Its head turned, weaving in the air. *Oh god. It smells me.* Conor grabbed an earthworm, hustled over to the ravens' perch, held out his hand to Kawla, the golden-billed bird.

She regarded the worm. Her eyes glittered at Conor. Regarded the worm.

Conor held his breath.

Kawla looked up at the ceiling, over at Nergal. She wasn't going to take it.

A swishing noise. The snake was moving.

Conor closed his eyes.

Something sharp poked his hand. He didn't want to look. But he did.

The white-billed bird—the death bird—stood immobile. Kawla's golden bill, however, was chomping. She threw her head back to swallow the earthworm, then she opened her beak and sang.

It was almost the same croaking and mewing as Crakk's song. But it was the most beautiful music Conor had ever heard. "Yes!" He pumped his fists in the air, did a touchdown dance.

"You did it! You did it!" Ashling danced over to Conor and hugged him.

"The snake is coming," Nergal said. "My lady, send them back now."

Conor wheeled around. The snake was ten feet away,

staring right at him, tongue flickering. *How is this fair?*

"My lady," Nergal said more urgently. "The boy has won, but there is a living snake coming for him. You must pay attention."

Boop-boop-boop . . .

"Give me that." Nergal grabbed the phone, snapped it closed, and tossed it to Conor.

"How dare you?" the Lady said. Nergal pointed at the snake. "Oh dear. And I suppose it's hungry, isn't it?"

The snake put its head down. It oozed forward, undulating across the stone floor.

"Kill it, boy," the Lady said. "You have the power of life and death now."

"He can use that power but once," Ashling said.

"I thought you didn't know anything about the Birds." *She's a liar,* Conor thought.

Ashling's eyebrows nearly peaked up. "It just . . . it just makes sense. Really, Conor-boy, doesn't it? Make sense, I mean?"

"You're so clever, Ashling, pet," the Lady said. "Oh dear, I suppose I should send the boy back now. But this is so exciting."

The snake eased closer. Conor stepped closer to Nergal, which somehow seemed safer. "So I can stop whatever the Death is, right?"

"Yes, dear, you can," the Lady said. "As long as it's replaced by another. And from the Uí Néill, of course."

Conor forgot about the snake. "What?"

"Of course, silly." The Lady tittered. "Haven't you figured that out? Someone from the Uí Néill still must die at the appointed time.

"And when that time comes, you will decide who it is."

Chapter Nineteen

Some kind of emotion pumped through him: Was it despair? Anger? Hatred?

Conor figured he'd start with anger. "You never said a word about me having to choose the Death. I was supposed to *stop* it. How am I supposed to choose? There must be a million O'Neills."

"I wondered if you had explained, my lady," Nergal said.

"I didn't see you explaining anything," the Lady retorted. "Always the disapproval. Conor, Declan, whoever you are—even I, even the Birds, we cannot stop death entirely. And of course you have to choose someone near you, at the appointed time, after you're back in the World. You cannot point vaguely across the ocean and hope to hit an Uí Néill. You must point at a specific person." The Lady beamed at him. "That snake is very close, dear."

Conor felt he could personally stomp the snake. "I'll kill someone by *pointing*?"

"Well, no, dear, fate will do the killing. You need not

concern yourself with that. You merely, you know, direct fate. By, as you say, pointing."

Conor would have slumped to the floor if there hadn't been a snake coming for him. Ashling put her hand under his arm to hold him up. He twisted away from her, enraged, betrayed. "Did you know about this too? You did, didn't you?"

"No, no." Her face was all twisted up, like she was about to start crying. Or pretending to cry, anyway. "I didn't know, I honestly didn't."

She'd let him waste all this time, risk *dying,* because he'd thought he could prevent the Death. But now the Death could happen any minute, and she knew he'd never have the courage to point at anyone. He'd let the Death happen as fated, and she'd get her new life.

She was getting back at Declan, maybe, for making her die so many centuries ago.

She *was* a monster.

He'd picked up a tarantula. A *tarantula!* He'd figured out what to feed the golden-billed bird all by himself. And now what . . . Let Glennie die? Kill someone else in his family to save her?

The snake was closer—he could hear it. *Me. The Death will have to be me.*

The snake was five feet away. He took a step toward it.

"No!" Ashling squealed. "My lady, get him out of here! Please!"

"But this is so interesting," the Lady said.

The snake raised its head off the floor and eased forward, smooth as molasses. Its head touched Conor's knee. Its tongue flicked. He could see the energy building. It was going to lunge.

"My lady," Nergal's deep voice said. "Enough."

"You are such a spoilsport, Nergal." The Lady sounded aggrieved. "Oh, all right. Let's see . . . to join your phone friend, I think." She made a gesture that Conor only saw out of the corner of his eye because his attention was on the snake—its empty eyes, its massive body . . .

Everything slid sideways. Conor closed his eyes so he wouldn't puke.

A rush of cold air. Voices in the wind.

The smell of canned vegetable soup.

A shriek, followed by a thump.

"How the heck did that happen?" Glennie sounded breathless. "One minute we're there, the next minute we're here."

Conor opened his eyes. Angela Timulty, RN, was crumpled on the floor in a dead faint, just visible in the dim light of Grump's hospital room.

"That was cool." Javier was peeking out from under Grump's bedcovers. "You popped in out of nowhere." He flung the covers back. "Hurry up. They're moving around down at the nurses' station."

Ashling and Glennie stepped over Angela Timulty, RN, and stood guard at the door while Conor helped Grump and Javier change their clothes. Safe in bed, Grump lay back on his pillows with a sigh. "So what happened with the Birds, kiddo?"

On the floor, Angela Timulty, RN, moaned and put a hand to her head.

"Tell you later," Conor whispered. "It's all fine."

"He was totally awesome." Ashling took Glennie's and Javier's hands, Conor put his hand on her wrist from behind, and they all disappeared. They hustled through the awakening hospital onto the dark street. The clock in the hospital lobby said it was just after four in the morning, a scant three hours after they'd scuttled by with Grump in the wheelchair. Time had slowed down while he was away—Conor chalked that up as one more thing he shouldn't believe but did.

Nobody felt like flying, and anyway Ashling's belt and cloak strips were long gone. In a stroke of luck, they came upon an empty bus waiting at a stop, doors open while the driver talked through his window to a police officer. They sneaked onboard, invisible, and soon some visible passengers boarded, too. The bus took them halfway home before turning off in the wrong direction.

They walked the rest of the way, a long, silent, invisible trudge. There were enough people on the street to make talking unwise. Conor had nothing to say to anyone anyway.

Especially to Ashling. She wanted Glennie dead, and she'd known exactly what that golden-billed bird offered.

She'd lived in the Other Land for sixteen hundred years—how could she not know? Her life had been cut short in a horrible way, and she'd had all that time to plan revenge. She wanted him to kill his own sister, and that was that.

She was a monster.

Javier climbed up to his bedroom using the fire escape. The one at Conor's house was so squeaky that Conor and Glennie let Ashling fly them in Conor's open window. Then Glennie tiptoed off to her room.

"Conor-boy," Ashling said. "I didn't know." Her hair was floating, and her ears hadn't reappeared yet.

Conor didn't trust himself to talk to her. He got into bed.

He didn't think he'd ever be able to sleep, considering what he had on his mind. But the next thing he knew his father was pounding on the door. "Hey, Con, it's ten thirty in the morning. You've been in bed twelve hours! You wanna come get Grump with us or what?"

"You kids look awful," Mom said when Conor and Glennie made it downstairs. "Are you feeling all right?" She put a hand to Glennie's forehead. "I knew I shouldn't have let you go to that hospital. They're such germ pits."

"We're fine, Mom." Conor poured himself some granola. Glennie handed him the milk.

"You still worried about Grump?" Dad said. "I'm telling you, he's fine. They're releasing him in an hour."

"We know he's fine," Glennie said. "We're tired because we stayed up too late reading."

Leave it to Glennie to say the one thing a parent would want to hear.

Glennie. Conor watched her crunch her granola, reading a comic book about magic rats. Dad always said she was going to be president someday. Glennie said she was going to be an international crime-fighter.

Either way, he couldn't let her die.

Grump? Mom? Dad?

How about an aunt? A cousin?

Maybe a total stranger was the way to go—some O'Neill he didn't even know. Before they left for the hospital, Conor consulted his map of the neighborhood. There seemed to be an O'Neill he'd never met three streets to the west. Maybe he'd go there that afternoon and check the guy out.

Point at him.

Ashling never emerged from her cupboard before they left for the hospital. That was fine; he didn't want to see her. On the way over in the car, he got a text from Javier:

So? Wut hapnd?

Tel u 18er, Conor replied.

The hospital didn't want to let Grump go because he, too, looked dreadful. But Grump insisted, and the doctors thought his heart would be okay as long as he took his pills. Plus, they were short-staffed because Angela Timulty, RN, had been ordered to take an extended vacation—she kept insisting that three people had appeared out of thin air in a patient's room.

An aide brought a wheelchair. "Had to get this from the next floor down." He helped Grump to stand. "Our extra one disappeared overnight. I swear, you gotta nail things down in this place."

"Sort of stupid to nail down a wheelchair," Glennie said.

"Glennie," Mom said in a warning voice.

Grump winked at Glennie and held her hand all the way to the car.

When they got home, Conor and Glennie helped Grump into his half of the house. He refused to go to bed, so Mom installed him on the couch with pillows everywhere he could possibly need them. She left Conor and Glennie to get him some lunch—he insisted on Honey-Glazed Nutsos.

"So, kiddo," Grump said through a mouthful of cereal, "what happened?"

"Wait," Glennie said. "I'll go get Ashling."

By the time she returned, holding the door for the invisible banshee, Javier had arrived. Ashling reappeared with an eager, pleading look in her eye, but Conor ignored her and went to make peanut butter sandwiches. She sat down on the floor next to Grump's couch, saying not one word except "Good day" when Grump greeted her.

Conor took his time over the sandwiches—he'd rather die (maybe really) than tell anyone about his new dilemma. Back in the living room, he used peanut-butter mouth as an excuse not to talk while they ate. Glennie and Grump filled Javier in on their journey to the Other

Land and what happened before Conor went in to meet the Birds.

To Grump's dismay, Glennie kept calling the Other Land "the Underworld"—apparently, she'd been very impressed by Nergal. "He has lion feet," she explained.

Conor finished his sandwich. Everyone turned to him, expectant, and he knew the time had come.

He told them everything that had happened. Plus the kicker: "And now I have to choose who dies."

Grump's reaction was predictable. "It's simple, kiddo. Choose me."

Conor shook his head. "There's an O'Neill I don't know three streets over. I'm going over to look at him. Maybe he's sick or something."

"You're going to kill a complete stranger?" Glennie said.

"Better him than someone I know." But she was right, wasn't she? Tears formed in Conor's eyes. This was impossible. No one could expect him to make this decision. It was too hard.

Glennie looked like her peanut butter wasn't agreeing with her. "Did we ever find out who the Death is supposed to be?"

Conor blinked back his tears and, without meaning to, found himself gazing right into Ashling's blue eyes. The eyes of a young girl who'd waited sixteen hundred years for a new life. Whose old life still nudged at him, half memory, half dream.

Ashling didn't blink, didn't let her gaze slide away. "It doesn't matter who it is. Conor's going to choose someone else." Her chin lifted. "I *want* him to choose someone else."

Easy for her to say. She knows I'm not going to be able to choose, and then it'll be Glennie anyway. She'll get just what she intended from the start. He broke away from her blue eyes, pretended there was something interesting in the alley outside the window.

He felt Glennie watching him. "Holy macaroni," she said quietly. "It's me, isn't it?"

Grump slapped his hand hard on the couch. "That's IT!" he roared. "We're not losing another little girl in this family. Conor, you're pointing at me right now, do you hear me?"

Somebody opened the door behind him, but Conor didn't care who it was. "No!" he shouted back. "I'm gonna find an O'Neill who's really, really sick and wants to die. And I'll decide when I'm good and ready, because"—he gulped air—"I'm the hero."

"He can't do it right now anyway," a deep voice said. Conor whipped around to see Nergal leaning on his lion-headed staff in the doorway. The Babylonian lord of the dead was wearing a green tracksuit under an oversize purple raincoat, big black rubber boots covering his lion feet. When he turned around to shut the door, his behind wiggled weirdly. After a puzzled second, Conor realized that Nergal had stuffed his tail into his pants.

"What are you doing here?" Ashling snapped. "Did you think I couldn't handle this Death by myself?"

"May I sit down?" Nergal asked. "It will require releasing my tail."

"It's a free country." Grump pointed to an armchair. "Want a peanut butter sandwich?"

"No, thank you. We may not eat." Nergal took off his raincoat and reached into the back of his pants to pull his tail out before sitting down. Tail draped over the arm of his chair, he hauled off his big boots to reveal his paw-feet. "Ahhh." He leaned back and flexed his leonine toes.

Javier gurgled. "See?" Glennie said. "Awesome, right?"

Nergal raised his eyebrows at Conor. "Are you going to introduce me to your friend?"

"Uh, yeah. Javier, this is Nergal, Babylonian lord of the dead. Nergal, Javier. The friend I phoned about the spiders."

"How do you do?" Javier said in a faint voice.

"Ah-ha!" Nergal gave Javier a broad, warm smile. "The knowledgeable one. You saved your friend's life, dude."

Javier blushed. "Why can't you eat?"

Nergal beamed at him. "What an intelligent question. Part of the answer is that we don't eat because we don't have to, much as we may crave it at times." He watched Glennie—pale, but determinedly nonchalant—pop a potato chip into her mouth, and kept staring at her while she chewed it. "But also, one mouthful would make me mortal."

"Sort of like Ashling not touching Worldcraft." Glennie crammed in another chip and chewed as if her life depended on it.

"Yes, but the effect of clothing—or anything we touch—ends when we stop touching it. Food becomes part of us, and the effect is permanent."

"What's so bad about that?" Glennie asked, spewing crumbs.

"Well, the lion's feet would be inconvenient if I were mortal, to say nothing of the tail," Nergal said. "And . . . forgive me, I am used to being myself. I have no wish to be like you."

"So," Javier said. "If Ashling ate, like, a potato chip—" Glennie waved a chip enticingly.

"She would become mortal, but for a banshee this would be especially unfortunate. She would be unable to fulfill her quest, and she would be so distraught that she would rush to end her mortal life. She would wind up like . . . Perhaps she has told you about Maeveen?"

Ashling buried her face in her hands.

"Who's Maeveen?" Javier asked.

"We saw her in the Underworld," Glennie said. "She screams a lot."

"But . . . Persephone," Conor said.

Nergal averted his gaze from Glennie's potato chips. "I beg your pardon?"

"Persephone. She ate three pomegranate seeds in

Hades and she had to stay there three months out of every year. But the rest of the time she could come back to this world."

"The Persephone tale has been embroidered." Nergal clearly didn't approve of embroidery. "Hades is the Underworld, of course, and there is no food there. Utter nonsense, typical of the Greeks. Like putting coins in their mouths to take them to Charon, as if the Underworld had any use for coins."

Javier had been silent, pondering. But now he spoke up: "What if she ate human food—I mean, food from this world—when she'd already keened for the Death? That would keep her from going nuts, wouldn't it?"

Nergal shook his head. "Part of her charge is to escort the Dear Departed to the Underworld. She cannot do that as a mortal."

"But what if she ate when she got there?" Javier persisted. "If she turned mortal there, wouldn't she . . . I dunno, go back into the system? Like, get reborn?"

"Possibly. But you disappoint me, boy. I just told you: There is no food in the Underworld, and there never will be. We cannot take Worldcraft home with us, at least not on our persons. And even if we could, food spoils there at an exceptional rate, rotting to nothing within minutes. Something to do with the vagaries of Underworld time, I believe."

Javier-silence, of the grumpy variety. Then: "Why can't

you do whatever you want? Aren't you, like, gods or something?"

"Oh, no." Nergal waved the thought away. "Demigods, at most. We have to follow the rules."

"But who made the rules?"

Nergal smiled. "Well, now, that's the question, isn't it? We're not even exactly sure what some of them are, notably the ones that govern death and rebirth. That's why we're so careful about our records—we keep seeking a pattern. But if there is one, we've failed to find it."

"The mysteries of death." Glennie had eaten an entire large bag of potato chips in five minutes. She looked sick.

Nergal sighed. "I get tired of that phrase. Sometimes I think we use it as an excuse for not trying to find the answers, not taking a chance. We are too comfortable as we are, perhaps."

Ashling slumped against the couch, woebegone. "Nergal, why are you here?"

"Ah." Nergal brightened up. "I am here to acquire . . . phones, I think you called them. We believe they could be useful to us, although I personally hope we don't have to have the little *boop-boop-boop* men in them. And since I'm here anyway, I thought I'd stop by and see if you understood how your death choice will work."

"I could figure it out," Ashling said. "I am the smartest of all the—"

"Yes," Nergal said. "But a truly smart person seeks

information from every possible source. I—if you will pardon the boast—am a very good source."

"So what do we need to know?" Conor's heart lifted. Maybe there was a way out of this after all.

"The main thing," Nergal said, "is that you will not choose the time of the Death, merely which person is to become the Dear Departed. The Death will draw near; Ashling will feel it coming and begin to keen. If you are nearby, you will point at the person you designate. If you do not hear the keen or do not take immediate action, the Death will proceed as originally fated."

Glennie opened another bag of potato chips.

"Do you know when the Death will be?" Conor asked Nergal.

"No."

"So I have to stick close to Ashling all the time and make sure there are lots of O'Neills around."

"Yes."

"I don't get why you're the one making all the decisions." Glennie selected a potato chip, scrutinized it, and put it back. "It's *my* death we're talking about."

"The Lady chose me to challenge the Birds," Conor said. "And the Birds said it's my decision."

"Maybe I *want* to be the one. Did you ever think of that?" She turned to Javier, eyes unnaturally bright. "The Underworld was awesome. It's got Nergal, plus a guy with a dog's head. Plus, I made friends with a tiger."

279

"Get that thought out of your head right now," Grump said. "You're not going to be the one, and that's final."

Glennie folded her arms tight over her chest, playground scowl in full bloom. The effect was somewhat diminished when she gave a tremendous burp.

"Excuse you," Conor said.

"Shut up, Pixie."

"He does not like to be called 'Pixie,'" Ashling said. "He likes to be called 'dude.'"

"Glennie," Conor said, "you wouldn't stay in the Other Land forever, you know." ("If you are fortunate," Ashling muttered.) "You'd get a whole new life and you wouldn't remember this one at all. You wouldn't be you."

Glennie shrugged, getting paler by the minute.

"You might wear too-short jeans and a too-big orange polyester T-shirt," Javier said. "And lumberjack boots."

Glennie gave him a dirty look. "So what?"

"You might be a total wimp like me," Conor said.

Glennie burst into tears and hurled herself at him. Shocked, he patted her back, her arms around his neck, her fluffy pink headband sticking uncomfortably in his ear.

"Conor." Grump's chin was quivering. "I turned my back and my little Jeannie died. Let me save Glennie. Please, kiddo. Please."

Conor pushed Glennie away. "I need to think."

Nergal leaned forward. "You could make this go as you wish, you know," he said to Ashling. "You could fly the little girl away so no one is around when the Death comes."

Ashling nodded.

Nergal patted her knee. "But you will not do that, will you?"

Ashling gave a long, wet sniff. "I want it to be as he . . . as they would wish."

"I'm not a little girl," Glennie said. "I'm ten. Little girls are nine or younger. And it's *my* death we're talking about here."

"This is a great sacrifice Ashling is making." Nergal was looking at Ashling but Conor knew who he was really talking to. "She has wished for a new life ever since she lost the old one. Eternity is a terrible thing, if you're not born to it like me. Even I have to work hard to stay interested."

Conor contemplated his surroundings. Ashling's bowed head. Glennie, brave but panicky. Grump, lying back on his cushions, Arctic White.

It was too much. "Why does it have to be so hard?" he burst out. "How come *every*one has to lose? It's not fair."

Ashling shook her head. "No. It is not."

"I sometimes think unfairness is the only pattern there is." Nergal began pulling his boots on again. "But, fair or unfair, I know you will all do the right thing. Conor, dude, I am not sure what a *wimp* is, but I think you are not one of those." He stood up to tuck his tail back into his pants. "Now. Where may I shop for phones?"

"Do you have money?" Javier asked. A reasonable question, Conor thought.

"Yes," Nergal said. "I have been here before. Where do you think we got our computers?"

Javier's jaw dropped. "You have computers? What kind?"

"Laptops," Glennie said. "Super-old tan ones."

"I thought you couldn't touch Worldcraft," Javier said to Nergal.

"Ah." Nergal smiled. "Worldcraft negates some of our more—er—*mysterious* powers and attributes. Conor will tell you that the Cailleach had to take off her laptop before she could attack him. But computers are a tremendous help in our everyday activities. I hope cell phones will prove the same."

"Okay," Javier said. "But how do you get them there? You said you can't carry stuff in."

"I must have a mortal with me to carry the phones." Nergal raised his eyebrows at Javier. "That mortal would, of course, be home before his parents knew he was gone. Would you take me to buy phones, boy? Perhaps you would like to see the Underworld for yourself."

Javier beamed.

Conor wondered if the Adventure Boys had a badge for this.

Chapter Twenty

Three streets west of 36A Crumlin Street, at 42 Kaicey Street, lived one Richard O'Neill. That afternoon, when Grump was taking a nap, Conor hauled Glennie and Ashling to this Richard O'Neill's front door.

"What are we supposed to do now? Set a trap for the poor guy?" Glennie asked. She kept insisting that she was looking forward to the Underworld. But when a spider dropped down from Grump's ceiling after Nergal and Javier left, she didn't snag its thread on her finger and chase Conor around with it. She took it outside and deposited it on the railing, then erupted in tears.

"I'm not going to let you die, Glennie," Conor had said as she snuffled and snorted. He repeated that now, sitting on the stoop at Richard O'Neill's house.

"I'm *supposed* to die," Glennie said. "It's not right to choose somebody else."

"The Three are in charge," Ashling said. "They say it's up to Conor. What is supposed to happen is whatever he decides."

She didn't call him "Conor-boy," he noticed. She sounded formal, as if they'd just met.

"That's right," he said. "I outsmarted the Birds, so I get to say."

The fact that he agreed with Ashling seemed to encourage her. "Conor, I did not know about this choice they have given you. I did not."

"I don't want to talk about it."

"How could she know?" Glennie said. "She never saw the Birds in action before."

"She's lived there sixteen hundred years. You're telling me she never met those Birds?" He was talking as if Ashling wasn't even there, which was rude. He wanted it to be rude.

"I had met the Birds, Conor, had even cared for them. But I never saw anyone make the challenge—it hardly ever happens. I knew only what the Lady told us about their powers."

"That makes sense," Glennie said.

"It was the Lady who fooled you, fooled us all," Ashling persisted. "She's tricky. I warned Davey O'Neill of that very fact when he was in the hostel."

"Hospital," Conor said. "So now what? You hang around to see if I wimp out and you get my sister as your Death?"

She was silent, head bowed. Then she whispered, "I don't know what I want."

"Conor, you're being a jerk," Glennie said. "It's not Ashling's fault. She did her best for us."

They'd all done their best.

"You were trying to do something good," Glennie said softly, "but you were trying to stop death. And we can't. Death comes no matter what."

Ashling straightened, sitting beside him, and met his gaze. The sun was warm on his face. *Like Beltine, the bench by the stone wall.* Her smile was the same as it was then.

Every bit as sad.

Richard O'Neill opened his door. "Hello there. Nice to see you again." Because, of course, it was the Richard O'Neill from the hospital emergency room, complete with the three-legged cane and the oxygen prongs in his nose. "To what do I owe the pleasure?"

"I'm doing a genealogy project for school," Conor heard himself say. Glennie shot him an admiring look. "Do . . . do you know who your ancestors are?"

Mr. O'Neill adjusted his oxygen prongs, thinking. "I know some. Listen, would you kids . . . I mean, would you want to come in? Your mothers probably tell you not to go into strange houses. Mine always did."

"Don't offer us candy," Glennie said. "I'm sure it'll be fine. I mean, your last name *is* O'Neill."

"They know where we are," Conor lied, just in case. "If we don't come home, they'll know where to find us." *And maybe you'll be dead anyways,* he thought. Anguish washed over him.

Richard O'Neill's living room had a saggy old couch and two easy chairs, all covered with nubbly bedspreads. In the room beyond, the dining room table and chairs were piled high with books and newspapers. French doors overlooked a tiny, cluttered backyard, an easel set up in front of them.

Unlike the furniture, the art on the walls was dust-free and in good condition: landscapes, people, flower arrangements, all painted in bright colors.

"Ohhh," Ashling said. "Lovely wall pieces."

Mr. O'Neill gave a half smile that was the same thing as a blush. "They're mine. I used to teach high school art. I don't do that anymore. Don't even paint." He jerked his head at his wheeled oxygen tank, which rolled along beside him like a dog at heel. "I get too tired."

They all sat down. Mr. O'Neill told them to call him "Richard," but did not offer them anything to eat or drink, so that was all right. Conor borrowed pencil and paper— "Not exactly prepared, are you?" Richard said—and got the names of all the ancestors his host could remember. That took about ten minutes, and then they all sat there.

"So, any of my ancestors sound familiar?" Richard asked.

"No," Conor said. "But my grump will know them, I bet."

"Oh, yeah. Davey will know."

"You should have listened to what he told the Cailleach," Ashling said.

"The Cailleach?" Richard said. "There's somebody around here who says she's the Cailleach?"

Dead (or at least terminally ailing) silence.

"She doesn't just *say*—" Ashling began, but Glennie kicked her. A kick doesn't hurt a banshee, but it gets its point across.

Conor tried a carefree laugh. It came out "Ha! Ha!"— neither carefree nor really a laugh. "It's this old lady who dresses up. Ha! Ha!"

"And for some reason your grandfather was telling her his ancestry?"

"She . . . she likes genealogy, too. Ha! Ha!"

"Do you like your life?" Glennie asked, getting to the point.

"Strange question." Richard ruffled his hair—oddly, the same way Conor's dad did. "To be honest, I was hoping for better."

"Why do you have that thing in your nose?" Ashling asked. "And that . . . that metal object."

"Oxygen tank," Conor muttered.

"Oxen sank?" Ashling said.

"Emphysema," Richard said. "From smoking. I was okay until I hit fifty-five. But now look at me."

Ashling waggled her mouth a bit, trying to fit it around *emphysema*.

"So," Glennie asked, "do you wish you were dead?"

"Glennie!" Conor wasn't close enough to kick her.

The question seemed to interfere with Richard's breathing. "What the heck . . . kind of a question is that?"

"She didn't mean anything by it," Conor said. "These things kinda come out of her mouth, you know?"

"I know, I have a younger sister, too. But I gotta say, that didn't seem like a question that just popped out."

Ashling was whispering to herself, still trying to conquer *emphysema*. In her distraction, her braid rose slowly into the air.

Richard O'Neill started coughing so hard his breath came out in wheezes. Conor leaped up in alarm. "Mr. O'Neill . . . Richard . . . is there something I can get you? Water?"

Richard nodded, trying to catch his breath. Conor found the kitchen beside the dining room, and hustled back with a coffee mug full of water. Glennie, meanwhile, started pounding Richard on the back whether he wanted her to or not.

"Enough," he gasped, trying to sip the water and slopping it down his front. "Thank you . . . Miss . . . O'Neill." He refused her kind offer of a Fruity Fooler.

They waited while he got his lungs under control. He put the mug down with a shaking hand. "All . . . right," he wheezed. "Who . . . or what . . . are you?"

"We really are the O'Neills from Crumlin Street," Conor said. "Ashling, though. She's, well—"

"Banshee," Richard wheezed.

"Another who knows the old tales," Ashling said approvingly.

"And somehow . . . you, the O'Neills of Crumlin Street . . . have met the Cailleach at the door . . . to the Lady's realm."

"It's sort of Nergal's realm, too." Conor couldn't believe he was saying this to a complete stranger. "He seems to have a lot to say about what goes on."

"He's Babylonian," Ashling said.

"And we met Charon," Glennie said. "He's Greek."

"Why don't you . . . tell me everything?" Richard O'Neill wheezed.

So they did, although they stopped abruptly before the part where Conor started trying to find other O'Neills.

Richard, who had enjoyed the tale so far, turned serious. "So now you're here, asking about my genealogy and whether I wish I were dead. Am I right in thinking that you'd like me to volunteer for death duty?"

Conor couldn't believe he was sitting in somebody's living room, asking him to die so he, Grump, and Glennie could stay alive. *How did I get here?* Five days ago, his biggest worry was a nonpoisonous spider, slightly bigger than a pencil eraser.

"As you can imagine, kids," Richard was saying, "this will take a little thought. My inclination, frankly, is to say no. I may not have the life I expected, but I do enjoy things. Cheeseburgers. Movies. Talking to my grandkids on the phone. The Red Sox, most of the—"

"You have grandkids?" Glennie didn't look happy to hear that.

"Yeah, but they live in California. I hardly ever see them." Richard played with the tube to his oxygen tank. "Cheeseburgers aside, I won't say I'm not tempted to end this life and start another. You don't have any idea when this would happen, I guess, right?"

"No," Conor said. "We won't know until Ashling starts to keen."

"Let me think about it," Richard said. "If I hear a keen start and I want to be the one, I'll try to make it to your house. I'll use that alley by the Wilsons' if you want to come meet me."

"I don't know that we'll have that much time." Conor got up. "But it's better than nothing. Thanks for listening to us, Mr. O'Neill . . . Richard. We're sorry we disturbed you and . . . everything. Don't worry about this, okay?"

Richard stood up, too, teetering. He steadied himself on his oxygen cart. "I haven't decided, you know. I might—"

Conor shook his head. "Forget it. Please. We're sorry we came."

"But Conor-boy," Ashling said. "Perhaps this man *wants* to die."

Conor felt as if the Cailleach was draining him again: cold, exhausted, discouraged. He followed Glennie to the door.

"Don't worry . . . kids," Richard wheezed after them. "Something will work out."

Conor waved and led Glennie and Ashling down the coldest, loneliest street in the world.

"Richard O'Neill's not going to be the Death," Conor said, back at Grump's.

"Good," Grump said. "This is a family matter."

"He's family," Conor said.

Grump gave him the Davey O'Neill Special, the look that said, *Clever, kiddo, but we both know you're full of it.*

And he was full of it, Conor knew. He pounded the arm of his chair with his fist. "There's *gotta* be a way out of this. Like, a way to get the Lady to choose someone else."

"You tried that already, Conor-boy." Ashling was sagged up against the couch, sad as an old ragbag. "You've tried everything. It comes down to a decision."

Or no decision, Conor thought. Which, of course, would be a decision.

Javier rapped on the door and stuck in his head. "Can I come in?"

"Join the Death watch," Grump said. "Want a soda or something, kid?" No attempt at Spanish. Conor supposed this was a change for the better—especially for Javier— but somehow it felt like Grump wasn't himself.

"Got any juice?" Javier asked, virtuous. He was happier

than Conor had ever seen him—bigger, somehow, and glowing just like Dad when he talked about the City Council.

Nergal came in, too, carrying three large shopping bags from Digital Outlet. He looked dazed. "Did you know there was a thing called television?" he asked Grump.

"It's a brain drain," Grump said. "Radio and something to do with your hands, that's the ticket."

Grump sounded so cheerful, as if he were getting ready to leave for Ireland or something. *He's so sure I'm going to point at him,* Conor thought. *And then we'll never see each other again. Doesn't he care?*

"Did you get your cell phones?" Glennie asked Javier.

Javier rifled around in one of the shopping bags. "And chargers and . . . look, headsets! So they can use their computers and still talk to each other on the phone."

Nergal leaned against the mantelpiece next to the picture of Jeannie. "I've never seen anything like that place. When I bought our computers, I went to a little store and that was all they had."

"I'm going be the Underworld's technology adviser," Javier said, glowing. "Nergal's hauling me and the phones over there in a week or so."

Ashling sat up straight. "You can take food with you. I can eat it and become mortal."

Nergal looked as if he might cry. "We can try, child, but you would have to be right there when we arrived. You

292

would almost certainly be off in the World, waiting to keen for your latest Death. We cannot predict when you would return."

"I'll eat it when I come back with my Dear Departed."

"It will have rotted away to nothing within minutes. You know that."

Ashling sagged all over again.

Javier made a visible effort to hold himself in. But he just couldn't. "Nergal got me a new cell phone," he said to Conor, trying and failing to keep his voice to a whisper. "He'll call me when he needs advice. They're going to *pay* me."

"How will they do that?" Conor asked.

"He will have an account in his name, and we will add money to it," Nergal said.

"But . . . how?"

Nergal smiled. "One of the mysteries of death."

"I'm *so* going to MIT," Javier said.

"Have you decided what to do about the Death?" Nergal sounded as if he were asking about the weather.

"We went and talked to a man with *empty seed mask*," Ashling said in dejected tones. "He may wish to die. But most likely not."

"*Emphysema,*" Conor said.

"The time draws nigh," Nergal said. "It must be soon— Ashling has been with you several days."

Conor's stomach clenched like a fist. Glennie looked sick, too.

"I put my will and stuff on the kitchen table," Grump said.

"Thanks." Conor's brain was a hunk of meat loaf.

"Conor," Grump said, "I love you. I will always love you, even if I don't remember it. Glennie, too. You know that, right?"

Conor couldn't speak.

"We know, Grump," Glennie said.

Conor's tongue loosened itself. "Grump. I can't do this. You're asking me to kill you. I can't do it."

"C'mere, kiddo." Grump patted the sofa beside him. "The rest of you talk amongst yourselves."

Conor sat down next to Grump.

"Kiddo, I know it's hard for you to imagine. But we all gotta keep moving, and there's only one more step for me to take. I won't tell you any lies. I'm nervous about this one. But . . . I dunno, it feels right to me."

"You're in okay shape, Grump. This Richard O'Neill guy—"

"Kiddo, I know Richard O'Neill, and I happen to know he still enjoys a good cheeseburger. Anyways, this ticker of mine could shut down any minute."

"Grump, I'd never see you again."

"Ah, who knows, kiddo. A few years from now, you hear there's a kid across town blowing stuff up, that'll probably be me."

Grump leaned his head back on the sofa and closed

his eyes. Conor watched him, imagining him dead. The thought froze his soul.

Nope. Nope. I'm choosing Richard O'Neill. If Ashling started keening for the Death, he'd run for the alley by the Wilsons' house. Maybe he'd get close enough to point even if Richard O'Neill was still in his house.

That would be murder, he thought. *But I don't care.*

"Well, this is cozy." Conor's dad came through the front door, fresh from politics and a beer with his buddies. "Where's your mom?"

"She was in before," Grump said. "I think she's taking a nap."

"I don't blame her. You kids look pretty bleak, too. Heck, Grump looks better than you do."

Nergal stepped away from the mantelpiece, a foot and a quarter taller than Dad. "Good afternoon, sir."

Dad had to tilt his head to see Nergal's face. "Good afternoon. Who are you?"

"I am Nergal."

"We met last night," Grump said.

"Oh, at the hospital." It wasn't a question, so they all let it fly past without an answer. "How do you do?"

"I do fine."

Dad let his gaze travel down Nergal's massiveness to the overstuffed bags at his feet. "Been shopping?"

"Cell phones," Nergal said. "For my business."

"Oh? What's your business?"

"Uh," Nergal said.

"Recycling," Grump said.

The residents of South Boston said Brian O'Neill could talk with anyone. Sure enough, Dad had no trouble at all chatting with Nergal, Babylonian lord of the dead and recycling tycoon. Nergal had no idea what recycling was and it took him a while to catch the hints Conor and Grump kept feeding him. But Dad didn't notice.

"Well, Pop," Dad said at last. "You're looking pretty good. I guess you'll live."

"Come sit by me, Brian." Conor got up, and Grump again patted the cushion next to him. "I don't see enough of you."

"You see me every day, Pop." But Dad looked pleased and sat down.

Grump grabbed his son's hand and held it, which was a shock to everyone but mostly to his son.

"You sure you're feeling all right, Pop?"

"Never better, boy." Grump squeezed the hand. "You're a good kid, you know it? I'm sorry I spent your college money. Really. You shoulda gone to Boston College, and it's my fault you didn't. Lotsa stuff's my fault."

"I'm going to have Moira take your temperature," Dad said.

But Mom, when she arrived, found that Grump's temperature was perfectly normal. "He's fine, Brian. Stop worrying." She surveyed the group. "There are people here I don't know."

Conor introduced Nergal. ("He's a recycler, Moira," Dad said.) And then Ashling. ("I told you about her. She's the . . . uh, pen pal.")

"I'm from Ulster," Ashling said. "Which is in northern Ireland."

"I've heard of it." Mom pointed to a moving dot on the kitchen wall. "Oh, Brian, that big wasp got in here again. I've had it with the humane approach. Get it, will you?"

"No!" Conor and Glennie and Ashling cried.

Dad grinned at Nergal. "Conor thinks when you try to kill something it'll get mad and come back and get you. Apparently, he's convinced his sister and his girlfriend now."

Conor wished Dad would stop saying *girlfriend*.

"Conor's theory is not always untrue," Nergal said.

"Well, it's untrue in this case." Dad fingered several of Grump's model-building magazines to see which one had the right heft. "I'm going to get that sucker, and when he's dead he's going to stay dead." He found the perfect magazine and rolled it up.

"For practical purposes," Nergal said, "and specifically at this place and time, that might be accurate. Taking a broader view, however—"

Whap! Dad missed the wasp by a mile. It buzzed angrily and looped the loop, then darted to another patch of wall, this time in the dining room.

"Oh, Conor." Ashling's face was stretching.

The Mississippi quarter was in his pocket. He held it out to her.

She shook her head, whispered, "Too late." He could see through her shoulder.

He grabbed her hand and headed for the door.

Glennie and Javier followed.

"Wimps," Dad said. *Whap!* "Drat. Stay still, you little creep."

When they were out on the sidewalk, Ashling ran around into the alley between the houses. Glennie started to follow, but Conor held her arm tight. "Anyone who sees her as a wraith will die. Keep your head down."

The Mississippi magnolia quarter dropped onto the ground. *When the Death comes I'll put it in somebody's mouth for Charon,* he thought, distracted.

But whose mouth would it be?

The wasp must have been nearly dead, because there was the keen. It wailed of lovers torn apart forever, mothers bereft of babies, the universe wondering where it had gone wrong.

"What the heck is that?" Dad yelled from inside the house.

Across the street and down the block, O'Neills and their neighbors poured out onto the sidewalk, everybody asking the same question. It was a perfect spring Sunday, so even when Ashling had stopped keening, nobody went back inside—they stayed out there and caught up on gossip. Even Grump came out, Nergal courteously giving him his arm.

Glennie saw their cousin Katherine, who lived four doors down. The two girls greeted each other with squeals, as if they hadn't walked to school together two days before. They settled themselves on the hood of someone's car.

Conor leaned against the house, waiting for Ashling to join them.

"That shrieking thing was cool," Javier said. "So that's what happened to her at school that day, right? Because of the moths. And that's why you attacked Jon on the bus."

Down the street, people were yelling. There was a ripping, screeching crash. A motor revved, powerful and loud.

A blue sedan, moving fast, ricocheted off a parked car and kept coming.

Boom! It sideswiped a red minivan.

Kept coming faster.

Conor moved out to the sidewalk, saw it all in one glance: Even though Glennie and Katherine were watching the car along with everyone else, somehow it didn't occur to them that they should move out of its way.

It occurred to Mom, halfway down the block in the opposite direction. "Glennie!" she screamed, and started to run.

Glennie turned to see what her mother wanted, and saw the expression on Conor's face. She jostled Katherine's shoulder and shouted something, but Conor couldn't hear what she said.

Because Ashling was wailing again. *Never again, never again, my love, my dove, oh gone, you're gone . . . gone . . . gone . . .*

Richard O'Neill hobbled down the sidewalk, mouth wide open as he struggled to breathe, his three-legged cane in one hand, oxygen cart in the other.

Time slowed. The wayward car came barreling toward them. Mom tripped on uneven pavement and almost fell headlong, but steadied herself and kept running.

"Conor!" Grump's voice behind him, breathless because the old man was coming for him just like Richard O'Neill. "Let me save my little girl. Let me . . . Please . . ."

Richard wanted to be chosen, that was clear. Or there was Katherine, another O'Neill right there in harm's way.

Or Conor himself. There was always Conor.

There was Mom, running down the sidewalk. If either he or Glennie died, it would be the end of her anyway.

Nergal was beside him. Because everything seemed to have slowed down so much, Conor had time to turn and consult him. "For everything," Nergal said, "there is a season."

"Conor," Grump wheezed, grabbing Nergal's arm to keep from falling over. "Do the right thing."

Mom launched herself in front of Glennie and Katherine.

If the car hit, it would get all three of them.

"Moira!" Brian was running now.

Conor's heart ripped in two. He closed his eyes.

And then he pointed.

Chapter Twenty-one

A chill wind arrowed up the street from the harbor and almost blew Mom's spring hat right off her head. She caught it in time, shivered, and struggled to button her coat. "Good thing we don't do all-night wakes anymore. I wouldn't survive."

"Pop would like it to be more of a party." Dad followed her down the steps from the cemetery. "I guess cupcakes will have to suffice."

"He talks like Grump's still alive," Glennie whispered to Conor.

He glanced back at the gravesite, with its heap of dirt and flowers. Grump didn't seem dead to him, either. Impossible that he was over there in the ground.

As they walked home, Conor went over it all in his head for the fortieth time. Glennie. Katherine. Richard O'Neill. Mom. Dad. The wayward car screaming by, missing everyone.

Grump clutching his chest and falling down. Grump lying on the sidewalk holding Conor's hand. Grump's last whisper: "You did the right thing, kiddo. See you around."

It didn't feel like the right thing. Nothing felt right—especially not what he'd done next, huddled there beside Grump's body, Ashling's Mississippi magnolia quarter on the ground by his knee.

He was weeping for Grump then, of course, but his tears were for Ashling, too. He'd been nasty to her, almost until the last minute, and still she let him choose the wrong Death. Now she was stuck for eternity with that crazy Lady.

Her hand on my heart.

Kneeling there beside Grump, he thought of Charon and the coin in a dead Greek's mouth.

Everyone was frantically waving down the ambulance. The only ones watching Conor were Glennie and Javier and Nergal. Even Glennie gasped when he lunged for her pocket, then stuffed a whole little pack of Fruity Foolers into Grump's dead mouth.

It was disrespectful, when you thought about it, and he didn't even know if it would work. As insurance, he put his head back and yelled to the sky—to Ashling, so she'd know what she was supposed to do with a pack of jelly beans in an old man's mouth. "Remember Persephone! Eat it before it's gone!"

Nergal had laughed. "Dude. You invented a new rule." He put his big hand over Grump's face and closed his eyes, at the same time making sure none of the candy wrapper was poking out of Grump's mouth.

Now Grump's house was empty except for assorted furniture, his three jars of peanut butter in Mom and Dad's pantry, Honey-Glazed Nutsos in the trash, and rocket parts in a cardboard box . . . how could that be anything but wrong?

"I still can't get my head around your girlfriend running away like that, Con," Dad said as they waited for the stoplight. "And that guy Nergal! I mean, he stays right by Pop while he's dying, closes his eyes and everything, and then he gathers up his stuff and walks off, never to be seen again. You'd think they'd stick around a minute or two, or drop by or call, maybe even come to the wake."

"Death upsets people," Mom said. "I mean, poor Nergal—he meets a man in the hospital and the man goes home and dies."

"Nergal didn't seem upset," Dad said. "Matter of fact, I think he was laughing."

Dad had been mad at the hospital at first—Grump's death had to be someone's fault, after all—but Grump's doctor told him the heart attack could have come any day. Father Ralph said it was Grump's time, and anyway Grump was the one who wanted to come home and eat Honey-Glazed Nutsos.

Everybody was mad at the guy in the rampaging car, even though it wasn't his fault, either. He'd been on new medication and had passed out at the wheel. He wrecked his own car and three others, but nobody got hurt.

Except Grump.

And, by extension, Conor.

He couldn't imagine how he'd get through life without Grump. His brain was fuzzy—he couldn't think, couldn't talk. All he could do was stare at his family and wonder which of them he should have chosen instead.

He was glad he hadn't chosen Glennie, anyway. She'd stuck right by him ever since, so kind and courteous that her mother took her temperature.

Mom had kept them out of school until after the funeral, which had been this morning. Everyone was coming back to the house for tea and cakes. Then life was supposed to go back to normal.

Conor stood in a corner of the living room, trying to be part of the wallpaper. But Mrs. Miller, one of the youth hockey coaches, noticed him anyway. "I hear you'll be trying out for us, Pixie!" She handed him a chocolate cupcake he didn't want.

"Uh. I guess."

Mrs. Miller leaned in close. "You're lucky, you know. Not every dad cares as much as yours does."

"I know."

"Not to speak ill of the dead, and Davey was a good, good man, but everybody knows his kids weren't his top priority. Your dad, now—"

The world went hot and red. Conor shoved the chocolate cupcake back into Mrs. Miller's hand, smearing chocolate on her sleeve. "Shut up. You don't know anything about Grump." He jostled past her, heading for the stairs.

Dad's heavy hand fell on him before he was halfway across the room. "Apologize," Dad hissed. "Right now."

Mrs. Miller scuttled over. "No, no, Brian. Jeez. I'm dumb as dirt. Really." She did look upset. "I'm sorry, Conor. What a stupid thing to say, today of all days."

The world felt not one bit better. "I'm not doing hockey," Conor said. "I'm not good at it and I don't like it."

"He doesn't mean that, Katie." Dad released him. "Go get some air, Con. We'll talk about this later."

How does he *know what I mean?* Conor slipped out the kitchen door and almost fell down the back stoop, because this was like Declan slipping away into the woods and for a second it seemed weird that there were steps and an alley. *I'm not Declan,* he told himself for the zillionth time. *Well, I'm sort of him. Or he's sort of me. Except neither of us is anybody but our own selves.*

It was so confusing he wanted to throw up. Instead, he walked. Somehow he wasn't surprised when he ended up at Richard O'Neill's wrought-iron front stoop.

"This time, I hope you'll let me offer you some tea," Richard said.

"I'll make it," Conor said. Richard settled down in his chair, oxygen tank by his side.

Richard looked awful, his eyes red, his skin yellowish.

When Conor handed him his tea, Richard's hand shook so much Conor had to put the mug down on the table for him.

Conor sat on the couch with the nubbly bedspread and let the silence hum like a blessing. Richard picked at invisible fluff on his gray flannel-covered knees. He took a deep breath, coughed, and focused his attention on the ceiling. "It should've been me. I heard the . . . banshee and I . . . tried to get there, Conor. I *was* there. Why didn't you choose me?"

Conor didn't know why, either. "For everything there is a season."

"That's no answer."

No, Conor had to admit, it wasn't. He sipped tea and tried again. "He hated the idea of me choosing a stranger. And he wanted to be the one to save my sister." Bitterness overcame him. "Nobody knows he did that. They think he just *died*."

Richard nodded. He used both hands to pick up his tea mug, managed a shaky sip, wobbled it back to the table. "Terrible spot . . . to put a kid in."

"I asked for it."

"You didn't. It was a trick. The Lady's trick."

Conor shrugged, too tired to argue.

That night, while they did the dishes, Conor told his father what Mrs. Miller had said about Grump's kids not being his priority.

"Well," Dad said, "she's not wrong."

Conor wanted to shout, *He died for Glennie!* But of course he couldn't. "He loved us," he said instead.

"No doubt about that." Dad put his soapy hand on Conor's shoulder, gave it a little shake. "You have the O'Neill Spark, he always said."

Conor closed his eyes, tears stinging.

"He was right. You're a smart kid, Conor. Go to BC, major in economics. I'm telling you, it'll be great."

Conor blinked his eyes dry. "Now you want me to major in economics?"

His dad's face was all glowy. "Well, you don't have to. But I've been thinking about this and, boy, if you major in economics, you can do anything. It trains your mind, you know? That's what my friend Jimmy said last time I saw him—he was an econ major. So you've got a certain logic, an understanding of how things work."

Conor looked at his father and saw the ten-year-old in the picture on Grump's mantel: eager, smart, yet clueless. "How things work? You mean like, why people die?"

His dad frowned. "No, no, no. Important stuff. The financial system. Markets. That may not sound so great now, but it will when you're grown up."

Conor remembered that he, age twelve, had once had the power of life and death. He probably was the only person in the world who knew who he was sixteen hundred years ago.

All by themselves, his vocal cords said, "Dad. I'm not going to play hockey."

"Tryouts in five weeks, Katie says."

"Dad." Conor took his father's glowy face in his two hands so he couldn't look away. "I'm. Not. Playing. Hockey. I don't like hockey. I'm not good at it. Maybe I'll try for Latin School—I haven't decided. But I'm not playing hockey."

His father pulled away from him. "*Maybe* you'll try for Latin School?" His O'Neill Blue Eyes were wild, like a Dál Fiatach raider with an ax in his hand.

Conor backed right off. "Probably, probably. Don't get upset." But then he remembered he was a hero. "Maybe not, though. We'll see."

"*We'll* see?"

"No. Right. *I'll* see."

The glow went out of his father's face. "You live in our house, you play by the house rules."

Conor hastened to explain. "I'm not saying I won't go to high school, or even that I won't try for an exam school. I'm just saying, maybe it won't be Latin. And"—*I'm a hero, I'm a hero*—"I'm definitely not playing hockey."

"What're you gonna do all summer, sit around and draw maps?"

"I'll go to summer school." *Huh? What am I saying?* "In art."

"Art?"

"It'll be something of my own. What these admissions people are looking for."

His father pulled out a chair from the kitchen table and plunked down with a heavy sigh. "Cripes." There was a long silence. Then: "Okay, listen. We'll talk to the folks at school. I guess there's all kinds of ways to get into BC."

Or not, Conor thought. But his vocal cords remained mercifully silent on that point. Heroes pick their battles, and college was five years away. Plenty of time to make up a new house rule before then.

He was actually glad to get back to school the next day. He didn't have to worry about Ashling transforming into a wraith and killing everyone, although he did have to lie to his classmates when they asked where she was. He said she'd gone home, which was sort of true.

"Do you think it worked?" Javier asked that afternoon on the bus. "Were the Fruity Foolers still in your grampa's mouth when he got there? Did Ashling eat them and turn mortal and get reborn?"

"Nerd alert," Andy Watson said. Conor had to admit, Javier did sound like he was talking about a role-playing game.

"Shut up, Andy." But that was Conor's vocal cords talking all by themselves, because his brain had frozen in horror. "Javier. Cripes. I just realized something. Something awful."

"What? What?"

"Let's say the jelly beans were still in Grump's mouth. Let's say Ashling ate them and it worked and she became mortal."

"Yeah. So. Good, right?"

Breathe. But he couldn't breathe. "She'd be mortal but she wouldn't be *dead.*"

Javier stared at him. "So . . . so she wouldn't . . ."

"She wouldn't get reborn. She'd be stuck there until she died, worse than if she was a banshee."

Javier-silence, now of the horrified variety. Then Javier said the only thing he could: "You did your best."

At home, in misery, Conor flipped through Trivial Pursuit cards and ate Fruity Foolers. Nothing made him feel better. He remembered the last thing he'd said to Ashling: "emphysema." That didn't seem like a very good last thing to say to someone.

"You did your best," Glennie offered.

He wished everyone would stop saying that.

April slid into May. In the dark of a Saturday night, Javier flew to the Underworld with Nergal and two large bags of cell phones. He came back starry-eyed but with no useful information. He hadn't seen Ashling or Grump, and Nergal wouldn't talk about anything except wireless communications.

Conor discovered an extremely large spider living in a corner of the game cupboard, and got Glennie in to capture it and put it outside. She rolled her eyes and called him a wimp, but she didn't tell anyone.

Richard showed Conor how to make a carnivorous spruce tree look like it could jump off the page and bite your nose.

Conor stopped working on his South Boston map because he knew where he was. He went to visit Boston Latin School and totally forgot to calculate the distance from the West Fourth Street Bridge. He also went to visit the arts academy, which didn't appear on any map anywhere.

He finished mapping the Land of Shanaya and moved on to Dragonia. Richard taught him to draw a dragon that couldn't decide whether to fry you or eat you raw.

Richard also taught him to figure out the correct scale of things on a map. He wrote down a formula that turned out to be algebra. Up till then Conor had thought algebra was good only for figuring the speeds of Train A and Train B.

Conor allowed himself to ace his next pre-algebra test. As usual, getting the answers right was easier than getting them wrong.

Summer school was awful, but also okay. And also totally awesome.

The classes were held at Glennie's school, so he and Javier could walk there. That was the okay part. Also, Javier was pretty happy with his computer science class, even though Olivia Kim was in it and seemed to need a whole lot of help with her homework. Javier even went to her house a couple times. He said he didn't really mind.

Conor's art class, on the other hand, was horrible. The teacher was nowhere near as good as Richard. He set up a still life for everyone to draw and then stared out the window and sighed while they worked on it. The still lifes were stupid—all fruit, not like dragons and carnivorous trees. Conor felt he was wasting his time.

The totally awesome part came in the middle of July.

Desperate for entertainment, Conor was turning a pear into a zombie peach-eater when the door at the back of the classroom opened and a deep voice asked, "Is this remedial math?" Conor whipped himself around so fast that his pencils and erasers and sticks of charcoal rained to the floor.

Nergal, Babylonian lord of the dead, had his tail stuffed into a red tracksuit under his turquoise raincoat.

The art teacher pried his gaze from the windows. "Dunno, man. Ask at the office."

Nergal smiled as if the teacher had been extremely helpful. "I did. They sent us to room"—he checked a slip of paper in his hand—"3-D."

"This is 3-C. So 3-D's across the hall."

"Thank you." Nergal winked at Conor and turned to leave, showing the class the suspicious and oddly active hump in the back of his raincoat. "He got hamsters in his pants?" whispered the kid next to Conor.

Conor was paralyzed. Why did the Babylonian lord of the dead need remedial math? As the door was about to close, a girl's voice from across the hall said, "What Greek math whiz noticed in 530 B.C. that the morning star and evening star were one and the same?"

"Pythagoras," Nergal said. "Smart fellow."

"Hey, man, where you going?" the art teacher cried as Conor ran for the door. "Your stuff's all over the place."

He made it into room 3-D with no recollection of opening two doors and crossing a hallway. He stood there staring at Ashling with a stupid grin on his face and not a clue what to do next. He certainly wasn't going to *hug* her, for cripes' sake.

She smiled back at him. Her red hair was chin length. She was wearing purple capri pants and a lime green Grateful Dead T-shirt.

"Sit there, please." The math teacher pointed to a seat in the third row. "Can I help you?" she asked Conor.

"He's Ashling's cousin," Nergal said. "Her return is a surprise."

"For the moment, her return is none of his business." The teacher wrote Ashling's name in a ledger and handed Nergal's slip of paper back to him. "Please leave. Both of you."

Conor sneaked another look at Ashling as Nergal swept him out the door. She beamed at him, so excited and happy he thought he himself might never stop grinning.

"How . . . ?" he croaked as Nergal shut the door behind them.

"Dude." Nergal put out his hand for Conor to shake. "Awesome to see you."

"How . . . ?"

Nergal smiled. "Your new rule almost worked. She ate the Fruity Foolers and became mortal, although not dead."

"Ohhhh." Conor slumped against the wall. "I was afraid of that. I didn't think of it until later."

"The Lady was, shall we say, annoyed. For a time, I feared that she would make the child live out her mortal life in the Underworld."

Conor groaned. "I'm so stu-u-pid."

"No, no, no, boy," Nergal said. "Yours was a very clever solution. It simply required follow-through." His smile broadened. "Also called bribery." He leaned forward and whispered, "Silly Mustache Brothers. I put them on her phone."

"She let Ashling go for a *cell phone game*?"

"She isn't really mean, you know—just bored. And even the Lady knows, when somebody invents a new rule, the rational response is to make it work."

Conor went back to art class, where he watched the clock until the bell rang. He and Ashling met in the hallway between their two classes. "The whole-number system begins with zero," she said by way of greeting.

"Glad to see you, too."

She put her hand on his heart. "Dude. You rescued me after all."

"Pixie-poop has a girlfriend," said Andy Watson, who was taking remedial math for the second time.

"Shut up, Andy."

Ashling was gazing into his eyes—probably looking for Declan, the sword-wielding hero with muscles and metal-working talent. Maybe she was expecting him to kiss her or something.

"Listen," he said. "I'm not Declan. I mean, I sort of am. I remember some things. But mostly I'm me. And, you know, I'm only twelve years old."

"I do not know how many years old I am." With absolutely no warning—shouldn't there be a beeping sound or something?—she leaned forward and kissed him right on the lips. The hallway erupted into hoots and catcalls.

Conor's ears got so hot it was surprising his hair didn't catch fire.

Kissing wasn't as gross as he'd expected, although close enough.

Ashling smiled at him. "When is the midday meal? I can eat food now. I want macaroni and cheese." Turning, she skipped down the hall toward the stairs.

"I'm not Declan," he repeated to himself as he followed her down.

It turned out Ashling was living in an apartment four

blocks away from Crumlin Street. Various demigods took turns staying with her when the Lady didn't require their services. Anubis, Egyptian protector of the dead, became adept with the vacuum cleaner, while Kisin, the Mayan lord of the Underworld, discovered that he was an excellent cook even though he couldn't eat anything. The Latvian goddess Mara did the shopping. She loved the scent of blue cheese.

Conor's parents were delighted when Ashling's chief guardian, one Nergal L. Babylon, revealed to them that she actually was a distant cousin. "I thought so," Dad said. "She's got the O'Neill Spark."

Conor was almost happy—the Declan part of him no longer felt guilty about Ashling's death, and the rest of him was relieved that she wasn't serving a life sentence with the Lady. But despite everything Javier, Glennie, and his own logic could tell him, he still missed Grump and wished he'd been able to save him.

"He would have died in a year or so anyways," Glennie said.

Didn't matter. Conor felt restless, like he'd left something undone.

Eighth grade started. Ashling was elected to the cafeteria committee. Conor tutored sixth graders in math and joined a study group for the high school exams. Ashling did not attempt to kiss him again and seemed to have forgotten she'd ever done it.

Javier totally crashed the office computer, then managed to rebuild it without losing everyone's grades, despite strong peer pressure to the contrary. He went to a dance with Olivia Kim that turned out to be a total bore. That's what he told Conor, anyway. And Glennie, who gave him a whole package of Fruity Foolers to remind him who his real friends were.

One sunny Sunday, everybody was standing around after Mass when Meghan O'Neill, Grump's eldest niece, hustled up to Mom with a young woman in tow. The young woman wheeled a baby in a stroller.

"Do you believe it?" Meghan said. "This is my Corey from Nebraska! And she's had a boy this time. Cutest little thing. Five months old next week."

Glennie and Ashling were right in there, poking their fingers out for the baby to grab, wrinkling their noses because he needed a new diaper. Conor wasn't too interested until he heard Meghan say, "He's got the strangest birthmark on the back of his leg. My dad says it's shaped like Ireland."

"They may run in families," Mom said. "Conor, what are you doing to that child?"

Conor was on his knees, lifting up the baby's stinky leg to see the birthmark.

Purple, with a red spot for Dublin.

Conor rocked back on his heels. The baby's nose had the barest hint of a bulb at the end. He thought the

O'Neill Blue Eyes had a glint to them, a hint of mischief.

There was no other sign that the baby knew who he used to be.

Still.

"I'd start making up some house rules right now," Conor told Grump's new mum.

Acknowledgments

This book takes liberties with Celtic religion. (Several religions, come to think of it.) I tried to be more respectful of everyday life, and am deeply indebted to my South Boston advisers: Kim Simonian (organizer supreme), Paul Williams, John Murphy, Jeannette Hurley, Alicia Jurus, and Mo Hanley. The staff and students of the Oliver Hazard Perry School also were of great help, and the fifth graders of May 2011 will find their first names sprinkled throughout the book. I'm grateful to Danette Vigilante for her advice about Javier. (Any mistakes or idiocies are mine alone, of course.)

Here in Maine, Conor's tale benefited from the sharp eyes of "beta readers" Seeta John, Catherine Nevin, Mia Vierthaler, and Sosha Sullivan. Lisa Heldke's Socratic dialogue was helpful as well as entertaining. Ed DePasqual provided rocket know-how. Friend Memorial Library is a researcher's treasure trove, thanks to Stephanie Atwater, Tracy Spencer, Nancy Randall, and interlibrary loan. And I would have keened and turned into a wraith long ago without my writers group: Ann Logan, Becky McCall, Gail Page, Kim Ridley, and Susa Wuorinen.

Copy editor Dan Janeck knows his way around a manuscript—a calming fact.

Shelly Perron is a friend and adviser beyond price.

Rob Shillady read and commented astutely on every friggin' draft.

It's impossible to express what Conor and crew owe to the mystical powers of Kathy Dawson, their editor at Dial Books for Young Readers. And of course Conor wouldn't exist at all without super-agent Kate Schafer Testerman.

As the ancient Irish would say, you all are totally awesome.